WHY SHE RAN

Why She Ran is the fourth novel, featuring criminologist David Dunnigan, by Irish author S.A. Dunphy, who has previously written works of non-fiction.

ALSO BY S.A. DUNPHY
After She Vanished
When She Was Gone
If She Returned

Why
She
Ran

S.A. DUNPHY

WITHDRAWN

HACHETTE
BOOKS
IRELAND

First published in Ireland in 2020 by
HACHETTE BOOKS IRELAND

1

Cataloguing in Publication Data is available from the British Library

Trade paperback ISBN 9781473699229
Ebook ISBN 9781473699212

Typeset in Sabon by Bookends Publishing Services, Dublin

Printed and bound in Great Britain by Clays Ltd, Elcograf, S.p.A

Hachette Books Ireland policy is to use papers that are natural, renewable and recyclable
products and made from wood grown in sustainable forests. The logging and manufactur-
ing processes are expected to conform to the environmental regulations of the country of
origin.

Hachette Books Ireland
8 Castlecourt Centre
Castleknock
Dublin 15, Ireland

A division of Hachette UK Ltd
Carmelite House, 50 Victoria Embankment, EC4Y 0DZ
www.hachettebooksireland.ie

For Deirdre. Without you, nothing makes sense.

PROLOGUE

THE HARPY AND THE GRYPHON

1

HE EARNED THE NAME THE HARPY WHILE STILL a corporal with the Special Boat Service (SBS) due to his fondness for the unusually shaped blade of that name. When he left to go freelance, he kept the moniker – in Greek mythology the harpies were monsters: half-human, half-bird, they were the personification of the oncoming storm.

He liked that.

His work with the SBS helped him forge links with a variety of people in high positions in the military, government, and the diplomatic corps, but he also made friends within the more shadowy realms of the private sector, particularly the euphemistically named 'security consultants' who offered mercenary services ranging from spying to assassination – unpleasant tasks committed by even less pleasant people acting on behalf of whoever was prepared to pay them enough.

And that was how he met the Gryphon.

He arrived at a residence in a wealthy Oslo suburb one evening in the spring of 2006. His instructions had been to eradicate the property's owner, and to leave no witnesses. It was not difficult to secure a plan of the house and grounds, complete with a schematic of the security system, and he relished the challenge of gaining access.

The moment he approached the electric gate at the rear of the walled garden he knew that someone had got there before him: the mechanism had been shattered and with a gentle push he was inside. A window on the ground floor hung open, and the house had that electric, nerve-jangling feeling buildings vibrate with when they are empty, although he counted six cars parked outside.

The whole place stank of death.

He found the first body, a maid, lying on the stairs and a second on the landing. A cursory examination revealed no obvious cause of death (there were no gunshot or stab wounds, no ligature marks or signs of broken necks), and he knew right away he was dealing with a fellow professional.

His intended target was sitting bolt upright on his bed, staring at the open doorway. He did not have to look closely to know he was not breathing. As the Harpy entered, a voice said from somewhere to his left, 'You move quietly for such a big man.'

The speech was light and unaccented, but something about its cadence spoke of Eastern Europe. The Harpy froze – he always carried a Beretta pistol under his left arm, and his usual Harpy knife in a scabbard behind his right hip, but there was no doubt he would be dead before he could reach for either. The available options were severely limited.

'You beat me to the prize,' he said, gently. 'I know when I've been bested. There's no need for us to fall out over it.'

'And the fact that I have you at a disadvantage,' the voice purred (he surmised it was perhaps a metre behind him), 'lessens your inclination to enter into a physical confrontation, I assume.'

'Call me a pragmatist.'

With slow, almost languorous movements a tall, slender man in a white shirt and black jeans stepped into view. He had blond hair framing a long, thoughtful face, and appeared to be carrying no weapons. There was about him, however, a sense of absolute confidence and latent violence that was almost like an audible hum.

'There are several bottles of very old and very good Scotch downstairs,' the blond man said. 'Why don't we have a drink while we discuss what should happen next?'

'We both know there are only two possibilities,' the Harpy said. 'I leave this house alive or you do.'

The blond man smiled a sad smile. 'Nothing says we cannot share a drink first.'

'What should I call you?'

'I am known as the Gryphon.'

2

THEY SAT OPPOSITE ONE ANOTHER IN THE dining room in a house full of dead people and they drank and talked. The intention as they went downstairs had been to prepare for the final confrontation but, for some reason neither could precisely identify, they felt no urge to enter into such a lethal altercation. The Harpy soon found himself thinking how comfortable he was in this stranger's company, and how he had not experienced such comradeship in a long time. At first he wondered if he was being lulled into a false sense of security, or if the liquor had been drugged, but soon he realised that was not the case, and in spite of all his training, he relaxed.

An hour passed, and then another.

He found himself speaking of his military career, of the good times and the bad, and the dark moments when he had wondered if he would survive and the even darker moments when he believed it didn't matter. The Gryphon told him about losing a friend during the horrific training rituals of Russia's Spetsnaz, and of a massacre he and his team had come across once in a village in Kosovo – in a voice that was almost a whisper he recounted finding a classroom full of dead children, and wondered how the universe allowed such things to occur.

'How can I mourn those boys and girls and still bring death to the people who work in this house?' he asked, real pain evident in his voice. 'The maid I killed – she was not a bad person. Yet I did not think about her family, whether or not she had a son or a daughter.'

'I do this job because I can and because people pay me well to do it,' the Harpy mused. 'I stopped thinking about the right and wrong of it a long time ago.'

The Gryphon narrowed his eyes. 'I do not believe you.'

'You don't know me.'

'Maybe you no longer allow yourself to be aware of it. But you *do* think about it.'

They gazed at one another across the table, and something passed between them.

Then they walked out of the house together, and did not part until death visited one of them in the form of a Yellow Man three years later.

3

THEY DIDN'T WORK FOR MONTHS. THE GRYPHON had a house on a small island in the South Pacific, and they went there and made love and drank wine and swam in the warm ocean. They didn't talk about their work; they had so much to learn about one another it just didn't seem important.

The Harpy felt like a teenager – he had joined the army when he was sixteen, so had never really had a relationship that lasted more than a couple of days. Now here he was in his late thirties having a giddy, head-over-heels love affair, and he found he just couldn't get enough of this man who had swept into his life and turned it upside down.

He wanted to know everything about his new partner: his likes and dislikes, what made him laugh and what made him cry. At the end of the second week, he said to the Gryphon, 'I don't want to leave.'

'I don't want you to either.'

'What is this? What are we doing?'

'I think we are being happy.'

And he knew the Russian was right.

When the rains came they understood they had reached a turning point. The Harpy made them a lunch of grilled fish, mango and flat breads which they ate with cold bottles of the local beer on their covered porch, watching the tropical rain come down in sheets, turning the sea into a seething mass of whirlpools and eddies. 'I hate how my life was before,' he said as they ate.

'You do not wish to work anymore?'

'I'll have to, sooner or later.'

'I can keep us for a time yet.'

'It's not that – I have money, Gryph. I don't need to do another job for two, three years.'

'So what is the problem?'

'We've run away. You know that, don't you? Just like Huck Finn and Tom Sawyer. Do you know those books?'

The Gryphon nodded. 'We don't just read Chekhov and Tolstoy. Mark Twain is well loved in Russia.'

'This has been wonderful, but it doesn't help us. Not in the long term. We need to go back to the world and get our lives in order.'

'How?'

'Do you want to continue being a paid killer?'

'You know I do not.'

'Neither do I. I want to open a bar.'

The Gryphon sat forward and peered at him, a bemused expression on his finely boned face. 'Have you ever worked in the hospitality industry?'

'Never.'

'Then your bar will probably fail.'

'Will you help me make it succeed?'

The Gryphon twined his long, almost feminine fingers about the Harpy's rougher, thicker ones. 'Where you go, I will follow.'

4

THEY BOUGHT A RUN-DOWN ESTABLISHMENT on the outskirts of Soho in London's West End and refurbished it themselves, consuming almost all of their combined savings. The décor was olde English pub, and they decided to specialise in minority ales, craft whiskeys and gins. The Harpy took on a chef called Mordechai, an Israeli who could work wonders with seemingly basic ingredients and seemed to welcome eighteen-hour shifts. Using his keen eye for cuisine, they developed a menu of traditional pie and mash alongside a daily special which usually involved one of the more exotic dishes they had encountered on their travels: a chicken tagine rich with saffron and apricots; a sweet but blisteringly hot Sri Lankan pineapple curry; a nasi goreng packed with prawns and punchy with chunks of red chili and fresh coriander, resplendent with a fried egg on top.

The first year they were open was like a beautiful dream. The Gryphon was determined the pub (which they called The Lion and Eagle in his honour) should feature live music, and three nights a week they hosted the cream of the city's folk-rock scene. The Harpy had memories of evenings that felt as if they would never end, where the songs hung in the air like clouds of melody and the smiling faces of the crowd seemed an antidote to all the pain and unhappiness the couple spent so much of their lives causing.

If 2007 was a dream, 2008 was a nightmare. The economy crashed, and their regulars chose to eat and drink at home. It broke the Harpy's heart to let Mordechai go, but he took it stoically, and asked them to call him if things improved.

Final notices from their suppliers began to stack up, and one night the Gryphon sat him down and said, 'Do you remember the first time we met?'

'Of course I do.'

'You said we had two choices: either I lived or you did.'

'What are you saying?'

'We found a third choice. We can do that again.'

'I still don't understand.'

'The Lion and Eagle can stay open or close on its own merits. Or we can find a way to help it along.'

'How?'

'We take on a couple of jobs a year – well-paying, only ending people we believe really deserve it. We work together and we work clean. No torture, no blade work, all quick, painless deaths. If we are clever, we can keep this place going and continue living as we wish to live. Hopefully in a year or two things will improve and we can leave the killing behind for good.'

He knew it was the only answer, although as he agreed he felt a chill. Later, he would wonder if it was a presentiment of what was to come.

5

THEY DID TWO JOBS IN THE LATTER HALF OF
2008. The Gryphon took charge of everything and placed
advertisements in the right places. There is always work for
people with the skills they possessed, individuals who can
promise results that are completely untraceable.

The Russian had perfected a technique that involved swift
blows to various pressure points that, if applied with enough
force and rapidity, could bring about unconsciousness and
death; he was also an expert in poisons. In their early days
together he told the Harpy that he could shoot and use
various edged weapons, but preferred to travel light. His
hands, and a wallet filled with syringes, darts and phials of
potent chemicals, were all he needed.

It did not take long for their reputation to spread, and by
the end of 2009 (they did four killings that year), their debts
were all paid off, and while the bar remained largely empty

except for a few die-hard regulars, both men felt things were looking up. Or at least, they told one another they were: they studiously avoided discussing the fact that The Lion and Eagle was still running at a significant loss.

In January 2010 they received a message via one of the Gryphon's deep Web accounts, requesting a face-to-face meeting regarding a potential job. This was not the norm (deals were usually done via encrypted emails and transfers from one numbered account to another), but a larger sum of money than either of them had ever seen offered was in play, and the message indicated that a kind of interview process was being implemented.

The Harpy's instinct was to walk away from the deal. 'I don't like it,' he told the Gryphon. 'It smells bad.'

'If we win this account, the money is enough we will never need to work again. We would be mad not to tender for it.'

'We shouldn't have to. Our track record speaks for itself.'

'If you want me to withdraw, I will.'

'I'd feel better if you did. I know it's a lot but … we've fought hard to have this life. I don't want to lose it. Or you.'

'You're right. I will let them know we're out of the race.'

There was a part of him even then that knew his lover was lying. When the Gryphon told him he needed to take a trip to meet a distiller a week later a voice in the back of his mind told him something was off, but he chose not to listen. A month passed and business began to improve. He was able to bring Mordechai back a couple of days each week, and they introduced a new lunch menu – their ploughman's, complete with chunky bread baked in their kitchen and a selection of pickles they produced themselves, was a huge hit. The Harpy began to feel things were on an upward spiral.

On the third anniversary of their meeting, he and the Gryphon booked a band they both loved, and with the bar not as full as it once had been, but with enough customers to break even, they toasted each other and talked long into the night of happier days to come.

When they went to bed their lovemaking was tender and sweet and delicious. Afterwards, a blissful sleep took them with a gentle caress.

Two hours later the Harpy was just drifting from one dream to another when the screaming started.

6

HE SHOT INTO WAKEFULNESS AND PEERED INTO the darkness, disoriented and wondering what the hell was going on. A shape coalesced before him like smoke and he saw that his partner – a man usually oblivious to fear and physical pain – was standing naked at the end of the bed, making a keening sound that was totally alien to him. The Gryphon was facing the Harpy, who had to blink and shake his head to ensure that what he was seeing was not some kind of waking nightmare, for his lover's abdomen had been slashed open diagonally and the Gryphon, still wailing in a pitiful manner, was trying to hold onto a mess of pink gut that had tumbled out.

The Harpy began to rise to go to his lover, but an intense pain cascaded over him – a pain so all-encompassing he blacked out for a moment. When awareness returned he looked down, and saw the bed he was lying in was heavy with blood. Pulling the sodden sheet away from himself, he confirmed what he already knew: his own mid-section had been neatly sliced open – he could perceive the lumpen shape of his own innards through the gash.

A normal person waking to such horrors would simply tip over into hysteria (a condition, it seemed, the Gryphon had submitted to). But the Harpy was not a normal person.

Two things happened at once: his training kicked in automatically, and information about the severity of the injury and the chances of survival ran through his mind in an almost objective manner; simultaneously he registered that he was weak to the point of near-paralysis, and the room began to swim.

It took all the will he could muster to wrest his focus back onto grim reality. He glimpsed at his bedside table, which seemed a vast distance away, and spied his mobile phone. He didn't know if he could get to it, but he would have to try.

With what strength he could spare, he tried to call out. 'Gryph.'

His lover continued to sob, oblivious to anything but his own misery.

So he tried a second time. 'Gryph, look at me.' *How did he manage to stand?* he wondered, but pushed the thought away – it didn't matter, anyway.

A pair of bloodshot eyes blinked open and saw him.

'Can you hear me?'

The question was greeted by a desperate nod.

'I think I can reach my phone. I'm going to call for help,' he said, his voice little more than a whisper. 'I might pass out again, so I need you to stay with me.'

The Gryphon shook his head. 'No good.' Blood seeped from the sides of the Russian's mouth as he said the words.

'I have to try,' the Harpy hissed, trying to sound reassuring. 'I'm *going* to try. We'll get through this. I promise you.'

'You don't ... don't understand ...,' the Gryphon said, the words sounding thick and wet as more blood flowed from his mouth. 'He's still here.'

As if being birthed by the darkness, a figure moved from the corner of the bedroom where it had been hidden by the curtains. The intruder was smaller than the two wounded men by several inches and slim to the point of being willowy. He was dressed in a beige suit with an open-necked shirt, and was carrying the Harpy's trademark blade loosely in his left hand (which he must have taken from the locked weapons room they kept at the back of the cellar). In one fluid motion he slashed the knife across the Gryphon's throat, a geyser of blood erupting from the wound in a vicious gout.

The Harpy would have screamed if he could – he made to lunge forward but the terrible injury he had sustained prevented him, and he felt his gut literally lurch and then he was on the floor, and blackness claimed him.

7

WHEN NEXT HE WOKE HE WAS FACE DOWN ON THE
carpet, which was wet and tacky with viscera.

'I'm going to move you,' a dry voice said. The words were
spoken with neither emotion nor inflection. 'It will hurt.'

He felt hands beneath him and a bright white agony
enveloped the world and he was gone again. He drifted
through time without direction. Disjointed scenes revealed
themselves amid the darkness and the pain.

'Here. Drink. You've lost a lot of blood,' the characterless
voice was saying.

Water poured down his gullet and he gulped, realising as he
did so that his mouth and throat felt like sandpaper. He tried
to move his arms, but could not. The world was spinning and
he leaned over and threw up a lot of the water he had just
drunk.

'Take some more. Come on.'

He coughed, spluttered and floated away again.

Noises brought him back to his body, and turning his head, he saw the intruder. His skin was sallow and his hair straw-coloured. *He is a beige man, a Yellow Man*, the Harpy thought.

As he watched, the Yellow Man lifted the eviscerated body of the person he had loved from where it had crumpled on their bedroom floor. He tried to speak, to plead, to threaten, but he could summon no sound – his tongue felt too large for his mouth and then he was gone again. In that last fleeting moment of awareness, he hoped he was dying.

He was not.

He seemed to snap from oblivion to wakefulness. Sunlight was streaming through the bedroom window and the Yellow Man was injecting something into his arm. Painfully raising his head, he saw that his upper body had been wrapped in clingfilm, which pinned his arms to his sides, but kept his bowels in place and staunched the blood flow. He thought he could see some form of dressing under the plastic wrap, too.

He swallowed, tried to wet his lips. 'What are you giving me?' It hurt to speak.

'Antibiotics. I did not intend for you to land on the carpet. You keep your home clean, but one can never be too careful. It would be better if you did not catch an infection – your recovery will be hard enough.'

The words chilled him. The only reason to keep him alive was to transport him somewhere, and that meant imprisonment and torture. He tried to think of who might be behind the attack, but there were too many possibilities, and his mind was still foggy. 'You are a coward. Why not just finish the job and have done with it?'

'Your survival, albeit in a compromised state, is part of the job.'

'I don't know what information your people want, or whether this is about revenge, but you won't get satisfaction from me. I won't scream and I won't beg.'

'We don't want you to do either. All you have to do is live.'

'I don't understand.'

'Your partner just did a piece of work for an employer of mine.'

Now his heart sank. 'A job he had to be interviewed for?'

'Yes.'

'I take it he did not complete the task.'

'He did exactly as he was asked to do.'

'So what was the problem, then?'

'Suffice it to say my employer came to believe he was a security risk.'

'He'd been doing this work for years,' the Harpy said through clenched teeth. 'He never would have broken confidentiality. You don't survive as long as he had by betraying trust.'

'That's hardly the point. My employer had to be sure.'

The Harpy felt tears building behind his eyes and did nothing to fight them. They ran down his cheeks in rivulets. The grief was followed by a rage so intense that he thought he may physically explode.

'I'm going to kill you,' he said, slowly and deliberately. 'I'm going to take you apart a bit at a time, and then I'm going to find your employer and I'm going to kill him.'

The Yellow Man sighed and shook his head. 'So be it. I will be waiting. But I should probably let you know that, while you were unconscious, I severed both your Achilles tendons.

That knife of yours, it really is a wonderful weapon. I must get myself one. I can see why you're so fond of it.'

The Harpy tried to move his toes, and found that he couldn't.

The Yellow Man saw the realisation in his eyes and nodded. 'As I said, you do have a lot of recuperation ahead of you.' He stood up and smiled without a shred of humour or warmth. There was something reptilian about him, something inhuman. 'I will call for an ambulance when I get to my car. My employer very much wants you to live. You are part of the message, you see. The international community of killers and mercenaries will hear about the death of your friend, and they will see you making your way painfully back to some form of health – though I suspect you may need to use a walking stick, and you'll probably be shitting into a bag from now on.' He looked at the prone man with cold, empty eyes. 'They'll hear, and they'll know that he won the account, and was paid in full – let's assume for his betrayal, which probably would have come sooner or later. Good luck in your convalescence. I do hope we meet again.'

And then he was gone.

The paramedics told the Harpy he was lucky to have survived such catastrophic injuries. He informed the police when they came that he had seen nothing, that the attack occurred while he was asleep and that he had woken wrapped up like a basted chicken.

He spent most of the next four months in hospital on the flat of his back, and a further two years in painful physical rehabilitation. He used the time to begin planning.

Part One

NORTHERN SOUL

Wilfred Hubert

It was all about appearance.

He learned that when he was a small boy at his father's knee. His old man was a confidence trickster, a con-artist who knew half a dozen ways of scamming gullible people out of their money.

'One thing you've got to remember, Willy, is that everyone wants to be liked,' he told his son when he visited him in prison. 'If they think you like them, they'll like you back, and once you're their friend, you can take, take, take. The secret is making them think they want to give it all to you.'

Hubert listened carefully, secretly thinking that his father must not have been particularly good at this part of his job, seeing as five women he had been selling insurance to (policies that existed only as fictitious ideas on pieces of paper his father had printed at the local stationery store in Winslow, Arizona, where they lived) had hired a private investigator to look into his affairs. It seemed to the boy, young and inexperienced as he was, that people rarely employed PIs to follow someone they liked.

Despite his doubts, the lesson stuck. He had never been a success at school. He was frightened of the girls (he lusted after them, but their disdain-filled looks each time he walked past told him all he needed to know about their feelings towards him) and the boys just ignored him. But he always hailed them cheerfully anyway, offering hellos and greetings that were ignored at best and responded to with a 'Fuck off, nerd!' at worst.

He kept to himself at lunch, burying his head in cowboy comics, dreaming of a world where he was sheriff of his own town. One day, he promised himself. One day.

As soon as he was old enough he told his mother he would not be returning to education – and as in all other aspects of his life, she didn't seem to care.

He was sixteen when he started working in the warehouse attached to the very stationery store his father used to create the paperwork for his insurance scams, and he made sure he was always punctual, neatly dressed and that he met everyone with a smile. No job was too menial and no request was answered with anything less than an enthusiastic 'Yes sir!'

He loathed them all, but they didn't have to know that, did they?

Within the year he was managing the warehouse. He used the extra money he received to buy stock in the company – he was never much of a socialiser, and he had started going to the library on Wednesday evenings, when it stayed open late. He borrowed books on economics and finance, and soon he thought he understood enough to begin building a stock portfolio of his own.

It started out very small, but little by little, it got to the stage where he was making considerably more money from his trading than from his day job.

Within four years he was on the board of the Winslow Paper and Card Collective (plc). A year after that, they made him chairman. He made sure coffee and freshly baked pastries were available at every meeting, and he personally wrote to and thanked each member of the board for attending (friendly handwritten messages that were sent out with the minutes).

The fact that he spat on the croissants and rubbed the notes on his genitals before delivering them to his secretary was another thing he kept to himself. Secrets, he was starting to realise, were one of life's pleasures.

All the while he expanded his interests. He spotted early that computers were going to be the next big thing, and invested heavily in Silicon Valley. He was not technically minded – he hadn't a clue how the machines worked, and wasn't really interested. What did interest him was the fact that every office in the world was soon going to have one of these contraptions in it, and that meant huge profits. His research taught him that the major companies who were constructing these gadgets had factored in something called 'built-in obsolescence', which meant you'd fork out hundreds of dollars today to buy whichever model was the top of the market, and within a couple of years the one you were using would be old hat and you'd be shopping for a newer, flashier package (that would probably do exactly the same thing your old one did, just with a couple of extra bells and whistles and some snazzier graphics).

Hubert recognised a scam when he saw it, but this was totally legal and therefore completely safe to get in on, so he did just that.

He made his first million before his twenty-seventh birthday.

His broker (a bespectacled geek who seemed to be constantly covered in a dusting of dandruff) took him out to celebrate. He didn't know how they ended up there, but at one in the morning, he found himself in a brothel in Phoenix. A selection of girls lined up before him, and the madame asked which one he wanted. He didn't have to be asked twice: one of them looked to be about fourteen, and he couldn't take his eyes off her. She reminded him of a girl he'd had very specific fantasies about in high school.

A girl who treated him with utter contempt.

'I'm going to call you Sindy,' he told his companion as she led him to her room.

This girl paid for the sins of her namesake. She was bruised and bloody when he was finished with her. The madame was furious, but a little extra cash soothed her mood. She even told him, as he left, that she hoped he would visit them again.

He did.

And he asked to see the same girl.

After his third visit the madame called security, and he was instructed never to come back.

But it was worth it.

He had shown Sindy who was really in charge.

She knew who the sheriff was now.

1

IN THE SUMMER MORNINGS, THEY WENT FISHING. Tuntuk, the Inughuit chieftain, taught Miley how to bait the hooks with rancid fish carcasses, the scent of which spread through the frigid waters, drawing all kinds of ocean life.

They would return with char, salmon and dogfish, and the women of the tribe would take this bounty with smiling eyes and joke that they had brought back a better yield the previous week – had they *really* been fishing, or had they been drinking beer in the bar of the Faringen Hotel?

Tuntuk would pretend he had been caught out, and Miley would fuss and act as if he was offended at the suggestion.

When the clan gathered for the meal that evening in the low-ceilinged, tobacco-stained community centre, he and Tuntuk, seated at the table reserved for elders, would be given the best of the fish – huge steaks and slices of fried roe served with potato dumplings and bowls of a steaming seaweed broth.

The conversation would wash over Miley – words in both Kalaallisut, the Inuit language, and English, for both tongues were spoken interchangeably on the reservation – and he felt as if he might burst with happiness.

He was home, perhaps for the first time.

Miley had arrived in Greenland in the company of David Dunnigan (whom the Inuit had dubbed 'Mighty Warrior', a comment on his dogged determination and brusque manner rather than his physical prowess), a criminologist who worked as a consultant for Ireland's National Bureau of Criminal Investigation (NBCI). They had travelled there following a tip that suggested Beth, Dunnigan's niece, who had been abducted eighteen years previously while in his care, may have been trafficked there to work at the fish-processing plant which employed most of the local people (as well as a large contingency of what amounted to slave labour, the bulk of which had been trafficked in). The information had proven to be accurate, but sadly the trail was cold, and Beth long gone.

Dunnigan returned home, still searching for the child (who would now be a grown woman) he still blamed himself for losing. He had found her, finally in a brothel in Galway, having followed a trail of clues which had been largely provided by the network of homeless people his friend and mentor, the crusading priest Father Bill Creedon, saw as his congregation. It was a painful reunion, but the family were reunited after almost two decades apart.

Miley, though, had chosen to remain. As part of their quest two members of the Inuit tribe had died, murdered by corrupt police officers in an attempt to frame Dunnigan and his associates and prevent them from discovering the truth, not just about Beth, but also the organisation behind her abduction and subsequent movements, the shadowy After Dark Campaign. Miley had loved both of the deceased Inuit – Quin'ta as a brother, and Leeza ... well, he had been *in* love with Leeza, and he believed she had felt the same about him.

He stayed on the ice partly out of a sense of duty. Quin'ta had been like a son to Tuntuk, and Miley was his replacement: the young man would still be alive if Dunnigan had not come to the tundra and started what had turned into a small war. Miley wanted to make amends in whatever way he could.

But his reasons were selfish too. This was a place where his 'condition' was invisible. And he could not walk away from that.

After the meal there would be singing and story-telling, and through the songs and myths Miley learned the history of these people who had opened their homes and their hearts to him and given him something he had wished for all his life – the chance to be a full, independent, contributing member of the community.

No one on the res seemed to notice that he had been born with an extra chromosome, and the words 'Down syndrome' were never mentioned. That he was fully capable of doing everything the other members of the tribe did was never in question. It was as if he had gone to sleep and woken up without the defining features that marked him out as different.

When he looked in the mirror he saw the same face that had always peered back at him, and he realised the Inughuit saw it too, but did not register it as belonging to someone with a 'disability'. To them, he was a man like anyone else.

And to Miley, that was a dream come true.

2

ONE DAY TOWARDS THE END OF THAT YEAR THE Northern Lights turned blood red.

Miley sat on the tiny balcony outside the flat he shared with Tuntuk, wrapped up in his furs, a cup of black tea clutched in his hands, watching the strange phenomenon. He had seen the aurora many times since coming to the ice, and though this was different from the usual display, he thought little of it.

Two days later, though, he was hunting with his friend Ummpo, a squat, stoic young man who said little but meant every word. Through his binoculars Miley spotted a female seal two hundred yards ahead of them. He motioned in the direction, and Ummpo, who was a skilled marksman, trained his telescopic sight on the target. The rifle shot sounded as if reality itself had been punctured, so deep was the silence out on the snow plain. Miley saw the explosion of red as the bullet struck the animal just below the base of its skull. He gave the thumbs up to signify a kill, and the two hauled themselves up and began to trudge towards their reward through the powdery, freshly fallen snow.

When they got to the mound of white fur, now speckled with scarlet, they saw that it was, indeed, a female, and that she had been in the process of giving birth to a pup – the youngster was half out of her, and was in breach, the tail flippers protruding from the birthing canal. Unconcerned, Ummpo grasped the baby by the tail and hauled it out – pup or not, it was protein, and hard won. Miley was not paying attention: he was putting his binoculars back in their case, and hearing his hunting partner gasp, he looked up, puzzled. His friend had tossed the seal pup away and was standing back, aghast.

The tiny animal was already dead, but that was not what had upset the Inuit. The baby seal had two heads.

'Leave 'em both,' he said, stalking away in disgust.

'Why?' Miley asked, genuinely perplexed.

'That's bad karma right there,' Ummpo said without looking back.

'It looks like dinner to me,' Miley muttered.

'Let the polar bears have it,' Ummpo said tersely. 'Come on. This place bad for hunting. I know a better one.'

It took them three hours to shoot a much smaller seal.

3

MILEY WENT TO THE COMMUNITY CENTRE FOR
breakfast a fortnight later to find a crowd gathered around
the carcass of a musk ox, which was stretched on a tarp in
the middle of the hall. These strange-looking animals, which
resembled long-haired bison with unfeasibly large heads and
huge curved horns, were a major source of food and furs for
the tribal people. They were usually a dark, russet brown
colour. This one was pure white.

Many of those gathered were speaking in hushed voices,
and Miley could see from their expressions and body language
that here was more ill luck. Something dark seemed to be
stalking the Inughuit.

Tuntuk was speaking quietly with Showashar, the tribe's
shaman. He motioned with his head at Miley, and the three
men walked out into the dim sunlight. 'Bad omens,' Tuntuk
said without preamble. 'Something wrong. Showashar says
this about you.'

Miley raised an eyebrow. 'I don't understand, Father.'

'Evil things are happening across the sea,' Showashar said, taking a bottle of cheap whiskey from the inside pocket of his parka and helping himself to a deep gulp. 'There is bad trouble, and you are needed. I have been told in a dream.'

Miley shook his head. 'I made a promise to my Inuit father,' he said. 'My place is here.'

'Your Irish family needs you. There is work for you to do. The spirits tell me of much weeping and pain and only you can help.'

'My Inuk family needs me too. There is always tears and anger across the sea – my work is on the snow with the ice people. I am staying here.'

And he walked away, leaving Tuntuk and Showashar gazing after him.

Showashar's dream

He'd had the sight since he was a small child.

His mother said his grandfather had it too, and his grandfather before him. It was, she said, a great gift.

Why, then, did Showashar hate it so much? Perhaps it was because it never seemed to bring him good news. He never woke from a dream in which the tribe's hunters returned with a bumper catch of fish, or where the government granted them more land. He never received messages from the other side about a joyous birth or a fortunate wedding.

It was always death. Always destruction.

When he was a boy the ghosts would trouble him even during the day. As he walked across the ice with his mother they would be watching him from snowbanks – the spirits of those who had lost their lives to the cold over the countless years.

This terrified him because he did not know how to make them go away, so he would hide behind his mother's broad back and close his eyes and hope they would leave him alone. Mostly they did, but sometimes one of them would have a message, something he was supposed to tell the living.

This, his mother informed him, was his duty.

When he was older he learned that drinking dulled the gift. It made the shapes of the dead less coherent, and if he drank enough, he barely dreamed at all.

The dreams, you see, were the worst. When he was awake he could ignore the voices, but in his dreams he was trapped – they could find him easily, and show him things. Dark and foul things.

It was in a dream that the old man came to him.

In the Inuit culture, living to be old is a blessing. In a climate that threatened to take your life at any moment, to live to be old meant you were wise and had a lot to share with your community. Your knowledge and skills meant others could live.

Yet this creature was not a being of life. Showashar knew instinctively that he was a being whose every breath was spent on death.

In his dream he saw a place he had never been before – a land of rock and sand and heat. Like an eagle he flew low over the desert, like a skua over the ocean waves, skimming the surface as if searching for something.

His soul flew here and there, and suddenly he found what he was seeking – walking over the cracked and parched earth was the man Showashar's people called Mighty Warrior: the policeman, David Dunnigan. He was dressed in light green trousers and a rough shirt, and his hair was cut very short and flecked through with grey.

It had only been a little over a year since the shaman had seen him, but that time had taken its toll on the detective. He looked tired and worn. Hovering above, Showashar saw that the criminologist was making his way towards a walled compound that was about a mile distant.

The Inuit zoomed ahead and saw that the compound was heavily guarded: many men and women with automatic weapons patrolled the yard. Something drew him to a window on the ground floor of a low building, and he passed through like mist. There, in the centre of a vast room, attached to many machines, lay a skeletal figure, a dried shell of a body with eyes that spoke of hatred and malice. Those eyes – there was an evil intelligence at work in them that was horrifying to behold.

No words were spoken, but the shaman knew the creature's name: he was called Frobisher.

As Showashar became aware of the dying man, so this being turned its gaze upon him. In an instant, the shaman saw worlds of pain and suffering and torment, and he knew that this was an evil of great artifice and guile, and that Dunnigan did not have the power to vanquish it.

The only thing that could overcome this creature's wrath was someone whose heart was open and warm and free from hate.

As his consciousness fled back to his sleeping body, Showashar knew that the one person who could help Dunnigan defeat this terrible creature was Miley Timoney.

4

LATER THAT NIGHT MILEY TALKED TO TUNTUK, who had taken him as his son, about why he felt so strongly. 'At home, people didn't see me as a real person, father. For many years I wasn't permitted to live freely. I couldn't work or drive a car or be who I wanted to be.'

Tuntuk sat on the sagging, ragged couch in the living room of their cluttered flat on the reservation, land the Greenland government had granted to the tribe, mainly because no one else wanted it. 'How they stop you being the man you want to be?'

'My parents gave me to the state when I was very young. I was locked away in institutions.'

Tuntuk lit a hand-rolled cigarette and offered the tobacco pouch to Miley, who shook his head. His adoptive father always offered him a smoke, even though he always refused;

it was considered disrespectful and selfish not to offer – a person could always change their mind, after all.

'But you come to my country with the Mighty Warrior – you his friend. You his ... his captain, yes?'

'Yes,' he answered after pondering for several long moments. 'Davey was ... *is* my friend. He got me out of those institutions and helped me to make a life for myself.'

'He see you as a real person?'

Miley thought about that. 'Yes. I believe he did.'

'So not all the people from your home blind, then.'

'No. But most of them are.'

Tuntuk asked: 'All these other people who not see – they your friends?'

'No. I didn't have that many friends.'

'They people you give a damn about?'

'Not really, no.'

Tuntuk looked at him directly, a predominately toothless smile spreading across his walnut-brown face. 'Why you care what they think, then?'

Miley laughed, but with little humour. 'I couldn't give a toss what most people make of me,' he said. 'But don't you see, Father – my *parents* gave me up. My own mother couldn't bear to look at me. I wish I could say that doesn't matter, but I'd be lying. It does.'

The old chieftain sighed and, reaching over, took Miley's hand. 'Wherever you be – in Dublin, on the ice, under the ocean or on the moon – *I* am your father and the Inughuit are your people. We love you and we hold you in our hearts. That never, ever change. We honour you always, every day. Understand?'

Miley nodded, tears streaming down his face. 'I understand.'

Tuntuk squeezed his hand and offered him the tobacco.
Laughing despite himself, Miley shook his head.

'All the more for me, then,' Tuntuk chuckled. 'Wanna watch *Star Trek*?'

'Yes please.'

So they did.

5

BEFORE GOING TO BED THAT NIGHT MILEY DUG
out his smartphone, which he had felt little desire to use since
making Greenland his home, and plugged in the charger.
The following morning he switched it on and sent Dunnigan
a text. Knowing how reticent the criminologist could be, he
copied it to Diane (Dunnigan's estranged partner) and their
friend Father Bill also:

> *Sorry it's been so long. How r u? Let me know things are ok. Life is*
> *good here. Best, Miley.*

He sat and gazed at the phone for a while before realising it
was the middle of the night in Ireland, and that it would most
likely be many hours before he received a response. He put
the phone in the drawer of his bedside locker and went to get
breakfast.

*

Later that day Tuntuk asked him to make the ninety-minute journey in to Faringen to pick up some books for the reservation's schoolhouse. As usual when someone was making a trip to the nearest town, many members of the tribe had demands for one thing or another (coffee, whiskey, oatmeal, sugar and a bundle of old newspapers from the convenience store, which the proprietor kept for Kumuqq, the tribe's news junkie). Miley fuelled up one of the snowmobiles and, the money safely stowed in a sealskin wallet, headed for what he no longer thought of as civilisation.

*

It was two months since he had been in Faringen, its single rutted and pitted street lined with mismatched, weathered buildings. The town's convenience store, which was really a small supermarket that sold everything from snow shovels to tins of beans, would provide the bulk of the items he had on his list, so he visited there first.

The store had three aisles of shelves loaded with goods arranged in no order Miley could ever discern – clothes pegs sat beside plastic bottles of vegetable oil, salted fish shared space with black rubbish bags.

He was perusing the magazine rack, hoping to find an old *X-Men* comic (there were usually two or three out-of-date Marvel issues to be had), when the door to the shop opened and two men in stained overalls came in. Miley didn't recognise them, but he knew from the aroma that they worked at the fish-processing plant and were probably off shift just long enough to have visited the bar at the hotel. He returned to his comic book while one of them went to the back of the store and picked up some cans of Heineken, while the other barged past him, reaching for a copy of *Guns and Ammo*.

'Get out of my fuckin' way, dumbo,' the man said, thumping him with his shoulder on the way to the cash register.

Miley felt his heart drop. His initial response (one that was deeply ingrained) was to ignore the comment and try to shrink in upon himself, all the better to draw no further negative attention. But this time, the shame was rapidly replaced by anger. It was a long time since he'd had to face this kind of abuse, and he was damned if he was going to just stand there and take it. He'd spent far too many years afraid to speak up.

Not anymore.

'I wasn't *in* your way, asshole,' he said slowly and clearly to the reeking plant worker, who was staggering drunkenly off to pay for his periodical.

'I must be hearin' things,' the vile man slurred, turning on his heel to face Miley, which caused him to wobble dangerously. ''Cause I was sure I just heard you call me an asshole.'

Miley sighed and put his comic down. 'Your hearing is fine, although your manners could use some work.'

He heard the tread of the other worker behind him, and almost instinctively slid sideways, avoiding the clumsy blow that was directed at his head. The man tried to lunge at him again, but he was off-balance, and the second punch went far wide and he crashed into a shelf loaded with bags of dog food.

Glima is a martial art developed by the Vikings during the heyday of their pillaging, and had been passed on to the Inuit when the Norsemen came in contact with them at some point in the Middle Ages. A mode of hand-to-hand combat, it is about using your attacker's momentum against him, and was intended as a last resort for warriors who lost their swords in the heat of battle. Tuntuk was something of an expert, and he drilled Miley for an hour every day in the various forms and routines of the discipline. Some of it must have sunk in, Miley mused, as he straightened up in time for the man who had insulted him to aim a kick at his mid-section, which he easily caught, twisting the leg hard to the left. The thug howled and pinwheeled with his arms, trying (and failing) to remain upright. Miley shoved, and sent him over flat onto his back.

The sound of a shell being jacked into a shotgun chamber brought them all to their senses.

'Get out,' Roger, the store-keeper said, levelling a sawn-off barrel at the trio.

Miley brushed himself down and stepped aside. 'You heard him,' he said to the two prone figures. 'Out you go.'

'Not them, boy,' Roger said. 'You. Get your handicapped ass out of my shop and don't fucking come back, d'ye hear?'

'But I've … I've got a list for the res—'

'I said get out!'

Feeling as if he had received a beating rather than avoided one, Miley ran from the store. He did not stop at the library to pick up the books for the school, just leapt aboard the snowmobile and pointed it towards the horizon. Tears froze on his cheeks as he drove, but there was no one to see them or hear his cries of anger and shame.

6

IT WAS DARK BY THE TIME HE ARRIVED BACK ON the reservation, and he was relieved to find that Tuntuk was not home. He went straight to his room and closed the door.

He had been a fool to think he could hide from who he was. He might be able to stay on the res for months at a time, but he would eventually have to go into Faringen, or even into Uummanaq, the closest city, and then reality would just be waiting for him.

He had been lulled into an illusion.

He lay on his bed and closed his eyes. He may have slept, he wasn't sure, but he was roused from oblivion by a buzzing coming from his bedside locker. For a second he didn't know what it was, but then he remembered the phone, and pulling open the drawer, he found he had a text message.

*

When Tuntuk arrived home from the community centre two hours later, pleasantly drunk from the local hooch they served occasionally, he found Miley sitting in the living room, a bag at his feet.

'I have to go home,' the young man said.

Tuntuk nodded. 'I know,' he said.

Part Two

DUE PROCESS

Gina Dunnigan-Carlton

She grappled with her anger now on a daily basis.

She had never blamed her brother for the loss of her daughter eighteen years ago, when the child had been taken off the street when she was supposed to be in his care. Gina knew enough about the world to understand that sometimes bad things happen to good people, and she grieved and raged and got on with her life, trying to find a way to reshape her world without the little girl who had been at the centre of it.

Part of that process meant leaving behind things that reminded her of what she had lost, and one of those things had been Davey, the twin who had more or less raised her, finding, in his clumsy, awkward way, an ability to give her the love and nurturing her emotionally neglectful parents seemed unable (or unwilling) to provide.

It had hurt her to do it, but she knew beyond all doubt that it was necessary. Davey had always treated Beth as a surrogate daughter, and she, in turn, had doted on her wonderful uncle. They had shared a rapport no one else could match. For Gina to survive without going insane, Davey had to go, for a while at least. She and her husband had moved to London, where they found jobs and lost one another.

When she finally came back to Ireland, she found her brother a changed man, a shadow of what he once was. The search for Beth had eaten him up. Everyone else and everything else, even the job he so adored, had been subsumed by his crusade to find out what had happened to her.

But then, beyond all hope, he had found her: damaged and traumatised, but alive. They could be a family again.

Except, somehow, they couldn't.

The horrors she had experienced wouldn't allow Beth to let anyone else in – anyone except her uncle, who seemed to be able to connect with her on a level (and Gina did not believe it was a healthy level) she could somehow understand and tolerate.

And now, after finding her little girl all these years later, it was as if she had lost her all over again. She had always believed that, once he had discovered Beth's fate, her brother would be finished with his quest and would try to rebuild his life. But this had not been the case. Somehow, during the chase, he had started to draw evil men to himself like fat, bloated moths to a flame. He had spent so long in their world, he had become part of it.

And Beth seemed comfortable and content in that shadow world with him.

Davey had gone to England to hunt a monster, and Beth went chasing after him. And now Gina knew, in an instinctive part of herself, that something awful had happened. She sat at the window in her kitchen, looking out at her empty garden, her mobile phone in her hand, waiting for it to ring.

Waiting to hear what had become of her child.

The child that had never really come back to her.

1

THE POLICE STATION AT HAWICK WAS LARGER than David Dunnigan had expected and busier than he would have thought too, for mid-morning. They brought his niece, Beth, in ahead of them and placed her in a holding cell while he and Diane Robinson were put in what was euphemistically called a 'family room', really little more than a large closet with a couch and tea and coffee-making facilities. It was windowless and grim and Dunnigan found it more than a little claustrophobic.

A female officer called Lisburn sat with them. She was a stocky woman with a low centre of gravity, her curly red hair tied into a loose bun, and she did her best to make small talk. Diane politely responded, while the criminologist paced the tiny space, glowering at the walls.

'I would like to see Beth, please,' Dunnigan said before half an hour had passed.

'That's not possible just at the minute,' Lisburn replied.

She spoke with a gentle Scots burr – Hawick sits about fifteen miles inside the Scots border.

'Why not?'

'The detectives will need to question her, don't you think?'

'My niece is a vulnerable individual. She is currently engaged in an intensive course of therapeutic treatment, and has just been through an abduction that can only have been deeply traumatic. As I understand it, she is entitled to an accompanying person.'

'I'll pass that information on to my sergeant, and I'm sure they'll bring in a psychiatrist or someone to have her assessed. But Elizabeth is here due to a very serious charge. For now, let the investigators do their work. She's quite safe.'

'I am a consultant with the Irish National Bureau of Criminal Investigation,' Dunnigan continued, refusing to make eye contact with the officer. 'I would think that inter-agency courtesy should come into play. She is my niece, after all ...'

'Which is another reason we need to tread carefully. You can't properly represent her as an advocate – you're too emotionally involved.'

'I've just assisted the London Metropolitan Police in solving a significant cold case.'

'Which we appreciate very much.'

'So when can I see her?'

'Mr Dunnigan, your niece is implicated in the murder of a police detective. I would love to be able to tell you that we can waive the formalities, but I just can't. Please sit tight and I'm sure you'll be able to spend some time with her in due course.'

Dunnigan had come to the UK as part of an investigation

into a series of murders committed by a shadowy figure known as Mother Joan, believed by many to be simply an online ghost story, and Beth, who was having some trouble readjusting since being rescued from captivity, had followed him.

Beth had been abducted when she was four years old. She and Dunnigan, who had doted on her as if she was his daughter rather than his niece, had been Christmas shopping, and she had been snatched from the street right under his nose. He had later learned that the child had been kidnapped to order by an organisation run by the criminal Ernest Frobisher. Dunnigan had been instrumental in shutting his operation down, a fact that Frobisher and his associate, the twisted psychiatrist Phillipe Ressler, were severely agitated about.

While in the UK Dunnigan found himself working with a member of the London Metropolitan Force, Detective Inspector Alfie Jones, who had been involved in the case since the 1980s. They had tracked the killer to Kielder Forest in Northumberland, where Jones had been injured during a confrontation between Dunnigan, the terrifying Mother Joan, and a Ukrainian gang who bore a grudge against the Irish criminologist.

Beth had become quite friendly with Detective Jones, and was visiting him in hospital when he had been murdered: Dunnigan and Diane had walked in to his room to find the place drenched in blood while Beth sat beside his bed, clutching the same type of hunting knife that had been used by the serial killer they had come to England to find.

Which, needless to say, did not look good for Dunnigan's niece.

The criminologist took a breath to retaliate, but Diane

placed a hand on his shoulder. 'Constable Lisburn is doing her best, Davey. Why don't you get some air? I'll stay here in case we're called.'

'Don't leave the station grounds, please,' Lisburn said as he stalked out.

As soon as he was outside the front door, Dunnigan took out his mobile phone and called his boss, Chief Superintendent Frank Tormey, a senior detective in the National Bureau of Criminal Investigation (Ireland's equivalent of the FBI).

'Chief, I'm in trouble.'

A heavy sigh came down the line. 'I've been informed,' Tormey said in a voice that sounded tired and strained. 'There's a shitstorm of epic proportions happening over here.'

'I'm sorry, boss. I ... I wish I could tell you things are under control, but they're really not.'

'The minister has asked me to travel over with a lawyer to see if we can straighten things out.'

'Thanks, boss.'

'Don't thank me yet. I don't know how much of a difference we'll be able to make.'

'I understand.'

'I'm not sure you do. Someone is going to have to go down for this, and I am genuinely afraid that wee girl is being chosen as the fucking sacrificial lamb by people whose paygrades are so far above mine I get a nosebleed even thinking about them.'

The line fell silent.

'You still there?' Tormey asked after several long seconds had passed.

'Yes, boss.'

'Did you hear what I just said?'

'I did.'

'They're trying to lay all this at Beth's feet.'

'I know.'

'I'm trying to tell you that I don't know how we're going to get her out of it.'

Dunnigan paused for a second, gazing around the carpark of the police station, feeling as far away from home and safety as he had ever been. 'That's the thing, boss.'

'What is?'

'I don't know that she *should* be got out of it.'

'What are you telling me, Davey?'

'I'm saying that I think it is perfectly possible Beth killed Detective Jones.'

And then they both sat in silence, on separate ends of the phone line, in different countries, as clouds gathered overhead and the shadows drew in.

Beth Carlton

She felt as if everything was falling asunder and she didn't know what to do about it.

It was like she couldn't trust her own memory. She had replayed the events in that room in the hospital a hundred times, but still she was none the wiser. For all the world it seemed that someone had hit a switch and put her into sleeper mode, and when she powered on again, a terrible thing had happened.

And now she was afraid. Afraid they would take her away from her family and friends, afraid that she would become a prisoner all over again, afraid that the life she had tried so desperately to rebuild since Davey had found her and brought her home would be torn away before she had even really begun to live it.

She was used to being strong – on the outside, at least. She had long ago learned the art of keeping her raw emotions inside, bottling up the pain and the anguish that had been her companions since the day the Yellow Man had plucked her from the street. She had taught herself all kinds of tricks to remove her essential self from whatever horrors were going on around her, taking journeys in her mind to the fantastical places her uncle had introduced her to in the countless storybooks and films and TV shows they had shared before she was taken. She found her imagination a powerful tool, and somehow, naturally, her mind had begun to wall off the worst of the experiences she was forced to endure.

When her memory did this, it was as if the awful stuff had never happened. And that helped her to function, to continue surviving.

Her therapist told her this was called 'repression', and had advised that it wasn't healthy.

Beth had laughed at that. What could possibly be healthy about dwelling on moments of utter debasement and despair? Repression, she firmly believed, was her friend.

But had it now turned on her and become an enemy?

As she sat in the interview room, Beth fought a rising panic and wiped tears from her eyes. She knew Davey and Diane were just outside, and she had no doubt her mother would come – probably Superintendent Tormey too.

But she had never felt so alone.

She decided to let the tears come, and cried bitterly and noisily for a while, placing her head on the table and simply letting go.

When she could cry no more, she sat up, straightened her clothes and dried her eyes, and made a vow that from that moment on, she would be strong.

And she would do her very best to remember. Whatever horrors those memories might bring. Even if they told her she had done what they seemed to think she did.

2

IT WAS EIGHT O'CLOCK THAT NIGHT BEFORE Dunnigan and Diane were brought into an interview room that was virtually identical to the ones Dunnigan used in Garda HQ in Harcourt Street in Dublin. A metal table that had years of graffiti scratched into its surface dominated the space, microphones protected by small cages of metallic mesh embedded in its structure to record conversations that may be used as evidence at a later date.

Beth was sitting on a straight-backed chair that was bolted to the floor.

Dunnigan's niece was twenty-three years old. Like her uncle, she was tall, slim and had long dark hair, which she currently had tied back in a ponytail. Her face, angular and intelligent, was peaked with exhaustion and unhappiness. A cardboard cup of tea, which appeared to be untouched, sat at her elbow.

The criminologist noted that Beth was dressed in a loose-fitting tracksuit: the jeans, t-shirt and jacket she had been wearing when they got to the station had been taken as evidence, soaked as they were in the blood of the man whose murder Beth was implicated in.

'How are they treating you?' Diane asked, reaching over and taking one of the girl's hands in hers.

'Fine,' Beth said, and her voice seemed to be teetering on the edge of tears. 'They've been nice, really. So far it's been good cop/good cop, but I know that can't last.'

'Can you tell us anything about what happened?' Dunnigan asked gently.

'Nothing I haven't told you and them already.'

'I know this is horrible, but can you try and tell us again? This is what I do, and I'm really good at it. There could be something you've missed, or noticed but didn't know was important. Just go through it for me one more time, and then I promise we'll talk about something else.'

Beth rubbed her eyes with the heels of her hands, and sprawled back low in the chair. 'I was sitting in the hospital room, chatting to Alfie – Inspector Jones. We were having a nice time – he was sharing some ice-cream with me.'

'Did Alfie maybe do something to upset you?' Diane prompted. 'He may well not have meant to, but he could have made a joke that triggered you …'

'I don't know …' Beth had her eyes scrunched shut, as if the act of remembering hurt her. 'I remember we were talking about the *Toy Story* movies – he was saying I should really see the third one of them, he said he liked it best. And then—'

They waited expectantly.

'Go on,' Dunnigan urged.

'I seem to have a memory of the door opening, but I can't be sure. Then it's like everything started spinning and I felt a bit ill, and when that stopped, I was still in my seat, but Alfie was ... his throat was wide open and there was blood everywhere and I had that big knife. It's *her* knife, isn't it?'

'Mother Joan's? Yes, I think it is,' Dunnigan said. 'Her name is really Hester Kitt and I think she is a very broken and very unhappy woman. Though a very dangerous one, for all that.'

'What I don't understand,' Beth said, 'is that Alfie told me she could have killed him in the woods, but that she didn't. He said it was like she decided to spare him. So why murder him now? And why did she leave the knife with me?'

'Do you think that's what happened?' Dunnigan asked. 'Hester Kitt did this?'

'No,' Beth sighed. 'I mean ... I'm not sure but ... I just don't know anymore.'

'When we came in, you had the knife in your hand and you were covered in blood,' Diane said. 'Can you remember what you did when you came out of that dizzy spell you told us about?'

Beth swallowed, as if the memory was a pill she had to force down. 'I didn't know where I was, at first, and I looked around and for a moment I thought I was still asleep, because the room looked so different – there was red on the walls and the ceiling and the floor. Then I saw Inspector Jones on the bed, and I saw the wound in his neck, and at that stage there was still a spray of blood coming out, kind of in puffs, like his heart was still beating and with each beat another cloud would come.'

Her voice cracked. 'I reached over to cover the cut, but it

was too big – I could see the bones in his neck and I tried to lift up his head to make it easier, but it was no good. I think I got blood all over me when I did that. Then I felt something resting on my knees and I looked down and it was the knife. I don't know why I picked it up, I just did. It was stupid, you don't have to tell me.'

'No one is saying you're stupid, Beth,' Dunnigan said, and he heard the resignation in his voice.

'Davey,' Beth said.

'Yes?'

'I … I liked Alfie very much.'

'I know you did, Beth.'

'But that doesn't mean I didn't hurt him.'

Dunnigan and Diane exchanged glances.

'I get confused, sometimes, and I get angry and when that happens I *want* to hurt the people I love. I don't know why that is and I wish it wasn't so, but it's the truth.'

'Are you trying to tell us you believe you killed DI Jones?'

'No.' She looked terrified, but the girl's voice was firm. 'But I don't fully believe I didn't.'

And they both knew she was telling the truth. Because they thought the same thing.

3

BETH SAID SHE WAS TIRED AND ASKED IF SHE might lie down.

Lisburn said they would continue interviewing her in the morning, and brought the girl to a cell where a bed had been made up. Before closing the door she said, 'I'm not locking it, because you're not under arrest. I'll be at the desk down the hall if you need me.'

Beth nodded and was asleep within two minutes.

Dunnigan and Diane went back to the family room, and the criminologist busied himself making tea. 'You don't need to stay,' he said when they were side by side on the couch. 'Go back to the hotel and get some rest.'

'You know I'm not going to do that,' Diane said. 'So stop being an arse and just let me be here for you both, okay?'

Dunnigan and Diane had been a couple (briefly) after he came to the Widow's Quay Homeless Project, as part of a missing persons case involving homeless people. Father Bill had taken him under his wing, and he soon started volunteering at the Project, where Diane, a former counsellor and medic with the Irish Army Ranger Wing, worked as a receptionist and therapist.

The two had begun a tentative relationship, but the criminologist's ruthless dedication to his work and to finding Beth made it impossible for them to remain as anything other than friends. When Dunnigan did finally rescue his niece from a brothel in Galway, Diane had done her best to support him and the girl as they began to rebuild their lives. While the two were no longer an item, they remained close.

'What are we going to do?' she asked him after a while.

'I don't know,' he said, deadpan.

'Our girl half believes she did it.'

'Yes.'

'Why didn't you tell her she's wrong?'

Dunnigan sipped his tea and thought for a moment. 'Why didn't you?' he shot back.

Diane blinked. 'Tormey's coming?' she said, changing the subject. 'With a lawyer. Maybe they'll know what we should do.'

'I really hope so,' Dunnigan said. 'But I also agree that someone has to pay for this. Jones was a good man and, my friend, no matter who killed him, he's dead because he tried to help me.'

They fell asleep with their half-drunk mugs of tea in their hands, exhaustion finally catching up with them. Mercifully, neither of them dreamed.

4

DETECTIVE CHIEF SUPERINTENDENT FRANK Tormey arrived the following lunch time with a sharp-faced female barrister named Jacqueline Hardiman who was on retainer with the Department of Justice and who looked as though there was a bad smell permanently wafting just below her nostrils.

Tormey was tall and lean. He wore a rumpled grey suit, his greying hair trimmed to a functional crew-cut. With his thick, bushy moustache and slow, purposeful speech it seemed like he had stepped straight off the page of a cowboy novel by Louis L'Amour. After they had spoken to the officer in charge, Hardiman spent an hour reviewing the evidence, at which point they gathered in a meeting room at the rear of the station.

'What this all boils down to is whether or not Beth Carlton murdered Detective Inspector Robert Jones,' the barrister said, her hands steepled in front of her as she spoke. 'In that regard we have some points that go in our favour and some that very much do not. In fact, as things currently stand, I would say they are evenly weighted.'

'Jacqueline, could you quit grandstanding and tell us if you can get the wee girl off?' Tormey said, looking supremely bored.

'My job coming to this god-forsaken part of the world is to prevent a diplomatic incident,' Hardiman said glibly. 'The minister does not like the idea of members of his most decorated police force getting involved in complex and confusing murders concerning members of their family. I *will* resolve things satisfactorily, one way or another.'

'That does not make me feel any better,' Tormey drawled.

'The case hangs on a conflict of evidence,' Hardiman continued. 'Ms Robinson and Mr Dunnigan claim to have seen Dr Phillipe Ressler, a known associate of the criminal Ernest Frobisher and a fugitive from several international police forces. His presence in the vicinity of a violent death would, in itself, wrap the whole thing up, but for one rather inconvenient point.'

'Which is?' Dunnigan asked.

'We have no concrete evidence he was there, only your testimony. The CCTV systems in the hospital appear to have malfunctioned for a period of about fifteen minutes around the time DI Jones was murdered.'

'All of them?' Tormey spluttered.

'Yes. It looks like someone re-routed the power away from the camera system. This means there is no footage of anyone entering, leaving, or moving about the hospital for a little over a quarter of an hour yesterday.'

'We saw Ressler,' Dunnigan snapped. 'He was dressed in hospital scrubs that looked to be splattered with blood. Surely our sworn affidavits would hold some sway. I am a member of the Bureau and Diane is a former member of the defence forces.'

'Which would be wonderful but for some extenuating circumstances,' Hardiman said. 'The fact that you are a member of the accused's family, and Ms Robinson here used to be in a sexual relationship with you. If we add to that the fact that she has acted as a casual therapist and occasional babysitter for Beth since you found her in some kind of Eastern European knocking shop, we are chipping away at the validity of your evidence quite profoundly.'

'You're saying our statements aren't worth the paper they're written on,' Diane said wearily.

'I would never be so dismissive,' Hardiman said. 'But yeah, kinda. What does go in your favour is the fact that the cameras malfunctioned. It's so convenient it lends credence to your story.'

'Unless you propose that Davey here did it himself to allow Beth to act unimpeded,' Tormey said.

'Doesn't make sense,' Hardiman retorted. 'Beth was already in the hospital, and there is footage of her waiting outside DI Jones's room. If you give me time I'm sure I could construct an argument for Dunnigan sabotaging the system, but it would be a tenuous one.'

'So that works for us,' Dunnigan said. 'What else have we got?'

'Your niece is simply not helping herself,' the barrister went on. 'She has not said she did it, but she hasn't exactly said she didn't, either. I need her to be *much* more proactive in her own defence. I am looking for absolute certainty: *I did not murder my good friend, DI Alfie Jones!* Right now all I've got to work with is a frightened, slightly crazy-looking young girl with a history of trauma and a record of mental illness. She is not a sympathetic figure.'

'Beth was abducted as a child and forced into slavery,' Dunnigan said through gritted teeth. 'How much more sympathetic can a person be?'

'Oh, a hell of a lot. Ms Robinson, I need you to go and get her some proper clothes. Former prostitutes in tracksuits don't play well on the stand. If this goes to court I want her to seem civilised and conservative. Shop with that in mind, okay?'

Diane just looked at Hardiman, seemingly having lost the power of speech.

'And we haven't even got to the forensic stuff yet. The blade used to virtually decapitate DI Jones was a vintage leuku knife, a woodsman's tool commonly used as a survivalist weapon in mainland Europe. I see from my notes that this is the signature weapon used by a serial killer Mr Dunnigan came to the UK to track down, a Mother Joan. You're with me so far, Mr Dunnigan?'

'I'm doing my best to keep up,' Dunnigan seethed.

'Excellent. Now, am I right in my understanding that Beth Carlton had some previous dealings with this Mother Joan character, because you decided to take her with you while you investigated a possible murder she committed in Cork?'

'Yes.'

'This is usual practice among your detectives, is it, Chief Superintendent Tormey, to bring their relatives along as they review homicides?'

'It is not,' Tormey said, looking at the barrister with a hard stare.

'Well, it seems to be business as usual for Mr Dunnigan, because here he is in foggy London town, and he has his niece with him again. This time she manages to be abducted – for a *second time*, which, quite frankly beggars belief – and he abandons the case and hightails it up north to find her. While in the scenic county of Northumberland he and the lovely Beth tangle with Mother Joan again, and while they're at it wipe out an entire gang of mobsters.'

She looked at Dunnigan and gave him a wry smile. 'That's twice you and Beth had dealings with this rather nasty serial killer, and twice you walked away unharmed. A cynical mind might just rationalise that you and she had developed an understanding. A *relationship*.'

'What are you insinuating?' Dunnigan snapped.

'Mr Dunnigan, if I were insinuating, I would be a lot more oblique. I just outright told you that it looks as if you and Beth were in league with this Mother Joan character, who somehow managed to escape justice despite being within your grasp countless times. But the detective who dedicated the last two decades of his life to hunting her ends up dead, his throat cut by her blade. Which is found in your niece's hand. Can I be any more up front than that?'

'I thought you were here to help us,' Dunnigan said, exasperated by now.

'I am. But I need you to see how it looks and how a prosecuting attorney will present the facts. Mother Joan is a suspect, and police are combing the countryside looking for her, but that does not take any of the focus away from Beth. Surely you can you see how damning it seems?'

'Of course I can.'

'And it gets worse. Forensics have had a close look at the knife. They pulled three sets of prints from it.'

'Okay,' Dunnigan said, dreading what he was about to hear.

'The first set belongs to Hester Kitt, whom I believe is your old friend Mother Joan.'

'Yes,' Dunnigan agreed. 'You said there were three.'

'The next belongs to DI Jones, and looks as if they're from defensive movements. Basically, he tried to grab the knife as it came at him. There are slash marks on both his hands, so that tallies.'

'And the third is Beth,' Diane said.

'Yes. On the blade and on the handle. But there's one more thing.'

'What?'

'The lab took some cloth fibres from the strip of leather that winds around the grip. They were trapped under the binding. The boffins managed to find a match to these strands without having to look very hard at all.'

'Go on,' Tormey said. 'Put us out of our misery.'

'They come from the pocket of Beth's parka jacket,' Hardiman said. 'Which makes it look for all the world like she brought the knife in with her.'

Tormey, Dunnigan and Diane gazed at one another, aghast.

'Now that doesn't prove anything,' Hardiman said, seeing the shock on their faces. 'I'm going to tie them up with every kind of legal barrier and dirty trick I can bring into play. Our case hinges on that missing fifteen minutes of CCTV tape and the fact that you both saw Phillipe Ressler. I have an army of interns flying in tomorrow to interview everyone we can confirm as being in the hospital yesterday, to see if any of them can testify to Ressler's presence too.'

'It's all circumstantial,' Dunnigan said. 'No one saw Beth kill him.'

'No, but we have a murder weapon – it's not quite a smoking gun, but it's not far off.'

'There's no motive,' Diane said. 'Beth loved Alfie.'

'But Mother Joan, who they will argue Beth was in thrall to, had a powerful motive to kill him. I'm not going to sugarcoat it, people. We have a fight on our hands.'

'They can't hold her any longer,' Dunnigan said. 'They need to charge her or let her go.'

'I'll put it to them,' Hardiman said. 'But you better be prepared: they might just call your bluff and arrest her, and where are we then?'

'We're fucked, that's where we are,' Tormey said.

And they all knew he was right.

5

AFTER SOME TOING AND FROING, THEY DECIDED to release Beth.

'We are letting her go under your supervision and recognisance,' Lisburn told Dunnigan and Tormey. 'I am going to need her to hand over her passport, and I would appreciate it if you stayed locally and kept us abreast of your movements. Beth is part of an ongoing investigation, and we will most certainly want to talk to her again. Probably sooner rather than later.'

'She came here using a driving licence,' Dunnigan said, taking the document from Beth's bag and passing it over. 'She doesn't have a passport.'

'Probably for the best under the circumstances,' Lisburn said.

Dunnigan ignored the comment, and went to get his niece.

*

They had rooms in a Travelodge on the outskirts of Kielder Forest, a forty-minute drive away, and the criminologist thought he had never been so happy to see a bed, albeit a rough and not particularly comfortable one. He was taking his shoes off when there was a knock on the door.

It was Beth. 'Can I come in?'

'Of course.' He stood back and she entered with halting steps.

'How much trouble am I in?' she asked, sitting on the bed.

'The Irish government have sent a highly qualified and very able barrister to argue our case.'

'*My* case.'

'We're in this together,' Dunnigan said. 'We are a family. If they hurt one of us, they hurt all of us.'

'You haven't answered my question. How serious?'

'A man is dead. A good man. My friend, and yours too. So yes, it's serious. But the best people we could have are working on it.'

She looked up at him and he was powerfully reminded of when she was a small child. Sometimes it was as if a door opened between them and he was gazing into the past, before things had got so complicated and confused.

'Do you think I'm innocent?'

He ran his fingers through his hair and sat beside her on the bed. 'I don't think you would have ever consciously wanted to hurt DI Jones.'

'But d'you think I did it?'

He put his arm around her shoulders. 'I don't know, Beth.'

She laid her head against him. 'I don't, either. I've tried to remember – tried and tried and tried. But I just can't. Sometimes I recall how I was feeling when bad stuff happened, even if I pushed away everything else. But all I remember about being with Alfie was that we were laughing and having fun.'

He put his arm around her and hugged her tight. 'It might come back and it might not,' he said. 'I'm not an expert on how that kind of stuff works.'

They stayed pressed close to one another in silence for a long time. Then he said, 'Guess what I do know, though?'

'What?'

'It doesn't matter to me if you did it or not.'

And she believed him.

6

HE HADN'T BEEN ASLEEP MORE THAN AN HOUR when someone was knocking on his door again. He was sure it would be Beth, troubled by night terrors, but to his surprise he found Tormey standing there in his shirt sleeves, a bottle of Scotch clutched in one hand and two glasses in the other.

'We need to talk, Davey.'

'Come on in. I was only sleeping anyway.' Dunnigan went back inside, leaving the door open to admit the detective.

'Have a drink,' Tormey said, half-filling one of the glasses with the amber liquor. 'It's called Clan Fraser and it's bloody good stuff – they make it locally; you can't get it in Ireland.'

'You know I'm not much of a drinker, boss.'

'I am not fucking drinking alone tonight,' Tormey said, plonking his behind on the edge of the bed. 'Now sit down and at least pretend to keep me company.'

Dunnigan perched on the room's single chair and took the glass he was offered. 'What's wrong, boss?'

'I've just got off the phone with our legal counsel.'

'Ms Hardiman?'

'The very same.'

'How's the case going?'

'Now, that is a complicated question. You see, we are faced with a rather knotty problem: what we know to be true and what we can legally prove to be true.'

'I see. I think.'

'No one really believes Beth could have killed Jones, not on her own, anyway. The cut that finished him was so deep and was performed with such ferocity, a girl of her size and weight just couldn't have done it. The lab guys have just come back with their full report, and I have to tell you, any doubts you might have had about whether Beth delivered that blow would appear to be legitimate.'

'Well – that's *good*, surely.'

'You'd think. What they're arguing now is that Beth was in league with someone. Maybe Hester Kitt, maybe Ressler, maybe parties as yet unknown. The argument seems to be that she smuggled in the knife and lulled Jones into a false sense of security while someone bigger and stronger snuck in and did the killing.'

'So they're painting her as an accomplice.'

'Yes, they are.'

'But Hardiman can make mincemeat of that, can't she?'

'Our loyal defender is suggesting we cop a plea. Beth gives them whoever it is she was working with in exchange for the state granting her diminished responsibility due to temporary insanity. She'd have to serve a term in a psychiatric hospital, but Jacqueline says she'll get her somewhere that closely resembles Walt Disney World.'

'But she wasn't working with anyone. Ressler drugged her or hypnotised her or ... or *something*.'

'There were no detectable drugs in her system, Davey. They did a blood test – she gave them permission.'

'We can't allow this.'

'Do you remember what I said about Beth being served up as the sacrificial lamb? Well, here we are.'

Tormey drained his glass and poured another. Dunnigan had barely touched his, but he topped him up anyway.

'We cannot win,' Tormey said, 'not with the information we have. The London Met and the Home Office want their pound of flesh. Beth is going to be locked up, Davey. They're going to build a case and arrest her within the next few days. I'm sorry.'

Dunnigan, in a reflex action, took a gulp of the Scotch. It was smoky and savoury and burned his throat, but he swallowed and took another mouthful.

'What am I going to do, boss?' he asked, his eyes watering as much from the devastation he felt as the whiskey.

'Run,' Tormey said, looking into his glass. 'Take that wee girl and disappear.'

Dunnigan could scarcely believe what he was hearing. 'I don't understand.'

'We're on the border with Scotland,' Tormey said. 'It's a big country with large areas that have barely any people. Lose yourselves in it.'

'But won't you get into terrible trouble?'

'Nothing I can't handle. Listen to me: I can't sit back and watch Beth suffer any more. I don't have a fucking clue what happened in that room, but I cannot believe she had anything to do with it. I've been doing this job for a lot of years, and this feels very much like a stitch-up. We know Frobisher ran a medical company that controlled an awful lot of private psychiatric hospitals. I would have a genuine concern that placing Beth in a secure psychiatric facility would be putting her right back into their grasp. God knows what influence that man still has.'

Dunnigan felt himself getting cold – he hadn't thought that far ahead, but Tormey, practical as ever, was thinking tactically.

'Take her and get far away,' the chief superintendent continued. 'Who knows, maybe giving her some space and time will help her to remember what happened in the hospital. It can't hurt, at any rate. I'll deal with the fallout and see if I can get to the bottom of what took place. Fuck it, I've climbed as high as I'm going to in the NBCI anyway.'

'I don't know what to say.'

'Don't say anything,' Tormey said, standing up (a little unsteadily). 'Pack your gear and clear out.'

Dunnigan nodded. 'Thanks, boss.'

Tormey paused at the door, his eyes watery all of a sudden. 'You were always a fucking liability anyway,' he said gruffly. 'Look after that wee girl. I'll find you when I have things in order. In the meantime, don't get caught. Now get out of here before I change my mind.' And then he was gone.

It took Dunnigan all of five minutes to throw his few belongings into a bag. Then he went to wake Beth.

7

HALF AN HOUR LATER THEY WERE PLACING THEIR bags into the boot of the blue Vauxhall Astra he had rented from Hertz. He had paid for a week, which gave him three more days' use of the vehicle, and he figured they might abandon it somewhere along the way and then take public transport as far as they could. Or something. He hoped a more solid plan might form when he got on the road. For now, he just wanted to put some distance between the two of them and Hawick.

Dunnigan was closing the boot when he heard a familiar voice behind him. 'Where do you two think you're going?'

Diane, dressed for travel and with her own bag slung across her shoulder, was watching them ruefully.

'Away from here,' Dunnigan said, firmly. 'Now please, go back to bed and pretend you never saw us.'

'Where are you going?'

'Better you don't know. You'll have plausible deniability.'

'Do *you* know?'

'Tormey said to go somewhere unpopulated. I think he means the Highlands.'

'Really? And what do you expect to find in the Highlands? Do you know anything about the terrain? How are you going to eat? Where are you going to live?'

'I'll work that out when I get there. Beth can google it as we drive.'

'Oh for God's sake, Davey. You haven't a notion. You'll be recaptured within forty-eight hours and then not only will Beth be in trouble, you will too. Step aside. I'm coming.'

'Diane, I am not going to allow this.'

'Davey, move out of my way or I will put you on the flat of your back, and you know I can.'

Heaving a bitter sigh, Dunnigan did as he was told.

Beth clapped her hands in delight. 'Yay!' she said. 'Road trip!'

8

DIANE INSISTED ON DRIVING, WHICH IRRITATED
Dunnigan even more.

'You know I hate being a passenger,' he said. 'And you are
a terrible driver anyway.'

'Shut up, Davey,' Diane said kindly.

They had been on the road for an hour when they came to
a bridge that crossed the River Teviot. Diane pulled over and
rolled down her window. 'I'll just be a second.' She activated
the lever beside her seat to release the bonnet and got out,
taking a penknife from the pocket of her jacket. After a few
minutes of tinkering in the engine's interior she walked to
the railing of the bridge and dropped something over into the
water below, then returned to the driver's seat.

'What was that?' Beth wanted to know.

'The GPS from the sat nav. It can be used to locate us, and
we don't want that.'

'No, we don't,' Dunnigan agreed.

'Okay guys. I'm going to need your phones and any electronic devices.'

'The police took my phone,' Beth said.

'Of course they did, sweetie,' Diane said. 'Come on, Davey. Hand yours over.'

'Why?' Dunnigan asked suspiciously, pulling an old Sony from his pocket and giving it to her.

'Because you might as well be carrying a tracking device,' Diane said, and threw the handset over the railing and into the water below.

Dunnigan watched his phone disappear into the blackness. It took him a couple of beats to register what had just happened, and when the reality finally sank in a cascade of rage and bitterness crashed over him with such ferocity he found he couldn't speak. This, however, did not last. When words came, they poured out in a surge so rapid they were almost incoherent. 'I cannot believe you! I use that phone for ... for ... for so many things. Podcasts and reading and keeping dates and records and ... Diane Robinson, I did not give you permission to do that.'

'Davey?'

'I am speaking now. It is my turn.'

'Davey, give me your laptop.'

'You are not throwing my laptop away. I will not allow it. I've had it for years – I'm not giving it up.'

'Do you want to get caught, Davey? Do you want to see Beth locked up?'

He stopped, panting from his tantrum, sweat beading on his forehead and tears streaming down his cheeks. 'No. You know I don't.'

'Then I need the computer. If we take it with us, we might as well just ring Lisburn now and tell her where we are. It amounts to the same thing.'

Dunnigan got out of the car, went to the boot and took out his beloved laptop as well as an external hard drive on which he stored vast libraries of books, comics, movies, TV series – a lifetime of collected materials that had kept him company during bad times and good. He had few other possessions, and these he valued above almost everything else. Except for Beth. He reminded himself of that as he held the devices to his chest.

'You can hang on to the hard drive,' Diane said gently. 'There's no way to remotely trace it.'

Feeling a little better at this news, Dunnigan silently put the storage unit back, then walked to the railing and, without pausing, dropped the computer over. This accomplished, he sat back into the car.

'I know it hurts, but it had to be done,' Diane said.

'I don't want to talk about it,' Dunnigan replied.

They drove on into the night.

Wilfred Hubert

He first met Ernest Frobisher at a party in New York.

He had been hearing about the man for years (he was known as a ruthless operator, his financial machines devouring weaker companies and spitting them back out, stripped down and leaner than before, usually operating on a skeleton staff or else subsumed into one of his many other interests), and was curious to meet him.

The event was held in the penthouse suite of the Glasshouse Hotel, overlooking Central Park. The room was full of gorgeous women carrying trays loaded with glasses of vintage champagne, a celebrity chef was carving transparently thin slices of Iberico ham off an enormous leg, and there were mountains of beluga caviar being demolished by the already drunken captains of industry in attendance. A visit to the bathroom showed him similar mountains of cocaine on display there – all needs were catered for.

Hubert found Frobisher standing at the back of the room. In the days before the cancer took him he was tall and very thin. He always wore a three-piece pinstripe suit, a gold watch-chain running from a buttonhole to the waistcoat pocket. What little hair he had was cut very close to his skull, and was jet black.

There was about the man a palpable menace, but what struck Hubert the most was the predatory way he watched his guests. Hubert had seen a documentary once about great white sharks, and Frobisher's eyes reminded him of those giants of the deep: they were completely soulless, twin pools of hate – and hunger.

He considered not introducing himself, but thought he had better pay his respects. And he was curious. What harm could an introduction do, anyway?

'Mr Frobisher?'

Those black pools turned to survey him. He felt himself drowning, for a moment.

'Do I know you?'

Frobisher's accent was odd: he couldn't place it – it was a little bit English and a little bit Irish, as if he had spent equal amounts of time in both locales.

'I'm Wilfred Hubert. You invited me. I just wanted to say thank you.'

'One of my office bitches sent out the invites, so no need to thank me.'

'Oh. Sorry for bothering you, in that case.' He turned to go.

'You're the tech investor.'

Frobisher had heard of him, after all. He didn't know if that made him happy or scared him witless. 'Yes.'

'Let's have a chat.' With a motion of his head, he bid Hubert follow him to a small room equipped with a desk, a computer and a couple of chairs just off the main party area. As he sat down, a sallow-skinned man with fair hair and a cream-coloured suit closed the door behind them, and came to stand at Frobisher's elbow.

'You seem to have a pretty good grasp of the technology markets,' Frobisher said. 'It's an area I'm anxious to break into.'

'I can give you some tips.'

'I didn't ask for tips, Hubert. I want you to come and work for me.'

'I work for myself, Mr Frobisher. Thank you, but I'm doing fine as I am.'

'That wasn't an offer. If you earn your keep within twelve months, I'll cut you loose and you can go your own way. I *might even owe you a favour. If you don't prove a worthy employee, I might have to get cross. I promise, you wouldn't like that.'*

'Are you threatening me?'

'Yes.'

'I think I'd like to leave now.'

'Andrews, what is our friend Hubert's dirty little secret? The one he cannot afford the world to know? Everyone has one. Tell us his.'

'Mr Hubert likes violent sex with underage girls.'

'Well, Mr Hubert, aren't you the dirty, dirty little man?'

Hubert felt something very cold creep into his gut. It might have been fear and it might have been anger. It might even have been guilt. He had never been good at identifying his emotions. He was far better at pretending to be a human than actually being one. *'What do you want from me?'*

'Are you slow or something? I've already told you: come to work for me for a period of twelve months. Build my tech portfolio into something really fucking special, and then you can be on your way. Unless I need you again, which is entirely possible.'

'And if I say no?'

'Andrews here probably has pictures of you fucking a ten-year-old, and these images will find their way into the hands of the editor of one of the less reputable gossip magazines your countrymen seem to enjoy so much.'

The Yellow Man watched impassively.

'Oh, and I might have him remove one of your testicles and make you eat it. Just because you have pissed me off. Did you know you can survive an experience like that? It's very painful, but not at all lethal.'

Hubert thought he may throw up.

'*I think your options are pretty clear. Refuse me, and your life as you know it is over and you live what's left of it in disgrace with only one ball. Or come and work for me, go to a lot of parties and have all the adolescent pussy you can handle. I'll pay you well and you can do your own trading in your personal time. I think it's a pretty good deal. What do you say?*'

His life was never the same again. He hated to admit it, but after the initial shock wore off, it was way better.

9

AT SOME POINT DUNNIGAN SLEPT.

He woke several hours later to the staccato sound of Diane pulling up the handbrake. It was day, and the rather grim sight of a large rubbish skip that had once been yellow but was now mostly rust-coloured was all that could be seen through the windscreen.

'Stay here,' Diane said. 'I want to make certain we're out of range of any security cameras.' She pulled the hood of her jacket up and got out.

Dunnigan looked at the clock on the dashboard of the Vauxhall: it was 9.42 a.m. 'Where are we?' he asked Beth, who looked as if she, too, had just awoken. She was in an almost foetal position in the back, her knees pulled up to her chest and her woollen jumper stretched down to cover them, like a blanket.

'At a truck stop,' the girl responded. 'I hope she's happy the coast is clear, because I'm starving.'

Dunnigan stretched and made to reach into his coat to get his phone, only to remember that he no longer had one. Muttering darkly, he turned on the radio and flicked through the stations, looking for news broadcasts. He found a few, none of which mentioned Irish fugitives, which was comforting.

Diane returned after a couple of minutes. 'We're clear. I have no doubt a dozen or more traffic cameras caught us on the way here, but I did my best to keep to by-roads and country lanes, so hopefully we'll have minimised our exposure as much as is reasonably possible. Now ...' she pulled opened Dunnigan's door and stepped back '... let's go and get some breakfast and, most importantly, some coffee, before I collapse in a heap.'

Diane had parked at the very rear of a large carpark situated behind a sizeable petrol station and diner. As they walked towards the eatery Dunnigan asked her, 'What's our location?'

'Just north of Dumfries. There's a forest park called Galloway about an hour from here. I thought we could use that as a base of operations for a few days while we get sorted.'

'What do you mean by *sorted*?'

'If we are going off-grid we need a lot of gear.'

'What kind of gear?'

'Davey, I've been driving the narrowest, bendiest back roads on the face of the earth all night. Can we just go inside and sit down and then I promise I will talk you through it?'

'Alright.'

The truckstop contained a shop – a kind of mini-supermarket – and a food court that had counters representing various well-known restaurant and fast-food franchises. Beth and Diane ordered full English breakfasts and coffee, while Dunnigan, after much deliberation, finally settled on scrambled eggs with dry toast and a pot of tea.

There was little talking for the next ten minutes as they applied themselves to their meal. When the plates were clean, Diane picked up her mug. 'Okay. Now that I'm feeling a little bit more human, we should take a look at our resources. How much money do we have between us?'

Everyone emptied their pockets, purses and wallets. The final tally was not particularly comforting.

'Four hundred and ninety eight pounds and thirty-six pence,' Dunnigan said. 'I have some cash in the bank we could draw down – there's an ATM over there.'

'Davey, you're a detective. You know perfectly well that you withdrawing all the funds from your current account would send a signal loud and clear that you're running. They probably don't know we've gone yet, but they will by tomorrow. Probably earlier. They would be able to pinpoint that the cash was taken from that very machine, and then all the subterfuge and recrossing our trail during the night would be for nothing. Four hundred and ninety eight is what we've got, so that's what we'll work with.'

They thought about that for a moment.

'You said you'd tell us what happens next,' Beth said.

'I did, didn't I?'

'Yes.'

'Well, the police know what we all look like, and they know what kind of car we're driving.'

'Obviously,' Beth said. 'But what can we do about it?'

'Change it.' Diane grinned.

'Change what?'

'All of it.'

Beth and Dunnigan exchanged glances.

'Let's go shopping,' Diane said, standing up.

10

THEY LEFT THE CAR WHERE IT WAS AND WALKED a mile back into the small town of Dumfries

Without much difficulty they found a pound saver shop. Diane handed each of them baskets. 'Go to the clothes section. Pick out clothes you would never usually wear – stuff as far out of character as you can find style-wise. Don't go for loud colours or stuff that's too bizarre – we don't want to stand out, we want to blend in, but as other people. Got it?'

'No,' Dunnigan said.

'Come on, I'll help,' Beth said, and took him by the arm. She chose tracksuits for each of them, his in charcoal grey with a blue stripe down the sides, hers in muted blue with pink piping.

'I'm not wearing that,' Dunnigan said.

'Yes, you are. What do you think of these trainers?'

'I don't have an opinion on them. Why do we need trainers?

Are we going to be running somewhere?'

'I have a feeling we're going to be running everywhere for a while. What size are your feet?'

'Nine. I'm not wearing trainers.'

'Davey, I refuse to argue with you. Grey or black?'

'Neither.'

'Grey it is.'

They met Diane at the checkout. She had already paid for her items, and handed Beth the wallet which contained their funds. 'I'll meet you across the road.'

'What's across the road?'

'A motor shop.'

Beth nodded and lined up to pay.

Diane was already finished when they got out, and they found her on the footpath, a box under her arm. 'This is every boy racer's dream,' she grinned, showing them a kit which, according to the text on the box, could be used to modify any hatchback car.

'Are you qualified to make modifications to vehicles?' Dunnigan inquired dubiously.

'Let's pretend I am,' Diane said, placing a reassuring hand on his shoulder.

'That does not answer my question.'

'Let's get back to the truckstop,' Diane said, winking at Beth. 'We've got some work to do.'

11

'NO.'

'It'll grow back,' Diane said, her tones gentle in a futile attempt to mollify him.

'I don't care. You are not cutting my hair – you know I don't like getting it done at the best of times, but in Dublin I have a barber I have been attending for years and he knows how I like the process to be conducted and you don't. Anyway, you don't know how to cut hair. You're not a barber, Diane.'

The pair were in a cubicle in the male toilets of the truckstop, and despite the fact that he had agreed to remain quiet and keep a low profile, Dunnigan was screaming.

Diane had been prepared for this (she knew Dunnigan struggled with change at the best of times, his OCD and personality disorder making such things a huge challenge), but even she was surprised by the level of anguish he was now displaying. She took a deep breath and pushed on. Anxiety or no, this was something that simply had to be done. 'What I propose to do does not require any degree of barbering skill,' she said, trying not to lose her temper.

'That shows how little you know. I have a cowlick *and* a double crown, and Mr O'Connor always comments on the fact that a lesser hairdresser would have real difficulty in navigating the challenges my hair presents.'

'I am going to navigate those challenges by shaving the whole lot off.'

'What did you say?'

'Hold still. This shouldn't take long.'

*

Ten minutes later Dunnigan stood in front of the mirror in the bathroom, looking dejectedly at his head, which was now covered in a dark stubble. Diane had made him put on the tracksuit and trainers Beth had chosen for him, and he had shaved off the beard he had sported since his trip to Greenland the previous year. As he surveyed himself, he had to admit that he was dramatically different to the long-haired bohemian he usually presented to the world. 'I look like a heroin addict,' he said, to no one in particular. He wished he had his poster of the Second Doctor to talk to. The thought made him feel even more lonely and homesick, so he stopped thinking it and packed up his shaving kit.

When he went back out to the food court he found that Diane and Beth looked vastly different too. Diane's blonde hair was now dyed jet black, cut short and styled into punkish spikes. Beth's, while still reasonably long, was deep red in colour. Beth was decked out in her tracksuit and Diane sported an oversized t-shirt and baggy shorts.

'What do you think?' Beth asked as he sat down opposite them.

'We all look horrible,' he sulked. 'I don't think I can put up with this for much longer.'

Diane reached over the table and grasped his arm tightly. 'I'm going to say this one time,' she said. 'And I want you to listen very carefully. This is not a game, Davey. If we get caught, Beth is going to be put in an institution and you and I are going to prison. Do you understand that?'

Dunnigan just stared at her.

'I know you find change difficult, but the second you made the decision to take her and run, everything changed. We cannot erase that or decide we've had enough – we've taken this road and we have to follow it to its conclusion.'

'You did this for me,' Beth said. 'I can't ever repay you for it, but I want you to know I appreciate everything you've done. A lot.'

'You don't have to thank us,' Diane said gently. 'This is the only course of action that makes sense. Getting you away from the chaos with the police and interrogations and the courts will give you a chance to remember what happened in the hospital, which we can then use to prove your innocence. And hopefully Frank Tormey can do something at his end to find Ressler or even Mother Joan or Hester Kitt or whatever we're supposed to call her, which would help too. But it is all going to amount to nothing, Davey, if you don't get yourself in order. Do you understand what the stakes are here?'

'Of course I do,' Dunnigan said, his eyes fixed on the table.

'That may be so,' Beth said. 'But you're struggling, and Diane and I can both see it.'

'There is one way out of this for you,' Diane said. 'Say

the decision to run was mine. You came along to try and persuade us to change our minds. Tell the police we gave you the slip and did a legger. You could even feed them some false information – say we've gone to Wales, or somewhere in the opposite direction from where we're actually headed. You wouldn't get into too much trouble. I bet Tormey could protect you.'

Dunnigan blinked at her.

'But if you want to do that, you need to say so now. This is a one-time-only deal. If you decide not to take it, you're in for the duration.'

'You know I'm not backing out,' he said quietly. 'Please don't suggest it again.'

Diane and Beth exchanged furtive glances.

'Fair enough. I won't. But Davey, I need you to listen to this next bit, and really take it in. You've changed how you look, and that's great, but there is another alteration I'm going to ask you to make, and it's going to be even harder for you.'

'What?'

'How you act – your behaviour – is as likely to give you away as your appearance. People will pick up on your manner. It stands out. I mean, people who were here this afternoon are going to remember the Irish guy shouting in the toilets, aren't they? It won't take very long for the police to work out that was you.'

'I'm sorry.'

'It's okay, but Davey – you have to practise keeping quiet. You've spent your life telling anyone within earshot the vaguest things that pop into your head. The consequences have never mattered to you before, but from now on, you have to care, because the fallout could be disastrous for all of us. Do you understand that?'

'Yes.'

'Good. Lecture over.'

Beth took her uncle's hand and squeezed it. He squeezed back but didn't make eye contact.

It was two days before Dunnigan opened his mouth again. Diane would have been lying if she said she didn't enjoy the quiet.

Beth Carlton

She had a memory of a voice.

It was speaking in an odd accent, one that reminded her of the kind of cod accents actors in old movies tended to use when they were playing a stereotypical French person, but it wasn't quite that either. There was a subtle difference – was it Dutch, perhaps? She had spent some time living in Amsterdam, so perhaps she was mixing it up.

The voice was speaking in English, its cadence almost sing-song. She couldn't make out the words, it was as if she was hearing them from inside a cupboard, or while she was underwater.

When she focussed really hard, going deep down inside herself, she had a sense of numbness, as if her body wouldn't work. She tried to dig deeper into that, but could come up with nothing else.

She closed her eyes, trying to step into the memory. When she reopened them in her mind, all she could see was red. It was as if the world had been draped in a scarlet shroud.

And all the while that sing-song voice continued, crooning words she could not hear.

She didn't know what it meant. But she knew it wasn't anything good.

12

THEY WENT BACK OUT TO THE CAR AND SLEPT for five hours.

Dunnigan was awakened by Diane shaking him. 'I need both of you to help me,' she said.

'What with?' Beth asked.

Dusk was falling, but the carpark was floodlit and as bright as day.

'I want to get back on the road, so we have to alter the car. These kits are pretty foolproof, but there are a couple of adjustments I want to make that are a bit more advanced. Come on, I'll tell you what to do.'

The skip hid them completely so they could work in privacy. Diane took all the parts out of the box and placed them on the bonnet of the Vauxhall. 'We're going to put go-faster stripes along both sides, and attach a fin to the rear end.'

Dunnigan blanched for a moment, but said nothing. Diane

waited, expecting another explosion or at the very least an acerbic comment about their actions invalidating his contract with the rental company, but no such outburst came.

'Just tell us what to do,' Beth said.

'You and Davey can work on the stripes,' Diane said. 'They're just stickers, so it's pretty foolproof.'

Dunnigan and his niece applied themselves to the task while Diane, using her penknife and a multi-tool that came with the kit, fixed a large and rather vulgar-looking black fin to the car, just below the rear window. Within forty-five minutes the hatchback looked like a very different machine to the one that had driven into the truckstop the previous day.

'One last thing,' Diane said, producing a Stanley blade. 'We're going to need a different registration number.'

The plate read: BD67SMR.

'What are you going to do?' Beth asked. 'Switch ours with another car?'

'Too risky,' Diane said, studying the plate on the Astra. 'I'd be spotted. No, I'm going to tinker with the numbers we've got. They're going to try to track us by analysing registrations that ping on road cameras, so I want to make sure ours doesn't appear. Let's see what we can do.'

Using the knife, she very deftly cut the front leg from the letter 'R' and pried it off, leaving a 'P' in its stead. 'That's a start,' she said, sitting back on her heels to survey her work. 'But it's probably not enough.' With painstaking care, she cut away the middle band in the 'B', leaving a slightly misshapen 'D'. The registration now read: DD67 SMP.

'It won't stand up to close scrutiny, but I hope we won't have this car for very much longer.'

'It's amazing, is what it is,' Beth said in admiration. 'I never would have thought to do that.'

Diane blushed despite herself and pulled a baseball cap from the pocket of her shorts. 'The description law enforcement have, and what will have gone out into the papers, is very particular. They're looking for two girls and a guy, driving a very specific car. Now we've got one girl, a guy and one individual – me – who could be a bloke or a girl – you can't tell at a quick look. The car is completely different, and has a different reg. It's all superficial and will fall apart if anyone checks carefully, but my plan is to get us out of here and away from prying eyes.'

Beth threw her arms around Diane. 'You're amazing. You know that, don't you?'

Dunnigan watched their embrace and hoped the disguise would be enough. Instincts developed over two decades of police work told him the hunt was already on – the police would by now be looking for them. And he wondered if others, with even more nefarious intentions, would be too.

Wilfred Hubert

The year he worked for Frobisher was the scariest, but also one of the most satisfying of his life.

The Yellow Man was his main point of contact – he usually only saw his employer at social functions – and he made it clear that there were targets that needed to be met. These started out as easily achievable: the stock he bought should give Frobisher a particular weighting in voting rights within a chosen company. To be able to purchase such a quantity, Hubert had to do some wheeling and dealing, but he was good at that. People within the industry liked and respected him, and he had many contacts who tipped him off when particular individuals wanted to sell in bulk.

As time passed, the demands became more challenging: Frobisher wanted to cause this particular company's share value to plummet so he could swoop in and force them into selling. This might mean buying in bulk and selling at an outrageous price; alternatively, Hubert had learned that whispering rumours about disagreements and indecision between board members could just as easily bring about poor share performance, and he knew just the right ears to whisper in.

Every time he came in on target, the next one was bigger, but so were the rewards. Money, of course (that went without saying), but there was so much more. His first bonus was an Aston Martin DB5 – he had mentioned to Frobisher in passing that he had always wanted one, and at the end of his first month, as he passed a file with a full report of their portfolio's performance to the Yellow Man, he in turn handed him a set of keys.

'The papers are in the glove compartment, all made out in your name,' he said. 'And you have an unlimited tab for the

next fortnight at Jack and Jill's.' This last was a highly illegal brothel Hubert favoured. *'Make as much of a mess as you like. Mr Frobisher has it covered.'*

The generous salary and the toys continued. The difficulties he used to face from brothel-keepers when one of their employees ended up slightly damaged due to his attentions were no longer a feature now Frobisher's name was attached to his. It made his leisure activities so much more pleasurable.

What struck him most of all, however, was how the job increased his reach and his influence. Previously, he might have to wait several days for a particular industrialist to make himself available for a meeting. Now that he was ringing on behalf of Ernest Frobisher, all doors swung open at the first push.

When the year was almost over, Frobisher called to see him in person. *'You've done yourself proud, Hubert.'*

'Thank you, sir. I've enjoyed working for you.'

'Good. Fancy staying on?'

'I'd be happy to listen to any proposal you might have.'

'Excellent. I'd like you to continue as a kind of ... let's call it a silent consultant.'

'I don't understand.'

'I want you to represent my interests in a number of different fields. To make sure my investments are yielding the correct quantity of fruit.'

'Okay ...'

'I just don't want anyone to know that you're working for me. It'll be our little secret.'

'I will be very discreet, sir.'

It was the beginning of his rise into the stratosphere.

Part Three

STOLEN MOMENTS

1

DR PHILLIPE RESSLER MADE CAREFUL PLANS FOR their return to the continent.

Ernest Frobisher, his employer and mentor, could no longer travel by airline, even those that provided the most audacious luxury — the cancers that ravaged his body had rendered him virtually paralysed, and he therefore required private transport. There were companies who were more than happy to provide jets with the medical facilities he needed, along with a private nurse. Such companies also offered complete discretion (for the right price, of course).

Money was, thankfully, something they had in ample supply.

Ressler believed this might be their last trip. The most recent blood tests he had carried out on his superior showed that the melanomas had metastasised again, and even though he had been using an experimental treatment he had personally developed that was yielding remarkable results, Frobisher was an old man. The psychiatrist believed it was only hatred that was keeping him alive. And even such unbridled fury could not keep him going for much longer.

And the psychiatrist was forced to admit, in the few moments of self-contemplation he permitted himself, that this saddened him. Love was not a word Ressler had ever used – he did not really believe an emotion so selfless and pure truly existed – but he had to admit he held Frobisher in high regard. There was a strength of character, a power the man held, physically compromised though he was, that was remarkable to witness.

Ressler hoped he would exhibit such authority when old age and physical morbidity caught up with him.

He had booked them into a suite in the Ritz in London, an olde worlde hotel that still believed in class and good manners. A private hospital would have been better, but his employer simply refused to countenance one. Two rooms on the top floor had been cleared and they now resembled a high-tech medical unit. As he entered, Ressler saw that Jessica, a nurse practitioner he'd seconded from Kaiser Care, a private health company Frobisher owned (although there were now several hedge funds and umbrella companies between it and him), was taking a reading from a blood pressure monitor attached to a figure lying prone on an orthopaedic bed.

'Thank you so much, Jessica. I will take up the duties from here. Why don't you go and have something nice for dinner, eh?'

The woman nodded and left without a word.

Ressler was aware he made her feel uncomfortable. He made a point of leaning in close when he clearly didn't need to, and said her name far more often than was required. When she was no longer needed to care for Frobisher, he thought he might bed her. He would use just enough tranquiliser to make her pliable. Or he might not use drugs at all – sometimes the fight was half the pleasure …

He walked briskly up to the prone man and picked up the clipboard Jessica had laid down. 'You are doing better today, I think, sir.'

'I wouldn't call it better,' a voice croaked. 'I'm rotting from the inside, Ressler. I've got more drugs running through my veins than blood, but I can still feel the bastard eating me away.'

Ernest Frobisher resembled a bundle of bones with brown, wizened skin stretched far too tightly over them. His hair and eyelashes had long since fallen out, and a weeping tumour had taken most of the left side of his face, which was covered with a piece of gauze through which an ochre black liquid continued to seep. The only thing about him that seemed alive were his eyes, which glittered with an evil, foul intelligence.

Most people found them terrifying. Ressler thought them quite beautiful.

'You will not be consumed before tomorrow, sir. I have a plane booked to take us away from here.'

'Where are you dragging my useless carcass now?'

'One of the places you are happiest.'

'Good. And the detective and his little whore?'

'They will be busy for a while.'

'That doesn't sound comforting.'

'I haven't informed you of the trap into which I have so cleverly snared them.'

'Really? Do tell.'

He did. He thought Frobisher would choke to death from laughter.

He enjoyed making his boss happy. It was good that he should enjoy these, his final days.

2

WHAT WAS IT THAT RESSLER LIKED MOST ABOUT Frobisher? He had often tried to work that out. It wasn't as if Ressler *had* to work for someone else – he could have been anything he desired.

Ressler knew he was a brilliant man. At one point when he was in college their psychology lecturer had brought in a number of different IQ tests and suggested the students give them a go (some of them would be administering tests just like these once they qualified, so it seemed sensible to have an understanding of how they worked).

When the tests were completed, they were instructed to hand their paperwork to the student on their right to have their score tallied. The girl who was totting up Ressler's seemed confused (she was never the sharpest tool in the box) and had to ask the lecturer for assistance. Finally, they both gave up – Ressler must have filled out the sheets incorrectly.

After class, he had gone to the psychology lecturer to find out where he had made the mistake (he was not used to getting things wrong). When he sat down and went through the scoring with him, Ressler discovered that the problem was that his scores simply could not be measured by the test. He had, literally, scored off the charts.

His lecturer, never having seen results like these, assumed there had to be an error.

Curious, the young medical student had paid to be privately tested by three different specialists, and the results were all the same. He was, in the most modest of terms, a genius. One of the testers suggested that he fit into a category that was only whispered about in psychological circles – people did not like talking about it because it smacked of certain philosophical and political ideologies that were seen as shameful in today's world.

'What are you saying?' Ressler had asked.

'That you are something different.'

'Different?'

'The philosopher Nietzsche wrote about people like you. You may be a new direction for our species. The next evolutionary step. A triumph in genetic development.'

Ressler had laughed at that. 'Doctor, my mother was an alcoholic depressive and my father was so weak he could barely stand upright on his own. I very much doubt their genetic legacy did anything other than give me obstacles I had to overcome.'

'I was just expressing a theory.'

The fact remained, he was gifted, both intellectually and physically. He graduated highest in his year, not just in his university but in the whole of Belgium. At university he drifted from one society to another in his first year, quickly becoming bored with each one. However, it was enough to show him that, should be apply himself even slightly, he could have ben a championship fencer, a professional soccer player (the coach of the team begged him to try out for Royal Antwerp FC) or an Olympic swimmer.

His professional career was similarly blessed: he was able to pick and choose the jobs he wanted, and when Kaiser Care, Frobisher's company, offered him a chance to test some ideas he had been tinkering with about conditioning and control on traumatised subjects, he jumped at the opportunity.

His success brought him to the attention of his employer, who invited him for dinner one evening in Dublin, where the company's administrative offices were located, and after that, he really didn't look back.

What was it about this man, Ernest Frobisher, that immediately captured his loyalty? Frobisher was a smart man, there was no denying that. Probably not as clever as Ressler (few people were), but he was mentally exceptional. He was entirely focussed on what he wanted, and was not ashamed to admit it. Ressler bored quickly with people who danced around their most deeply held desires and pretended to be what they were not. Frobisher displayed to the world exactly who and what he was. That was, in itself, very attractive to the psychiatrist.

As he got to know the man better, though, Ressler began to understand that what he really valued in his employer was the (from what he could see) absolute absence of a conscience.

As a practising psychiatrist, and one who had done a sizeable amount of research, Ressler had encountered many who were diagnosed as sociopaths, the term science now used

115

to describe those who appeared to shirk ideas of right and wrong and who, it seemed, did not experience guilt. From his work, Ressler concluded that most of these individuals did not truly meet the criteria. They may have had some blind spots in their personalities, but when truly tested they came up short. Given free rein to indulge their deepest fantasies, the majority just could not follow through. Frobisher, on the other hand, seemed to be a man without any such limitations.

It occurred to Ressler that working for a man of seemingly limitless wealth who was unimpeded by the social norms of right and wrong was a privileged position to be in. A powerful position.

He determined to take every opportunity it offered.

3

FROBISHER NO LONGER ATE.

All the nutrition he could cope with was pumped into him through numerous tubes that intersected with his body at different points – one went up his nose, another into his arm, another directly into his stomach. Other tubes took the waste product away. A catheter drained urine from his bladder and solid waste was voided directly from his bowel into a colostomy bag.

He was being eaten alive by three different cancers: colorectal cancer, small lung carcinoma and melanomic skin cancer. The morphine deadened the pain, but it was always there. He had learned to treat it as a companion, one he would much rather be parted from, but one he was stuck with, nonetheless.

He taught himself to welcome the pain, to embrace it. When the pain was gone, it would mean he was dead. And there was so much left to do.

He could no longer read, and television just bored and irritated him, so he had taken to living in his head. He had memories there he enjoyed replaying, and places he was happy to go back to. Frobisher found that, with practice, he could recall in precise detail places and things and events, and the life he had lived offered him plenty of sustenance when the physical world became unbearable.

He had thought about asking Ressler to help him end it, as soon as the criminologist and his gang of irritants were dealt with. It could be so easy: an injection into his IV tube with the right dose of the correct drug and he could just drift away.

But he finally realised that was just not how he was built. He would go down swinging. And anyway, there was still fun to be had.

As soon as that bitch Beth Carlton was back inside, Frobisher was going to send Ressler to visit her. And he'd make sure he was there too, via Skype or one of those new apps. He didn't want to miss a second of it.

Part Four

THE ONES
LEFT BEHIND

Liam Doyle

He had been surprised when they left him in charge of Moonlight Meadows, Ernest Frobisher's main Irish home. He had been chief of security, that was true, but he had also been the supervisor when everything had gone wrong. The strange detective and that woman, who he later learned was ex-Special Forces, had come, and despite his having a gun trained on them, they had got away and brought all kinds of shit down on Frobisher.

The police had arrived and started poking into everything, but by then, of course, Frobisher was long gone. The Criminal Assets Bureau had tried to claim the house, but after a year of wrangling they had failed. Liam received a letter several weeks later informing him that he was being left in charge of security and maintenance of the property, and while he had to admit it was a pretty boring job, it paid well and he was largely left to his own devices.

His duties mostly involved letting the cleaners in twice a week, walking the perimeter twice a day, and making sure the gardener (who had worked at Moonlight Meadows since Frobisher's father's time and operated to his own timetable) kept the grounds in reasonable shape. He slept on site every other day (his contract specified he needed to do this), but he didn't mind. He brought the mansion's biggest large-screen TV into the guest room, and began working his way through the American Film Institute's top 100 movies of all time, starting at the bottom (Ben Hur, which he was surprised to find he really enjoyed) and working his way up from there.

He was halfway through Clint Eastwood's Unforgiven, which was number 68, when the door to his bedroom opened and a man walked in. He had to do a double-take, so surprised was he. That's what he felt: not fear or shock or even anger – it was just surprising.

'What the fuck?' he heard himself splutter (he was drinking a can of Brewdog Punk IPA).

All the doors in the mansion were locked and the alarms had all been set, so there was no way this man should have been there, unless he was one of Frobisher's people – but even then, no one had the alarm codes except Liam, so that didn't make sense either.

The man was tall and dark and was dressed in a black t-shirt and dark jeans. He was, Liam thought, very ordinary-looking, as if he was not a real person at all, just a composite.

'I am looking for Ernest Frobisher. And the Yellow Man.'

He spoke conversationally, as if, in his world, walking into another man's bedroom uninvited in the middle of the night was perfectly normal.

'Where do you get off?' Liam said, feeling genuinely aggrieved. 'Get the fuck out of my house.'

'We both know this is not your house. You live in a two-bed apartment in Ranelagh that you share with a plasterer named Steve. Steve has a pit bull terrier, Spike, whom he hardly ever walks, and a girlfriend named Tracy, who works in a beauty salon where she specialises in those strange eyebrows women seem to like these days but men don't. You, Liam, have no dog and no girlfriend, and this is your job: you maintain Moonlight Meadows. Now, please answer me, because the next time I ask the question, I will also hurt you. Where are Frobisher and the Yellow Man?'

Liam had a gun, but it was (stupidly) in the drawer of the bedside locker. That being said, the intruder was still standing at the door, and his hands were empty.

'Why should I tell you?' Liam asked, placing his feet slowly on the ground and one hand on top of the locker. 'I've no loyalty to that sick fucker, but what's in it for me if I do tell you?'

'Your life,' the man said.

'You'll have to do better than that.'

'Your life with all your faculties and all your limbs.'

'That's the best you can do?'

Liam feigned a stretch, and then in a sudden rush made a lunge for the weapon, but his hand got no further than the handle. The man was suddenly not at the door any longer, he was right up beside him, and the hooked blade of a knife had impaled his hand and fastened it to the wood of the drawer.

It was perhaps the worst pain he had ever experienced, but he found that he had no air to scream, because the man had caught him by the windpipe, and was pinching it in such a way that he could not take in even the most shallow breath.

'I told you the next time I asked would hurt,' he said, almost sorrowfully. 'The next time will be even worse.'

And so began the worst moments of Liam Doyle's life. He told him that he didn't know where Frobisher was, and that the Yellow Man was dead. He told him the truth and he told him very early in the questioning.

But the man said he had to be sure, and the questioning continued. As he questioned, he worked with the knife. And with every answer, he cut a little bit of Liam away.

By the time he was finished, there was nothing of Liam left.

1

GINA DUNNIGAN-CARLTON WAS GAZING AT
Chief Superintendent Frank Tormey as if he had suddenly
started speaking in tongues. The policeman called to her
house in Greystones as soon as he got back from the UK,
having informed Lisburn that he'd been summoned home
on urgent business. He thought that, as Beth's mother, she
deserved to hear directly from him what was going on.

'You're telling me they're on the run now?'

'Yes.'

'And you advised them to do it?'

'I did, Gina, yes.'

She got up from the kitchen table and began to make a pot
of coffee.

'You don't need to do that, Gina, love, I'm fine.'

'Would you please be quiet for a moment and just leave me
be?'

The words were spoken quietly, but Tormey knew the woman well enough to understand the import they held.

Gina was the same height as her twin brother, and shared his slim build and shock of dark hair, which she wore in a short, boyish cut. Unlike Dunnigan, though, she was always immaculately turned out: today she was wearing purple skinny jeans and a black designer t-shirt, offset with green converse high-tops.

'Of course,' Tormey said gently. 'I apologise.'

Gina continued to spoon coffee into the pot, pouring boiling water over it, stirring, and then putting the plunger top on. She placed it in the middle of the table on a coaster, and then set out cups, spoons, sugar and milk. 'Do you have any idea where they'll go?' she asked finally, as she went to the cupboard and got out a packet of chocolate biscuits, which she emptied onto a plate. Her voice had a noticeable tremble.

'I suggested to Davey that they make for the wild places. Scotland has lots of them.'

'You told my brother, who has difficulty walking through the Phoenix Park, to hide out in the Scottish Highlands?'

'I'm *pretty sure* Diane went with them.'

'You're pretty sure?'

'She's disappeared too. It stands to reason she's with them.'

Gina nodded. 'That's something, I suppose.'

'She'll know how to avoid capture and how to survive off-grid. The Rangers are the best there is. She'll keep them safe until we can prove Beth was framed.'

Gina pushed the plunger down on the coffee and poured for them both. 'How are you going to do that?'

'I don't know. I thought you might be able to help.'

'I'm not sure I know Beth anymore. All she's done since coming home is push me away.'

Tormey poured milk and added sugar to his cup. 'I've been around lots of families in trauma,' he said. 'It's pretty common for them to turn on one another. We all have a tendency to lash out at the people we love, don't we?'

Gina sighed and shook her head. 'Are the police in Scotland looking for them?'

'I would imagine they've noticed they're gone by now. I'll probably get a call tomorrow.'

'And what will you tell them?'

'That I don't know where they are. Which is true.'

Gina suddenly realised she was crying. It happened without warning: one moment she was fine, the next tears were streaming down her cheeks. 'I'm sorry,' she said, between sobs.

Tormey pulled over his chair and put one of his long arms around her shoulders. 'That's okay, love. I'd think there was something wrong with you if you weren't upset.'

2

THE WIDOW'S QUAY HOMELESS PROJECT WAS
bustling with activity the next morning when Gina called
in. Tarpaulins, plastic sheets and dust covers were draped
over the floors and furniture and men with rollers and
paint brushes were busy applying undercoat to the walls in
the hallway as she entered. She could see more men and a
couple of women – she guessed they were from the homeless
community the project served – in the dining room engaged
in similar activities.

'Can I help you, miss?' A young man was behind the
counter usually occupied by Diane Robinson. He looked to
be about fifteen years old, and a tattoo of an unconvincing
cobra coiled around his neck.

'I'm looking for Father Bill?'

'He's out back. Want me to call him?'

'No, thank you. I'll find him.'

'Straight out the dining room and through the kitchen.'

'Perfect. Thanks a million.'

Father Bill Creedon was about fifty with short salt-and-pepper hair, a handsome face made more interesting by a nose that had been broken several times (Father Bill had boxed in his youth), and the broad shoulders and slim waist of a pugilist. He wore the clerical collar of a Roman Catholic priest, but he paired it with designer jeans and a soft leather sports jacket. He was known to be hugely unorthodox (he was constantly in trouble with the bishop and quite often the police), but he was beloved by the people he ministered to: the working-class citizens of Dublin's docklands and inner city, and the ever-growing population of homeless who flooded into Ireland's capital hoping to find jobs, accommodation and a new life.

Father Bill had become a surrogate father to Dunnigan, and he had been instrumental in helping her brother find Beth, providing much of the intelligence he had used to finally track her down.

The priest had grown up in the narrow streets around Dublin's waterfront, and remained very close to the gangsters who plied their trade there. Through the homeless community he also had eyes and ears everywhere, making him was a powerful ally for any detective.

Gina found him supervising two young men who were painting the rear of the building. The priest was dressed in paint-speckled overalls, a cigarette dangling from his lower lip. He grinned when he saw her. 'To what do I owe the pleasure?' he asked, giving her a hug and a peck on the cheek.

'I need to talk to you, Father,' she said. 'In private, if you don't mind.'

'Of course. Let's go to my office.'

When they were inside he closed the door and offered her a chair. 'Now. How can I help you?'

'Is the seal of the confessional still a thing?' Gina asked.

'It is.'

'And it means you can't tell anyone what I say?'

'Gina, I flatter myself to think we're like family. You don't need to invoke canon law to confide in me.'

'This is important, Father.'

'Well then yes, it means I cannot be legally coerced into sharing what you've told me.'

'Good. Bless me Father for I have sinned.'

Father Bill looked gravely at her. 'How long has it been since your last confession, Gina?'

'I don't know. Years.'

'It's never too late to come back to God. Now, tell me how you have sinned.'

'I have lost patience with my brother. I have been jealous of his relationship with my daughter. I have ... I have thought things and harboured resentments that were unfair and unworthy of our relationship.'

'Your brother can be hard work sometimes,' Father Bill observed. 'Are you maybe being a bit tough on yourself?'

'Is it usual for the priest to try and talk you out of your sins?'

'Sometimes we need to forgive ourselves as much as we need God to forgive us.'

'Well, let's try this one for size, then. I am carrying a secret, Father. I know of a crime and I haven't passed it on to the authorities.'

'Really?'

'Yes. Would you like to hear about it?'

'Only if you feel the need to tell me.'

And she told him everything that had happened with Dunnigan and Beth in the UK – about Beth apparently having killed the Welsh detective, and how she, Dunnigan and Diane were now in hiding.

When she was finished, he made the sign of the cross in the air. 'Gina, God forgives you for your sins. As penance, you are going to have a drink with me and we are going to try to work out what to do next. After that, you can go in peace and do your best not to sin again.'

'Thank you, Father.'

He took a bottle of Glenfiddich Scotch whisky and two glasses from a drawer of his desk and poured them both a couple of fingers. 'I know it's a little early, but after a story like that, I think we could both do with one, don't you agree?'

'I won't argue with you.'

They drank.

'Gina, I can't begin to imagine how you must be feeling.'

'Angry. Hurt. Confused. Frightened. I want to *kill* Davey. But I also know he didn't ask Beth to follow him, and he was about to send her home before it all went pear-shaped over there. I suppose the real reason I'm here, though, is that I know you spent time with her over the past few months. Do you think she could have killed this detective?'

The priest had another drink. 'One thing life has taught me, Gina – anyone can do pretty much anything given the right provocation. Beth had a *lot* of anger. And rightly so: she had plenty to be angry about. But do I think she would have taken a hunting knife to a man's throat, a man who, from what you've told me, was grievously hurt trying to protect her? No. It doesn't sound like the Beth I know.'

Gina took a sip of the Scotch and rolled it on her tongue. 'She attacked me with a knife once. Shortly after she came back. It's why she moved in with Davey for a bit.'

'I didn't know that. I'm sorry to hear it.'

'It was only a breadknife and she only barely marked me, but ...'

'Those are words no mother should have to say,' Father Bill said.

'I'm only making excuses, aren't I?' The tears came again and Gina clenched her eyes to try to staunch the flow.

'You have been through a terrible ordeal,' the priest said, reaching for a box of tissues he had placed at the corner of his desk, 'one that has gone on for almost twenty years. I think you're entitled to make all the excuses you want.'

Gina nodded and, accepting a tissue, wiped her nose. 'Father, I need to do something to help them. I am going to go crazy if I'm not kept busy. My twin brother and my little girl are in trouble, and I know Diane is a real badass, but I'm Beth's *mother*, for God's sake. I have to feel I'm being at least a little bit useful.'

'Have you spoken to Beth's therapist? What was her name ... Doctor Grantham?'

'Harriet. I didn't think she'd talk to me, doctor/patient privilege and all that. And the last time she was with Beth, Beth broke her nose. I doubt she's her favourite client, do you?'

'The worst she can do is tell you to fuck off,' Father Bill said. 'What have you got to lose?'

'Nothing, I suppose.'

'In the meantime, I'll see if I can find a few things out. The more heads we have working on this, the better.'

'Thank you, Father.'

'Like I said, we're family. No thanks necessary.'

Gina stood and he came around the desk and held her tight for a moment.

'It scares me that I think she might have killed that man,' Gina whispered into his chest.

'Gina, Davey has made enemies of some very dangerous and very bad people. Just keep that in mind.'

She stood on tiptoe and kissed his stubbled cheek, then walked out of the office without looking back.

As soon as the door was closed, Father Bill put the bottle and glasses away, and took an ancient mobile phone from the same drawer they had come out of. 'Tim Pat, it's Bill. Can I come over? I need your help.'

3

HARRIET GRANTHAM WORKED OUT OF AN OFFICE in a health centre on St Peter's Square, near Phibsboro, close to Dunnigan's flat. She was a handsome woman in her late forties, her long hair silvery grey. Gina winced when she saw the bruising around her eyes and the tape across the bridge of her nose. She knew it had been aquiline and well-formed and wondered if it would still be when the swelling went down.

'Thank you for seeing me at such short notice,' she said when they were both seated.

'Your message made it sound important.'

'It is.' And she told the therapist what was happening, sharing everything except that Beth was on the run.

'How can I help?'

'Chief Superintendent Tormey believes the British police are going to try to make a case against Beth based on her being, at best, a willing accomplice in the death of Detective

Jones. I was hoping you might be able to help me put together a plausible defence. You've been working with her for months. This man, Ressler, was present when the death occurred. Might he have coerced her into doing something ... something awful?'

'You understand that there are strict limitations around my sharing information with you?'

'Yes.'

'However, one of the instances that allows me some wiggle room is where my being candid will benefit my client's safety and wellbeing in the long term. I think this qualifies.'

'Thank you.'

'I think you are asking me two questions: number one, could Beth have either willingly cut this man's throat or facilitated someone else in doing it; and number two, might Phillipe Ressler have done something to compel her into doing either of the above, without her knowledge and against her will.'

'That's about it.'

Harriet Grantham scratched her injured nose delicately, wincing slightly as she did so.

'Gina, we are both living testimonials to your daughter's capacity and propensity for violence. In neither instance did she appear to have been particularly sorely provoked, but I think we need to keep in mind that we do not know what was going on in *her* head on either occasion. What may have seemed superficial to us could have been monumental to her.'

'I see. Or at least I think I do ...'

'When Beth attacked you, you had been putting pressure on her to see a therapist, something she very much did not want.'

'That's right, yes.'

'When she attacked me, I was talking to her about branching out, maybe going to some parties, having fun, looking for joy in her life: being a healthy, functional young adult – also something she very much did not want to do.'

'What if Detective Jones tried to make her do something she didn't want to do?'

'Mrs Carlton, we are all products of our upbringing. You are a teacher – I believe your father was a university lecturer. I am a therapist – my mother was a GP. Beth spent the bulk of her childhood around violent, abusive people. Her medical report shows she was very brutally treated – she has many healed fractures and is covered in scars. It is clear she lived for years in a world where physical and sexual abuse were used as a way of expressing anger. I think what you and I experienced was simply Beth telling us she wasn't happy.'

'But surely she knows that's not how things are done now she's back in the … the *real* world.'

'That other world is just as real, Mrs Carlton – to her, it may even be more real than ours. But yes, I think she does know the different behavioural norms. These outbursts happen in moments of extremis. When she's stressed or feeling cornered.'

'You're telling me you think she could have done it.'

'No,' Harriet said, raising a hand. 'Let's not get ahead of ourselves. In both our cases, Beth hurt us, but not seriously. She was sending a shot across our boughs, warning us that we were treading on dangerous ground. I believe Beth to be fully capable of violence, but I suspect she would be reluctant to use deadly force unless left with no other choice.'

'Maybe this was one of those occasions.'

'You tell me this Welsh detective was badly hurt trying to protect Beth?'

'Yes. He was shot and nearly died. Some very bad men had cornered them in a forested area in the north of England. They wanted to kill Davey and they were using Beth as bait.'

'And this man fought for her?'

'Yes, so Chief Superintendent Tormey tells me.'

'Beth places great value on loyalty. One of the reasons she so reveres your brother is his unerring commitment to finding her. In the world she was forced to live in, loyalty to your gang, your friends, your employers, was everything. It was rewarded. I find it hard to believe she would kill this man who took a bullet for her. It doesn't gel with what I know.'

'She was found with the knife in her hand, covered in blood.'

'You say she has no memory of what happened?'

'None.'

'This brings us to the next part of your question: could Ressler have manipulated her into the murder, or done it himself and left her with the smoking gun in her hand?'

'This Ressler man is a psychiatrist, isn't he?'

'Yes, and a very skilled one. He studied in the Netherlands and was quite well known on the lecture circuit in the late 1990s. As I recall he was doing some high-profile work with deeply traumatised patients, and was pioneering some experimental approach to psychotropic drugs. Of course, we now know he was also working for organised criminals, conditioning children who had been abducted and trafficked into the sex trade: making them obedient and pliable. Which is how Beth would have come in contact with him initially.

He was her "handler" when she was first taken. She has quite vivid memories of him.'

'Could he still have influence over her?'

'Yes – I have no doubt he would. But more significantly, Ressler is expert in the use of drugs – I remember seeing video footage that was recorded as part of a clinical trial. It showed him using a form of diazepam he had personally developed to soothe a patient who was in a really heightened state of stress. The man was extremely violent, and Ressler, very skilfully, administered a shot and within seconds he was following instructions and as timid as a puppy. Ressler could have given her something to immobilise her just long enough for him to commit the murder, leaving her with no recollection of it. Or he could have given her something that would have left her susceptible to his suggestions – she would have followed his orders mindlessly.'

'So why haven't the authorities come to this conclusion?'

'From what you've told me it's because there is no evidence Ressler was there. All they have is Davey's word, and he is Beth's devoted uncle, and therefore not a reliable witness.'

Gina nodded. 'Would you write a letter outlining what you've just told me?'

'Of course.'

'Is there anything else you can think of that might be useful?'

'Well, I told your brother this, but he didn't seem inclined to take it on board: Beth was convinced she had a suppressed memory, something from her time in captivity, that would bring great danger down on all of you if she remembered it.'

Gina looked puzzled. 'Did she give you any sense of what that was?'

'Only in dribs and drabs. I got the impression she had been witness to a crime or been privy to some kind of information that could be damaging to her captors.'

'I would have thought her ability to identify them was dangerous enough in itself,' Gina mused.

'Well, quite. This seemed more than that, though. I think this was something she was *told* to forget.'

'And do you think she remembered it, this terrible thing?'

'Yes. I think it's the reason why she never wanted to go to therapy in the first place, for fear she might inadvertently disclose something, and I suspect it's what caused her to assault me. I had taken her window-shopping in town, as I'm sure you remember, and I think she saw something that triggered her: a memory came rushing to the surface of her consciousness.'

'Do you know what that trigger was?'

'Oh yes,' Harriet Grantham said. 'She told me, in fact.'

'What was it?'

'Wilfred Hubert.'

Gina shook her head, puzzled. 'The American billionaire?'

'Yes. As I told you, I was chatting to Beth about age-appropriate things: people in their twenties go to dinner parties and nightclubs and music concerts. She told me she had been to a dance, once, and I asked her if she had enjoyed it. She said she hadn't. I inquired as to why. The shop window we were standing at was full of television screens showing Sky News, and at that precise moment, Wilfred Hubert was on the screen, so we had about fifteen images of him, in closeup. Beth was transfixed by them, and she seemed to be almost paralysed with fear. I asked her again why she hadn't enjoyed the dance, and she pointed at the screens and said, 'Because of him.' After which she smashed my face into the glass and ran away.'

'That doesn't make any sense,' Gina said.

'Doesn't it?'

'But how ...'

'We know your daughter was a sex worker in several different cities around the world,' the therapist said. 'It is not beyond the bounds of reason to suspect she could have been in contact with all kinds of men.'

'Come on,' Gina said. 'It's a bit of a reach though, isn't it?'

'Ernest Frobisher, though a less public figure before his disgrace, was just as wealthy as Hubert. And Beth knew him well enough to call him Uncle Ernest.'

'Is there anything we can do with this?' Gina asked. 'I mean, how does it help?'

'I don't know,' Harrier Grantham said. 'Don't they say that knowledge is power?'

'I have heard that, yes.'

'Hubert is in Ireland at the moment, which is why he was on the television. If your friend the chief superintendent knew what he had done, maybe he could bring some pressure to bear. I mean, if there is another person on the face of the earth with comparable wealth and influence to Frobisher, it's Hubert. Maybe he could be induced to call off Frobisher's goons for a reduced sentence. It's a thought.'

'I'm a primary school teacher,' Gina said. 'Do you think I should march into the boardroom at the Department of Finance and accuse one of the richest men in the world of using child prostitutes without a shred of proof?'

'Well, it would certainly grab his attention.' The therapist smiled.

4

THE CALL FROM THE OFFICE OF THE GARDA commissioner came at 6.45 a.m., while Tormey was shaving, the day after he returned from the UK. The instruction was succinct: get to the Garda training college in Templemore, where the commissioner's office was based, right away.

He made the drive in just under two hours.

The commissioner, a florid-faced man in his early sixties, was not in a good mood. 'Your special project has done a runner with his girlfriend and that psychotic girl he turned the world upside down to find.'

'Sorry to hear that, sir.'

'I'm supposed to believe this is the first time you're encountering this information?'

The room they were in was pristinely neat. Tormey (whose office looked as if a filing cabinet had vomited up its contents all over the tiny space) wondered how a desk so naked (it contained a desktop computer and phone) could have seen any work done on it at all. A framed portrait of Michael Collins looking stern in full military uniform gazed down at them from the wall.

'I cannot comment on what you believe, sir, but yes, this is the first I'm hearing of Davey making a run for it.'

'You know him better than anyone. I want you to link in with the search team in Hawick.'

'Respectfully, sir, I'm going to recuse myself.'

'Like fucking hell you are.'

'I'm too close to it, sir. I could not guarantee I'd be as helpful as I should be.'

The commissioner narrowed his eyes. 'Are you refusing a direct order from your superior, Chief Superintendent Tormey?'

'I am correctly using the chain of command to voice a valid concern about the order I have just received. Sir.'

The commissioner sat back, lacing his hands across his flat stomach. He wore the dark blue uniform his rank dictated, and he wore it well. Tormey had served under him when they were both members of the Murder Squad, a special unit set up to deal with the growth of organised crime in Dublin in the 1980s. He knew the man to be tough, intelligent, and fair. As long as you didn't cross him. If you did, he would go to the ends of the earth to make your life miserable.

'I have never understood your loyalty to David Dunnigan,' the commissioner said with something close to sympathy. 'He is not a real guard, he's a civilian consultant on a part-time salary. He was an asset once, twenty years ago, but that all ended when the girl was taken. All he has done since then is give you one headache after another. I am going to offer you some advice, Frank. Let him go. You are actively sabotaging your career and endangering your pension.'

'Beth has been framed,' Tormey said. 'There is no way she could have killed Jones and we know Ressler was in the vicinity. Whether you like it or not, Dunnigan is one of our own. Jacqueline Hardiman is trying to throw that girl under the bus and it's not right. Let me bring them home and let's put some manpower into sorting the whole mess out.'

'It would cause a political shitstorm. I can't do it.'

'No one needs to know.'

'How would you get them back into the country?'

'It wouldn't be the first time we went below the radar – remember the Birmingham thing in 1987? We've been trying to bring down Frobisher and the After Dark Campaign for thirty years, off and on. This could finish him. That would be one hell of a legacy to leave behind. God knows, the office of the commissioner could do with some good news these days after all the bad press it's had.'

'Tread carefully, Frank.' The commissioner bristled.

'You know I'm right.'

'I'm going to say this once: either fall in and help with the hunt or consider yourself on leave.'

'But sir …'

'This comes right from the top, direct from the minister: there will be no further investigation into Frobisher and no follow-up on this Ressler character. Countless hours have been wasted by the Forensic Accounting Unit in the Criminal Assets Bureau trying to unravel their affairs and it has got us nowhere. Whatever has gone down between David Dunnigan and the After Darkers is beginning to look a hell of a lot like a personal feud. Neither Frobisher nor Ressler are currently in the Republic, which makes them Interpol's problem. Jacqueline Hardiman was sent to the UK with you to settle a very challenging diplomatic problem, and she had almost done it before your idiot of a consultant and his special forces moll took the suspect and fucking well fled the scene. Now, I am going to ask you one more time: will you help find them before this turns into a scandal that will make the Malcolm MacArthur affair look like a schoolyard tiff?'

The commissioner was referring to a case which had brought down the Irish government. Malcolm MacArthur was a murderer whose arrest caused widespread public outcry when it came to light that he had been apprehended in the house of Ireland's attorney general, with whom he had been staying. The fact that such an amoral individual could be going about his murderous business while being housed by one of the heads of the Irish judiciary seemed utterly bizarre.

Tormey remained unmoved by the comparison. 'I will not aid in their apprehension, sir.'

'Then you are suspended without pay until I can work out what to do with you. Leave your gun and badge at the front desk.'

'Very well, sir.'

'Good morning, chief superintendent.'

Tormey stood. 'You're wrong about this, sir.'

'It makes no difference whether I am or not. We serve at the pleasure of the department. We have our orders. That really is the end of it.'

'Well, it shouldn't be,' Tormey said, and stormed out.

Wilfred Hubert

He didn't notice it happening, but one day he realised that his own interests and Frobisher's were no longer separate. He now headed up a vast empire Frobisher had more or less directed him to create, and he ran it as he saw fit, because ensuring everything he did benefited Frobisher in one way or another had become second nature.

A quiet voice at the back of his mind told him he was Frobisher's creature, but an even louder voice told him he didn't care.

He had everything he had ever wanted, and his employer rarely contacted him any more – Frobisher trusted him to do the right thing, which was surely a compliment in itself.

He became something of a household name: his role as an occasional commentator on various television and radio shows discussing aspects of the markets had blossomed into a second career as media personality, and to his huge surprise, this only caused his market share to rise even further.

He affected the appearance of a tacky used car salesman: a mahogany fake tan, ridiculously coiffured hair, vulgar wide pinstriped suits and chunky jewellery. He acknowledged the absurdity of it, knowing that people would look at him and he would remind them of someone they knew: a supermarket manager or the man who sold them their first home or the mayor of their town. They would remember him, and even if they didn't fully trust him, they would identify with his everyman persona.

He was a billionaire, but he was just like them.

The Republicans asked him to run for office, but he refused. He knew he had more influence on the periphery of politics.

He attended conferences on everything from climate change to Third World debt. Presidents and prime ministers sought his guidance on any number of difficult problems. And the advice he gave was always Frobisher's words spoken in Wilfred Hubert's voice.

If the pill he delivered was a tough one to swallow, he made sure to do it with a smile and a joke, for he remembered his father's advice: appearance is everything.

The media made fun of him, belittling him for his tacky clothes and orange skin, but at the same time they never failed to give front-page coverage to his every utterance.

And then an evening came when he went to one of Frobisher's parties. And a girl died.

Part Five

THE LAST PLACE
ON EARTH

Roderick Devaney

Since the police closed St Jude's Asylum, his life had gradually unravelled.

He had never been much of a drinker, but as what little money he had left was eaten up fighting the legal challenges mounted by the families whose loved ones he had destroyed (allowing them to be tormented by Ressler, used as guinea pigs in clinical trials), he found it was the only thing that gave him comfort.

He couldn't afford really good stuff, but (taste aside) the results were the same whether the bottle came from the top shelf or the bottom. He wanted oblivion, and that was what he got.

The Devaneys had once been respected in the west Cork village of Donbro, but now the name was mud, associated with medical malpractice and abuse. His lawyers had informed him that a charge of people-trafficking was pending – the police were in the process of putting together a book of evidence.

He might as well drink. He was on the verge of bankruptcy, and it looked very much like a lengthy stay in a correctional facility loomed large in his future.

He still owned a run-down house attached to the grounds of St Jude's. After losing the last lawsuit, he'd had to let go what remained of his staff. He couldn't hope to keep the place in any kind of shape on his own, and frankly, he didn't have the inclination to try. For the past month he had been living between the kitchen and a small lounge his father had once used for after-dinner brandies. The furniture still smelt of cigar smoke, and he somehow found the aroma comforting.

He had taken to sleeping on the couch – if you could call the alcohol-induced comas he now experienced sleep.

He woke from one of them to find a tall, dark-haired man standing over him. The man was dressed completely in black, and had a knife with a hooked blade held loosely in his right hand.

'I've got no money,' Devaney said. 'Take what you like of the furniture and the art. I don't care anymore.'

'I haven't come for that kind of compensation,' the man said.

What little accent he had was English, possibly with just a shade of the north – somewhere around Newcastle, Devaney thought.

'What do you want, then?'

'Information. I'm looking for Ernest Frobisher.'

'I never had direct dealings with him. I worked with his associate, a man called Ressler.'

'You were paid by a company directly owned by Frobisher. There must have been letters, invoices, statements …'

'Yes.'

'And where did they come from?'

'Several different places. London, Amsterdam, Dublin.'

'Where was the main office situated?'

'London, I think.'

'There must have been a phone number you called if you needed to speak to a representative.'

'Yes. But Frobisher is a fugitive now. As is Ressler. Kaiser Care, the company I worked with, has been sold. I very much doubt anyone will be able to help you.'

'You worked with these people for years. You must have learned lots of things about them.'

'It was a business arrangement, that was all.'

'Phillipe Ressler was your chief psychiatrist.'

'Yes. That was part of the arrangement when I signed the business over.'

'So you worked closely with him.'

'I was never involved in the medical end of things. My role was strictly managerial.'

The man moved so quickly, all Devaney saw was a blur of shadow and then he was beside him on the couch, and the hook of the knife was pressed against the narrow expanse of skin between the bridge of his nose and his eye socket.

'I am going to ask you a series of questions, Roderick. If I am not satisfied with your answers, I will start separating bits of your anatomy from your person, beginning with your left eye and working down. When I have finished on your left side, I will begin on your right. Do you understand me?'

'Perfectly.'

'Excellent. Now, tell me about the last time you spoke to Dr Phillipe Ressler.'

Devaney spoke quickly and in detail.

'Thank you, Roderick,' his interrogator said. 'I have learned a great deal from you.'

'I won't tell anyone you were here,' Devaney said.

'I know you won't,' the man said, and cut Roderick's throat with one swift motion of his blade.

1

THE COWAL PENINSULA IS ONE OF THE LEAST
populated areas in Scotland, and indeed, the United Kingdom.
It consists of a narrow strip of land jutting out into the Firth
of Clyde, and is a mix of mountain and moorland. The ruins
of Mesolithic tombs and sites of worship suggest that human
beings have tried to make a living on this land for thousands
of years, but the absence of little more than a smattering of
families on the modern landscape indicates that most find it
far too tough to bother.

The fugitives spent a week driving by night and hiding
during the day, slowly making their way further and further
north. Diane didn't want to risk the car being on the road for
too long at a time, so each journey was restricted to three-
hour blocks, and then only by the most rural of roads.

As they drove, Diane bought items she thought would
be useful: sturdy boots, rain jackets, sleeping bags, a good

hunting knife, a small gas stove and cylinders, an over-sized bag of rice, salt, sugar and tea, a first aid kit. She shopped wisely and bought as cheaply as she thought prudent but soon their funds were gravely compromised.

These precious items were all picked up individually and miles apart for fear of a large purchase arousing any suspicions – the trio knew they were being looked for, now. Their photos had been in the papers and news bulletins had mentioned their flight all week. Luckily, no one, it seemed, had recognised them. The efforts at concealment were holding up.

A book purchased at a petrol station on the outskirts of Glasgow contained a map that was shaded according to density of human settlement – the darker the colouration, the more people called it home. Cowal was almost white.

'That's where we're headed,' Diane told them over a lunch of stale pasties and builder's tea.

They arrived in Drumfairline, the largest village on the peninsula, in the early morning two days later. Diane parked on what passed for the village's main street. 'We'll stop here for a bit,' she said. 'You two stay with the car. I'm going to see what I can see. I'll be back soon.'

Dunnigan and Beth were by now well used to the former Ranger not always sharing her plans with them, and while they were not always happy with her reticence, they were too tired to care that morning, and simply nodded before going back to sleep.

A couple of hours later she was back, a swarthy man in overalls beside her. Dunnigan watched the two having an intense conversation, after which the man walked a wide circle around the Vauxhall, pausing to examine where the fin had been attached. He kneeled and checked the tyres, before standing and offering his hand to Diane, who shook it. The stranger stalked back up the village street, and Diane opened the driver's door and got in.

'What was that?' Dunnigan asked.

'I've just sold the car. Well, actually, I've part-exchanged it.'

'What for?' Beth asked incredulously.

'Something more appropriate to where we're going.'

*

The something turned out to be an ancient Land Rover that Rob, the man in the overalls, informed them was a former military vehicle. 'She won't do you wrong so long as you treat her well,' he said, handing Diane the keys along with a fifty-pound note.

'We don't have papers or a log book,' Dunnigan hissed to Diane.

'Which is just as well, because he doesn't want any,' she said whispered. 'Now remember what I said about keeping quiet?'

He snorted and sulkily helped Beth transfer their gear from the boot of the Vauxhall to the back of their new transport.

'It feels odd saying goodbye to that little car, doesn't it?' Beth said as she put the last bag in its place. 'It's been home for the past week or so.'

'You're starting to sound like me,' Dunnigan said.

'No need to be insulting,' Beth sniffed.

'Let's go,' Diane said. 'We're burning daylight.'

As they pulled out the gate of Rob's yard, Diane took an Ordnance Survey map from her pocket and passed it to

Dunnigan. 'You're navigating,' she said. 'I'm looking for a place called Glen Firmlainn.'

'Is that where we'll be staying?' Beth asked hopefully.

'That's where we're going to be leaving the Land Rover,' Diane said pleasantly, 'before we hike ten miles up a mountain.'

Dunnigan was sure she was joking.

He should have known better.

2

GLEN FIRMLAINN WAS, ACCORDING TO THE MAP, a viewing point, but it was so overgrown with bracken and gorse, it didn't look as if very many people stopped to avail of its charms. Diane parked and then scouted about until she found a narrow pathway leading to a flat area, just off the road. With Dunnigan calling directions, she was able to reverse the Land Rover down into this, and it was then possible to cover the vehicle with scrub and dead vegetation, so it looked like a large and untidy bush.

They then spent thirty minutes dividing their equipment between them and attaching it to three backpacks. Finally, they were ready to go.

'According to an old guy in the pub in the village, there's an old gamekeeper's cottage ten miles north of here, in a kind of clearing between two peaks. He's given me directions, but if he wasn't accurate, you should be prepared to sleep out tonight.'

'Do you suspect inaccuracy?' Dunnigan asked tentatively.

'Hope for the best, prepare for the worst,' Diane said. 'Now let's go.'

*

If Dunnigan and Beth had been in any doubt about their levels of fitness, the ensuing hike made things clear. Within twenty minutes they were both lathered in sweat, their lungs burning and their hearts pounding in their chests. Diane, who seemed completely unaffected by the climb (they seemed to be travelling uphill at a very steep gradient) finally stopped when her two companions fell two hundred yards behind.

'Here's the deal,' she said, once they had caught up. 'We'll go in thirty-minute blocks, and then take a five-minute break. Take some water, both of you.' She tossed them a bottle. 'It helps if you keep your eyes on the ground and take controlled breaths. Don't start panting, you'll hyperventilate.'

'I don't have enough air in me to hyperventilate,' Beth gasped.

'That's my girl – always so positive!' Diane grinned.

*

The next four hours were a hell of nausea, dehydration and muscle cramps. Dunnigan would greet each rest stop with delight, but they were over so quickly and he was back to the agonising trudge before he even had a chance to catch his breath. Just when he was about to proclaim that he could not take one more step, Diane said, 'We're here.'

With a moan the criminologist dropped to his knees and then onto his face. A crumpling sound to his left told him Beth had done the same.

'When you've both got your breaths back, I think you'll see that we are in a rather beautiful place,' Diane said. 'I'm just going to have a quick scout about. The map shows there's a spring near here, but I want to be certain.'

'You have a map?' Dunnigan groaned. 'Why were we worried we wouldn't find the place, then?'

'Because the cabin isn't on the map,' Diane said, her voice getting dimmer as she strode off. 'What kind of a fool would I be to hide us out in a cabin that's shown on the maps? We might as well book into a bloody hotel.'

Dunnigan didn't even bother to come up with a response. He just continued to lie on the rough ground, sweat drying into his back and the impossible weight of all his gear pressing into him from above.

*

He may have fallen asleep – he had a sense of time passing, but he was too exhausted to care. The sound of Beth's voice woke him.

'Oh my God,' he heard her say. 'Diane's not kidding. This is amazing.'

He rolled over and shrugged off his pack. The absence of this weight caused him to almost fall over again when he stood up – his body had become acclimatised to the burden, and for a second he felt so light he thought he might float away. Finally he regained his balance, and straightened up to look at their surroundings.

Behind him was a rough, low stone structure, the ancient slate roof of which was half missing. He saw that someone (it must have been Diane) had already begun to cover the empty space with layers of gorse bush, forming a dense barrier to keep out the elements. But it wasn't the building Beth was marvelling at.

Dunnigan was standing on a flat area overlooking what he thought was called a glen, a narrow fissure that ran between two mountain ranges. He reckoned the glen was about a kilometre and a half in diameter, and it was covered in heather and gorse, the flowers of which created an expanse that was mottled in green, purple and gold. Above all of this wheeled a sky that seemed to go on forever. As he stood there the sun was just beginning to dip below the horizon, and the heavens were deepening into a warm orange that bathed everything in its light.

'Supper's ready,' Diane said behind them.

And he knew that, as painful and frightening as the past week had been, they had found a new home.

3

THE DAYS FELL INTO A PATTERN DUNNIGAN WAS surprised to find both comfortable and comforting. Neither Dunnigan nor Diane pressed Beth on whether or not any memories were returning of those crucial moments in the hospital, but both hoped the solitude and simplicity of their new existence would help those buried experiences to become unearthed.

The cabin, a one-roomed, one-storey construction made of rough mountain stone and natural slate, was cave-like in that it never got too hot or too cold. They cleared it of all the detritus the elements had blown in (leaves, dead twigs, some desiccated animal droppings), and laid out their equipment to make a useable living space.

The stream from which they would be taking their water was one hundred yards to the east, and even though the liquid they drew from it tasted fresh and clear, Diane insisted every drop was boiled before they drank it in any quantity. They used the stove sparingly to conserve gas, and set up a firepit a short distance away from the cabin which they covered with fresh stones every time it was not in use, to avoid detection.

'I don't want to burn anything in the fireplace of the house,' the former Ranger told them. 'If we need to move quickly, I don't want there to be any sign we were here.'

She set up snares which caught rabbits most days, and constructed a very serviceable bow and arrow from a long, flexible branch and a length of fishing line she had bought en-route. With this she managed to kill a young deer on their third day on the mountain, and this meant meat would not be an issue for a couple of weeks to come.

They had the rice they'd brought with them, and the area proved rich with herbs, and edible leaves and flowers. Their meals were hearty, if lacking in variety.

'We can go into town when we run really low on rice and can't get fresh greens, but for now let's sit tight and make the best of what we've got,' Diane told them.

*

The hunting party came during their second week.

They had set up lookout posts at two separate points in the glen, and took turns manning them. From these they could see anyone approaching from about a mile off, which would give them ample time to clear the cabin and get to ground.

Dunnigan had just taken up his post early on a Wednesday when he spied three specks moving down a goat path to the west. He watched for thirty seconds to be sure it wasn't deer or goat, and then ran to tell the others.

Diane had drilled them in breaking camp, and they had the building empty of any trace of their presence in four minutes flat, the improvised roof coverings scattered in pieces about the area. They had excavated three boltholes an easy distance from their camp, and they made directly for them – six minutes after Dunnigan had spied the intruders the fugitives had disappeared, swallowed by the very mountain that was their refuge.

Dunnigan lay still, counting the seconds in his head. Twenty minutes ticked by before he heard them pass: muffled conversation, heavy tread over the bracken and scutch grass. One of them paused almost directly over his hiding place. The criminologist thought he could smell tobacco smoke, and the man's heavy breathing permeated the rock-lined cavern.

Dunnigan was sure they were discovered, and was preparing himself for the fight that was sure to follow when the man heaved a sigh, called something unintelligible to his comrades, and stomped off.

They waited fifteen minutes until they were sure the men had gone, before breaking cover and meeting at a pre-arranged spot on the mountainside.

Diane watched the line of men disappear over a ridge.

'Do you think they were looking for us?' Beth asked.

'Let me put it this way,' Diane said. 'When we got here, I saw no evidence anyone had been in the area for months. A couple of weeks after we arrive, and suddenly we have company. I don't believe in coincidences. I reckon they were definitely looking for us.'

'We should check on the Land Rover,' Dunnigan suggested.

'Leave it a few days, just to be safe, and then I'll go,' Diane said. 'For now, we lay low. Sleep out tonight, and we'll go back to the cabin tomorrow. I want to be certain they don't come back.'

That night they ate cold venison and wild herbs. Diane would not let them light a fire. They took turns watching throughout the night, and in the morning their sleeping bags and clothes were sodden with dew. It was a miserable, cold vigil.

But the men did not return.

Beth Carlton

She could remember the knife, how it felt in her hand.

She had a vivid recollection of the smoothness of the handle, how it had been carved from some kind of wood and contoured so it fit into her grip comfortably, snugly. When she focussed her attention on that sensation, she could also get a sense of the weight of the blade, surprisingly heavy, but not in a way that made it difficult to lift. The weight was, instead, almost comforting. It was as if the heft of the knife communicated that it was a serious, accomplished tool, made by a master craftsman and capable of fulfilling the task it had been built for with ease if wielded by the right person.

What followed this realisation was the sensation which she could sense right down the length of the arm, of the blade cutting. Of the gentle and sure slice of the knife's edge through something. And with each cut, warm fluid spilled over her hand. She could feel the ebb and flow of it.

That night, as they lay rolled up in sleeping bags under the open sky, she closed her eyes and saw the shroud of red, and heard that cooing, strange voice, and felt the blade in her hand and the solid reverberations of the steel passing through something.

And she knew what the something was. She was remembering what it felt like to cut Alfie Jones's throat.

The thought made her sick to her stomach, because along with the knowledge that she was doing this evil thing came the surety that she did not want to do it, but couldn't help herself.

And she could not understand how that was so.

4

'DO YOU THINK THEY'LL BE BACK?' BETH ASKED Dunnigan the following day as they filled water bottles from the stream.

'Who?'

'Who d'you think: the men we saw.'

'I hope not.'

'I hope not too. But that isn't what I'm asking. Do you think they will?'

Dunnigan screwed the lid on one of the bottles and dipped the next one into the cool water. They would bring the water to their firepit to be boiled, which made it taste smoky and insipid, but, as Diane pointed out, that was better than dysentery.

'I think they will have reported back to whoever sent them that there was no sign of us in the cabin, and that it has now been checked and therefore shouldn't need checking again. So no, I don't reckon they'll be back.'

'Really?'

'It wouldn't make sense that they would. They're probably using a grid system to search. They'll move on to the next section of the area.'

Beth punched the air in mock victory, and went on with her water collection. 'Davey,' she said again after a bit.

'Yes?'

'Surely it was the police.'

'What was?'

'The ones who sent them. You said they would go back to whoever sent them and report. Well, surely that would be the police.'

'Yes. Probably.'

Beth gave him a quizzical look. 'Probably?'

'Mmm.'

'What are you thinking?'

'I don't know. I could be wrong.'

'Yeah, but you're usually not.'

He put the lid on his second bottle and sat back on the grass, his legs spread out in front of him. In the sky behind Beth's head he could see a chough, a broad-winged, red-billed mountain crow, wheeling in the cross-winds.

'They weren't speaking English,' he said.

'Weren't they?'

'No. It sounded Eastern European. I mean, I know the UK is a melting pot of cultures, and you'll have police from lots of different backgrounds, but would they send an entire squad made up of only Ukrainian or Latvian or Polish police?'

Beth chewed on her lower lip. 'Doesn't seem likely, does it?'

'No.'

'So who were they, then?'

'That's exactly what I'm wondering.'

Beth stood up, putting the last of the filled bottles into her bag. 'Have you told Diane?'

'Do you really believe she didn't notice it?'

'Well, when you put it like that ... but surely you should discuss it with her?'

'Why? She knows; I know. What's to be gained by talking about it? We'll discuss it when we need to.'

They began to walk back towards the cabin.

'We can't stay here, can we?' Beth asked him.

'No, I don't think we can. We might have fooled that lot, but there will be others.'

The chough made its coughing, cackling call, and somewhere to the south, its companion responded, the cry carried on the mountain winds.

'I like it, though.'

'So do I.'

Beth laughed. 'No you don't. You miss your comic books and your nerdy films and the ability to order in a pizza.'

'I like the fact that you're safe and that no one is trying to kill us.'

'Not today, anyway,' Beth said.

'I'm taking it one day at a time,' Dunnigan admitted.

5

DIANE WENT TO CHECK ON THE LAND ROVER A couple of days later, and returned to tell them she had found it unmolested. Before returning to camp she took a drive into Firlow, the nearest town, and bought some carrots, parsnips, potatoes and pasta, as well as a pair of cheap binoculars, which she hoped would make their watches even more effective. Though they could ill afford it, she completed her shop with a couple of bars of chocolate – she had learned in the army that there is nothing like sugar to raise the spirits.

During the trip she checked every news broadcast she could find and scoured the papers – it seemed their newsworthiness had run its course. There was no mention of them.

Exhausted from the journey and her two long hikes, she slept like a log that night, and the following day Beth volunteered to take first watch, urging Diane to have a lie-in.

Slinging the new binoculars around her neck, the girl set out for the highest lookout point.

The sun was warm and there was a gentle breeze. It was a beautiful day, and she had a full belly and was well rested, but as she climbed the escarpment, Beth was suddenly overcome by a feeling of unease. It took her a few moments to realise that what she was feeling was the sense she was being watched.

Bitter experience had long since taught Beth to trust her gut, and without breaking stride she put on a burst of speed, and vaulted over the rock that was the cover for her lookout position. Bringing the binoculars to her eyes, she scanned the valley below.

At first she saw nothing. It was about 7.30 a.m., and there was lots of wildlife about: rabbits, birds and a family of red deer. The heather swayed easily in the breeze, and for a few minutes she thought she must have been imagining things.

But then she spotted him: making his way down the centre of the glen was a lone figure. Through the lens of the glasses, Beth could see that he was tall and lean, dressed in green-and-olive-coloured outdoor gear. He was moving with a fluid ease – Beth knew that, to reach this far, he had already climbed a good distance, but he did not appear to be fatigued at all. He had a light pack on his back and what looked to be a blackthorn stick in his hand, and as he got closer, Beth was sure she could hear him whistling. She only caught snatches of the tune – she couldn't place it, but it was definitely something she had heard before.

Her first instinct was one of horror – after her conversation with Davey, she had invented all sorts of possibilities as to who the men they had seen were, and all of them came back to the same source: Frobisher, the man who had abducted and kept her as a commodity to be traded and abused for eighteen years.

She, better than any of them, had witnessed the size and scope of his organisation, and had a true sense of how malicious and twisted he was. But also how determined. She had not said it to Davey, but if Frobisher had sent the men, they would *definitely* be back.

This was only one man, but that, in itself, was no indicator. Beth knew that one man could be more than enough – Frobisher had employed an enforcer people called the Yellow Man, and he was rumoured to have wiped out entire criminal gangs single-handed. Mother Joan, whom she and Davey had just encountered and whose blade she seemingly used to kill DI Jones, was another example of a one-person army, a killer who did not need any assistance.

So why did Beth not feel any such threat from this figure? The girl was torn – she should probably cut around and let Dunnigan and Diane know they had company, but something about the approaching man made her think he was not hostile. Their cabin was off to his right, but he did not seem to be headed that way. Instead, he was making a beeline for her position. Had he seen her before she had spied him? Was he genuinely just a lone bird-watcher, hoping to catch a glimpse of one of the recently reintroduced golden eagles?

Keeping low, she crawled out from behind her protective boulder and, using the scrub as cover, moved down the mountainside. Her plan was to flank him, cut him off, and try to gauge how much of a threat he was.

As she drew closer, she found there was something deeply familiar about the hiker. It was in the way he moved, his bearing, but then the tune he was whistling reached her again, and this time she identified it: Neil Young's *Heart of Gold*.

And then she knew who he was. In a flurry of joyful movement Beth sprung from her hiding place and rushed towards the hiker. 'Oh my God, I can't believe it's you!' she screamed in delight.

'I wondered when you were going to come and say hello,' Father Bill Creedon said, throwing his arms around her in a powerful bear hug.

6

'HOW DID YOU FIND US?' DIANE ASKED AS BETH made porridge for everyone back at the cabin.

She was clearly pleased to see the priest, who was a friend and mentor to all of them, and without whom Dunnigan would never have found Beth and rescued her from the clutches of the evil men who held her. But that did not negate the fact that, if he had located them, others could too. His presence meant their jeopardy was far greater than they had at first assumed.

'I sat down with your former captain, Sean Murtaugh.'

Murtaugh had been the head of Diane's regiment when she was a medic and counsellor in the Rangers, Ireland's special forces. He now ran a successful security firm, and Diane remained close to him.

'How did that help?'

'Gina called me to say you had jumped bail – well, she told me it was her idea, in fact. She knew Davey wouldn't last five minutes on his own, so she made sure you went with him, Diane.'

'You never told me that,' Dunnigan said, sniffily. 'You said you happened upon us by chance.'

'I happened to be walking in the hotel's carpark in the middle of the night with my bag fully packed? Come on, Davey!' Diane sighed.

'Anyway,' Father Bill continued, 'I spoke to Frank and he told me your starting point – I knew you were on the border of Scotland and the north of England. So Captain Murtaugh and I sat down with a map, and I asked him: if he was on the run in that area, where would he hole up? Right away he said he would get off-grid, make for the Highlands, and then it was a process of elimination. We narrowed it down to three spots that were the most probable. This is the second I've been to.'

'How did you know we wouldn't go to ground as soon as we clapped eyes on you?'

'Well, I reasoned, and Murtaugh agreed with me, that coming on my own might help – you would be less likely to be spooked by one man. And I sort of telescoped it was me by whistling a Neil Young tune as I plodded along. You all know I'm a big fan of good old Neil. Short of carrying a sign saying "It's me, Father Bill", I don't think there was much else I could have done. And here we are.'

'And I, for one, am delighted,' Beth said, handing everyone steaming bowls of porridge. 'Sorry, we don't have any honey or anything.'

'This is perfect, Beth.' The priest smiled.

'Next question: why are you here?' Diane pressed. 'I mean, you know I love you and it's great to see you, but unless this is a flying visit, you're one more person we have to hide, and that doesn't help us.'

Father Bill smiled gently. 'Ever the soldier, Diane.'

'I'm sorry, Father, but a soldier is what Beth and Davey have needed this past three weeks. I have to think practically if we're to stay ahead of them.'

'Ahead of who?'

Diane paused, and the expression on her face spoke volumes. 'You know it's not just the police hunting you, Beth, don't you?'

'It's alright, Diane,' Beth said. 'I know it. Davey and me, we talked it over.'

'The word is that Frobisher has put a bounty on you,' Father Bill said gravely. 'Scotland is a beautiful place, but it's just not big enough for you to hide in. They're coming. And you have to know: if I found you, they will too.'

'So what are we supposed to do?' Dunnigan asked. 'Hand ourselves in, throw ourselves at the mercy of the courts?'

'That would be even worse,' Father Bill said. 'Frobisher would make sure you and Diane would be killed in prison, and you know the influence he has on psychiatric care through Ressler – Beth would be right back in hell all over again.'

'So what are you saying?' Diane pressed him.

'Beth did not kill that policeman – you know it and I know it. It was all part of a plan to isolate you and put you at Frobisher's mercy. He sees Beth as his property. By framing Beth, he has levelled the playing field.'

'Jesus Christ,' Diane said, throwing her bowl aside half-eaten.

'I never thought of it like that,' Dunnigan said, an expression of enlightenment spreading across his face as if a beautiful truth had just been revealed to him. 'That's actually kind of brilliant.'

'We're fucked,' Beth said.

'No, you're not,' Father Bill said firmly. 'Now, I admit that, as long as Ernest Frobisher is alive, you will have no peace. He will spend his last cent and use his last breath tormenting you. I am in no doubt of that.'

'How comforting,' Diane said ruefully.

'It is, though,' the priest said. 'It makes things very simple.'

'How?' Diane asked, exasperated.

'There is only one way to end it.'

'And what's that?' Beth wanted to know.

'Turn the tables on him.'

'How in the name of God do we do that?'

'We stop running,' Dunnigan said, a smile on his face for the first time in many weeks.

'Exactly,' Father Bill said. 'You take the fight to him.'

'Are you suggesting that *we* start hunting Ernest Frobisher?'

'That is exactly what I'm saying,' Father Bill said. 'Now, is there a cup of tea to be had on this bloody mountain?'

*

'I'm not sure I can let all of you do this for me,' Beth said when they all had cups of tea.

'You don't have any choice,' Diane said.

'Everything that's happened is my fault,' Beth said, looking at her group of friends imploringly. 'I know you all care about me and I can't tell you how much that means to me, but I cannot let you throw your lives away. Maybe it's time to just

175

hand me in. If it stops them coming after you all, it would be worth it.'

'But it wouldn't,' Dunnigan told her. 'When Diane and I first went after Frobisher, we didn't even know he was the one who took you. When Father Bill caused the death of his enforcer, that was because of what he was doing to the homeless community in Dublin.'

It had happened on the Dublin docks. Frobisher had been shipping out large numbers of Ireland's homeless community, the vast majority of whom he had either abducted or duped into going along. His intention was to sell them into slavery abroad. Father Bill, in the company of some members of the Dublin criminal fraternity had learned of his scheme, and had arrived that evening to thwart it. And that was when the priest had come face-to-face with the Yellow Man. During this altercation, which Father Bill intended to settle with his fists, Frobisher's employee had pulled a knife, at which one of the priest's associates, in a fit or ire at such ungentlemanly conduct, had shot him.

'We're all in this for different reasons,' Diane agreed. 'Even if you'd never crossed paths with Frobisher, the rest of us would more than likely still be here.'

'Do you promise me that's true?' Beth asked plaintively.

'Scout's honour,' Father Bill said.

'I promise,' Dunnigan added.

'Me too,' Diane agreed, giving Beth a thumbs up.

And the cabin seemed a homely, comforting place, a safe harbour from the storm they all knew was gathering outside.

7

THEY COOKED GAME STEW THAT NIGHT, USING what was left of the deer (which Diane had smoked) and a hare she shot that morning with her bow. Dunnigan pointed out to her that Scottish mountain hare was protected, and she returned that he had been eating deer killed out of season without complaint so he should probably just accept he was sliding irrevocably deeper and deeper into criminality.

He agreed that he was, and they left it at that.

With the carrots, parsnips and potatoes Diane had bought on her last trip to town, the food was a real treat. Somehow, they all knew it was a celebration, a declaration that the truth had, in some twisted sense, set them free.

When the meal was finished, Father Bill took a bottle of Irish whiskey from his bag and passed it around. As they all took a sip, he said, 'Ernest Frobisher and Phillipe Ressler were last seen entering Berlin by plane.'

'How recently?' Dunnigan asked.

'The day after Beth was taken in for questioning about killing the Welsh policeman.'

'How do you know this?' Diane asked.

'I have friends in both high and low places.'

'More specifically?'

'I was in the seminary with the gentleman who is now chaplain of Gatwick Airport. He called in some favours. Frobisher uses a particular company who lease private jets. With his particular health needs he can't travel, even first class, on standard planes. A man like Frobisher isn't hard to track if you know what you're looking for. My friend tells me the flight he took was bound for Berlin Tegel Airport.'

'So he could be anywhere by now,' Dunnigan brooded. 'From Germany he could travel by road to Afghanistan if the mood took him.'

'It's a place to start,' Father Bill said. 'We'll pick up his trail there and see where it leads. If Afghanistan is part of our itinerary, so be it.'

'I hate to be a fly in the ointment again,' Diane said, 'but how are we going to get out of the UK? We have no money and no papers, and we are on the run from both the law and the criminal underworld.'

There was silence for a moment, then Dunnigan said, 'I think I know someone who can help us with the papers.'

'And I have money,' Father Bill said. 'And even better, I have access to it, seeing as how I'm not on the run. I'm just on sabbatical.'

'And something tells me that the last place either the cops or the robbers are going to look for us is where Frobisher is,' Beth grinned.

'Well my gosh,' Diane laughed. 'It seems we have a plan.'

8

QUINN ALDEN LIVED WITH HIS MOTHER IN A council house on a large estate in Streatham, in south London. Forty-three years old, he habitually wore t-shirts emblazoned with pictures from retro video games, usually in sizes that fought to contain his protruding belly. His thinning hair was teased and gelled into a style reminiscent of those favoured by the boy bands he forced himself to listen to (most of the girls he spoke to on various web forums seemed to enjoy them, so he tried to keep himself educated in their musical stylings).

If you asked his neighbours, they would have told you that Quinn Alden (or Quinny as he had been known locally since his school days) was unemployed. This, however, was not strictly true. He certainly availed of social welfare payments (in his own name and that of his recently deceased grandmother), but he earned a more than respectable living as a hacker, doing various jobs online (usually of a less than legal nature) for anyone who could afford to pay for them. These tasks ranged from adjusting personal data to suit a person's image (an up-and-coming politician might, for example, wish for a drugs charge garnered in their youth to be expunged from the records – Alden could make that happen) or even creating new identities for people and providing the necessary documents to support their existence in the physical world. These days, if the internet said you existed, then you did. It could, similarly, have you declared dead just as easily.

David Dunnigan first came across Alden under the guise of hacker_red during his investigation into the serial killer Mother Joan (when she wanted to turn herself into an online bogeyman, she turned to Alden to get it done), and he could therefore apply a certain degree of leverage.

So it was that Quinn Alden, aka hacker_red, opened the door with a rather grim scowl when the criminologist paid him a visit two days after the fugitives returned to civilisation. 'What you want this time, bro?'

Alden, for reasons best known to himself, affected a cliched and probably completely inaccurate 'street' dialect in conversation. Seeing as he was paler than Dunnigan (who gave the term 'fish belly' new levels of meaning), this seemed highly incongruous.

'I would like to employ you,' Dunnigan said, and without waiting for an invitation, pushed his way into the terraced house.

'I got no wish to be doin' any labour for you or your kind,' Alden said, closing the door and following his visitor into the small kitchen.

'What precisely is my "kind"?'

'I seen the headlines, dude. You a wanted man – you and them ladies. I could get in strife wiv the fuzz if I seen with you, bitch. You caused me enough grief last time. I don't want none of what you're sellin'.'

'How do you know that until you hear what I have to say?'

'Ain't nuthin' comin' outta your mouth I wants to hear.'

'I will pay you handsomely.'

Something passed across Alden's chubby face. It was only there for a millisecond, but Dunnigan saw it.

'Handsome, you say?'

'William Shatner levels of handsome.'

'Original series Shatner? Like, Season One?'

'Of course.'

'Alright. I ain't makin' you no promises, but I s'pose a sitdown won't hurt me none.'

*

'He wants to be paid in what?' Father Bill asked when Dunnigan called him on a burner phone an hour later.

'Bitcoin. It's a virtual currency. I don't fully understand how you even come by it, but I'm told it is one of the most valuable assets on the financial markets at the moment.'

'That's lovely to know, but it doesn't help. Tim Pat has offered to fund our excursion, and he has done so generously, but his donation is in cash, not Monopoly money.'

Tim Pat Rogers was an old friend of Father Bill's, and happened to be the head of one of the most successful and violent criminal gangs in Ireland.

'He doesn't have any tech people on his staff?'

'Rogers is old-school, Davey.'

'Okay.'

'So where does that leave us?'

'I think I'm going to have to call Toddy, Father.'

Toddy was a homeless man who had helped Dunnigan in the past. He had once developed algorithms for one of the larger social media companies, but the stress of the job had caused him to have a breakdown. His mental health remained delicate, and the criminologist hated asking him for assistance – but he had no choice.

'Okay. I'll see if some of my people can find him.' Father Bill was referring to the team he managed at the Widow's Quay Homeless Project.

'Call me as soon as you have anything. Being back in London worries me.'

'I'll make sure they know how important it is we speak to Toddy. He's usually somewhere around Pearse Street Station. I should be back to you within the hour.'

The priest was as good as his word, and fifty minutes later called the criminologist, who was sitting across the table from a glowering Alden, who had begrudgingly made him some tea.

'Toddy is familiar with bitcoin,' he said. 'He tells me he has mined it very successfully – does that make sense to you?'

'I know the term, although I'm not clear what it means.'

'Doesn't matter. How much is your contact looking for? Toddy says we can have as much as we want.'

'Really? We'll pay him for it, of course – you said Rogers is backing us, didn't you?'

'I did, but Toddy says he doesn't want any money. He insists he collects bitcoin for fun. He says it's a game.'

'In all good conscience, Father, I can't take that man's money.'

'I will make sure he's compensated in whatever way I can, Davey. For now, let's just get this done, shall we? How much is this counterfeiter asking for?'

'He says he wants thirteen bitcoin, which is the equivalent of a little over one hundred thousand pounds sterling.'

'Doesn't sound much when you say it fast, does it?'

'For this, Alden will set up untraceable identities for the four of us complete with passports, driving licences, work histories, credit ratings and even a numbered bank account in Austria.'

'I thought those usually existed in Switzerland.'

'Apparently that's too much of a cliché. This gentleman prefers to work with the Viennese, apparently.'

'Hang on a moment. Diane has Toddy on the other line.'

Dunnigan heard muffled conversation. Then, 'Toddy would like you to send him the details of the bitcoin wallet he's going to be transferring the currency to.'

'I'll pass you over to Quinn.'

'This is *hacker_red*,' Alden said, letting Dunnigan know he was unhappy with his name being used on an open line. 'I am going to read out a long web address, and it is important you get it right.'

*

Three days later it was done. Alden insisted on meeting Dunnigan at a particular bench on Platform 3 in Paddington Station. ('I can't have you keep on comin' to my crib, man.')

At eleven in the morning it was busy and Dunnigan had to wait for the bench in question to clear. As soon as he sat down, the hacker appeared as if by magic out of the crowd. He was wearing pink cargo shorts and a t-shirt with a faded, blocky picture of Lara Croft from the original *Tomb Raider* game.

With a flourish, Alden handed him an envelope. 'All the details there, broseph. Passports, licences, details of where you all is s'posed to have lived and worked – I've even set up LinkedIn accounts and social media pages for y'all. The BIC and IBAN for your account in Vienna is there – you set up, man.'

'Thank you.'

'As far as the world is concerned, the dudes and ladies in that envelope have lived long and pro-ductive lives. You owe me big, y'know what I'm sayin'?'

'I *paid* you big,' Dunnigan retorted, and left him sitting there.

The whole thing had left a bad taste in his mouth.

9

OVER THE NEXT WEEK THEY BOOKED TICKETS and flew separately to Berlin. They travelled on alternate days, and they used different airlines and the city's two airports: on Monday Diane flew to Berlin Schönefeld, on Tuesday Dunnigan landed in Berlin Tegel, on Wednesday Beth arrived at Berlin Schönefeld, and on Thursday Father Bill came through customs in Berlin Tegel.

The papers they had just bought worked like a charm, and no questions were asked and no alarms were raised.

Dunnigan discovered that Berlin overturned everything he thought he knew about German culture: it was architecturally beautiful – ornate, gothic buildings side by side with modernist Bauhaus structures, which should be jarring but somehow worked perfectly. The streets, laid out with common sense to make it one of the easiest cities in the world to navigate, were lined with cafés, bars, boutiques and art galleries to suit every taste, and the people seemed open, humorous and friendly.

Yet below this there was another layer of existence for those who wished to make themselves aware of it. For in Berlin you will find the Gestapo museum, a memorial to cruelty and madness on an industrial scale. At various points around the city hang plaques on walls to remember deaths and atrocities carried out in the name of politics, extremism and evil.

Berliners do not shy away from their past. They acknowledge it and get on with their lives. Dunnigan liked that. He could identify with it.

They had booked rooms in a reasonably priced hotel near Checkpoint Charlie, and using Google Maps they charted circuitous routes across the city using bus, rail and taxi to get from their respective airports to the location, just in case any eyes were watching them.

It appeared they had been successful, and Father Bill was congratulating himself on their very effective subterfuge as he checked in at the Gat Point Charlie Hotel. He left his bags in his room and texted the others to let them know he was going to the bar to have a drink, and they should join him.

As he passed reception, the lady at the desk called over, 'Mr Murphy, I have a note for you.'

Father Bill paused. 'You must be mistaken.'

'No, sir. A delivery boy left it after you checked in a moment ago. He said it was for the gentleman I had just finished dealing with, and that was you, sir.'

Father Bill forced a smile and took the note. The message was written in English on a plain sheet of unlined paper, and printed in Arial font in block capitals. It read: I NEED TO MEET. THE FOOD COURT, ALEXA, 10.00 A.M. TOMORROW. Below this was a phone number and the words: CALL WHEN YOU GET THERE.

Father Bill thought he might be about to throw up.

Part Six

A COLD WAR

1

'WHO KNOWS WE'RE HERE?' DUNNIGAN ASKED, his face even paler than usual.

They were all sitting around a table in the hotel's small bar. It was almost empty in the early afternoon, and the barman, busy polishing glasses, ignored them.

'I've told no one,' Father Bill said. 'Except Toddy.'

Dunnigan looked at the priest in disbelief. 'Why did you tell Toddy? I mean, what possessed you to do that?'

'I have asked him to set up an alarm system so that if we get into serious trouble, all we need to do is dial a number and Frank Tormey will know we're compromised. What Toddy has done is create a file system we can update with information that will be emailed to Tormey, so he can continue if we can't. The system has to be encrypted, and that can only be done by one of us – which means the signal needs to come from a server specific to our location – with that in mind, all I told

Toddy was that I was coming to Berlin. I didn't tell him where in the city, I gave him no address.'

'Well, it looks like he's told someone.'

'I don't believe that.'

'With the greatest of respect, Father, he's not in his right mind – he can't be trusted.'

'You trusted him to help find Beth, and he came through for you. I do not believe he gave us away.'

'Well, someone did. It looks like we're finished before we've even really started.'

'Will you two be quiet, please?' Beth snapped. 'For the love of God, this is not the time to be at one another's throats.'

Both men suddenly looked ashamed.

'Did you call the number on the note?'

'From the phone in the hotel lobby,' Father Bill said. 'If it's a real number, it hasn't been switched on. I got an out-of-service signal.'

'Where or what is Alexa?'

'It's a large shopping centre in Berlin's city centre,' Dunnigan told her.

'Surely the sensible thing to do is to have a look at it and see how best to manage this. Whoever sent the note, they're giving us ample time to prepare. Is that the behaviour of someone who wants to get the drop on us or wishes us harm?'

'Beware Trojans bearing gifts,' Dunnigan said.

'Like it or not, Davey, she has a point,' Diane agreed. 'Let's reconnoitre. It can't hurt.'

They left the hotel by separate exits and made their way to Alexa.

2

THERE HAS BEEN A MARKET AT ALEXA PLASZ SINCE
the sixteenth century. The building that currently houses the
mall is, like many similar constructs in the city, quaint and
charming. It contains a huge number of different shops,
restaurants and cafés, old and new, and is one of the most
popular shopping destinations in Berlin.

Dunnigan and his friends arrived on the street outside
Alexa at 6.30 a.m. and set up watch at the north, south and
west approaches (points they had chosen during their previous
afternoon's reconnoitre) – the eastern side luckily does not
have an entrance or exit, as the western has two. They had
all bought cheap burner phones for the occasion, in case the
ones they had purchased in the UK had been compromised,
and they kept in touch with one another by group text (the
burners did not facilitate group calls), flagging up anyone
who looked even vaguely suspicious.

There's a possible suspect just gone in from my entrance. Tall male wearing a fur coat and black converse.

Your fur coat has just left by my exit, Father.

Copy that.

At nine, Dunnigan sent out a group text message that he was going in. Making a point not to behave anxious or jumpy, he went straight in the main entrance to the mall, and rode the escalator to the food court, which was on the first floor. It was extremely busy – shoppers, workers and tourists were all enjoying breakfast at the multitude of tables and counters on offer.

The criminologist scanned the area, but nobody seemed out of place. He walked once around the perimeter of the hall, then took up a position by the lifts and waited. As he watched, he spotted Diane, Beth and Father Bill arrive at their pre-arranged spots and take up watch.

Dunnigan tried to order his thoughts as he monitored the ebb and flow of people. Who could have sent the note? Was it a member of the police force, from either Germany or the UK? Could it be someone sent by Frobisher to kill them – he knew contract killers could be an odd bunch, maybe this was the modus operandi of this particular assassin: first send you a note to arrange to meet so he could tell you in advance that you were going to die.

Maybe it was none of the above – could it be a big mistake? The person who delivered the note hadn't identified Father Bill, after all, by either his real name or his assumed one. Could they have been sent on a wild goose chase? It was certainly possible. He scanned the crowd again – still no one seemed a likely candidate.

At 9.30 a.m. precisely, the lift door opened and a slim figure stepped out, dressed in a bright red puffer jacket, the hood of which was pulled up. They walked with a purpose towards the food court, pausing for a moment to take in the area before going to an Asian tea shop, and ordering a cup. Puffer then went to a table at the southernmost edge of the court and sat down.

Dunnigan looked across at his friends, and saw that they had pegged the newcomer too. He made a gesture for them to stand firm and, taking his phone from his pocket, dialled the number from the note. He heard a ring, both in his ear and across the food court. The hooded person fumbled in their pocket and took out their phone, but Dunnigan hung up before they could answer.

He waved at Diane, Beth and Father Bill, and without any further pause strode across the court.

'I don't know what you want,' Dunnigan said as he pulled a chair up opposite the heavily jacketed person, 'but you need to know – I am walking out of here. You are surrounded. Now tell me what you're playing at before I lose my temper.'

'That's no way to greet an old friend,' a familiar voice said, and the figure reached up and pulled down their hood, revealing a tanned, grinning, long-haired and bearded Miley Timoney.

Dunnigan nearly knocked the table over trying to hug him.

3

THEY GATHERED AROUND THE TABLE IN THE
bustling mall, marvelling at how well Miley looked and
telling him how surprised and delighted they were to see
him.

He was lean and fit, but seemed older somehow, and there
appeared to be extra lines and wrinkles on his kind face. Yet
they would admit to one another later that there was a calm
and confidence about the young man that had not been there
before they left him in Greenland among the Inuit people he
had grown to love. It was clear he had matured and developed
in more ways than they could imagine.

He gave Beth, whom he was meeting for the first time,
a huge hug, and she, in turn, seemed almost in awe of him
– she had heard so much about this man, one of the few
real friends her beloved Uncle Davey had, not to mention
someone who had sacrificed a lot in the quest to find her.

Without her even knowing it, Beth had come to idolise Miley a bit.

'I seem to be asking this a lot these days,' Diane said, holding one of her old friend's hands. 'But how the hell did you find us?'

'I kind of had a feeling things weren't going well for you,' Miley began. 'Our shaman started to have bad dreams, and he told me I was wanted back home, but I didn't want to hear it.'

'You had your own life to lead,' Diane agreed.

'I sent Davey a couple of texts, but he didn't get back to me. But then, out of the blue, I got a message from my Uncle Frank.' Tormey was Miley's uncle. 'He told me what had happened – Beth being in trouble and you guys having decided to make a run for it. He said he needed me – that *you* needed me. So I got on a plane, and I travelled to England as fast as I could. I met Uncle Frank in London.'

'But he didn't know we were here,' Dunnigan said. 'How did you know to come to Berlin? And why all the subterfuge? Why didn't you say it was you in the note?'

'I started to get worried I was being followed. There's a guy I've seen a couple of times, and maybe I'm being paranoid, but I thought I'd better be safe – I didn't want to lead someone right to you, and I was worried the note might be intercepted. I pretended to be asking directions to Checkpoint Charlie when I went into your hotel, and I went right there and did some sightseeing right after I left your place, just in case. As to how Frank knew, I'll let him explain,' Miley grinned. 'He wants to talk to you.'

He took out his phone and dialled a number. 'Hi. Yes, I'm with them now, Uncle Frank. Will I give Davey the phone?' And he passed the handset over to Dunnigan.

'I have to tell you, Davey, you've done well.' Tormey's voice boomed down the line.

'Thanks, boss.'

'But I need you to listen, because I have some information that you might find useful.'

4

'I HOPED DIANE'S TRAINING WOULD KEEP YOU alive and ahead of your pursuers,' Tormey said. 'It looks like I was right.'

'She has been amazing,' Dunnigan said, smiling across at his former partner, who winked back at him. 'We never would have made it without her.'

'They've been combing the Highlands for you, and there are all-points bulletins out across both the UK and Ireland.'

'We saw some people in Cowal. Were they police?'

'Fucked if I know. They brought in trackers. Did they have dogs?'

'No.'

'Probably not our people, then. They might just have been butterfly spotters, you know. The wild places are full of oddballs.'

'Not these people.'

'Sure you gave them the slip anyway. I hear from young Toddy that Father Trendy is with you now too.'

'So it *was* Toddy who gave us away.'

'He didn't come to me. I sought him out. Told him I wanted to help you. He didn't believe me until Miley talked to him. He has a way of making people see sense, that young lad.'

'He does. I'm glad he's with us.'

'Make sure you keep my nephew safe, d'ye hear me? My missus would have my guts if anything happened to him.'

'What did you want to tell me, boss?'

'Oh yeah. I forgot with all this chit-chat. I've been doing some homework, calling in favours and knocking on doors. I think there's a chap in your neck of the woods you should have a chat with.'

'Do you have a name?'

'He's called Nathaniel Joel. He's from Clontarf, originally, so they tell me.'

'And why do you think I should talk to him?'

'He is – and this is all off the record, okay? – Joel is an officer with Irish Intelligence.'

'I didn't know we had an intelligence agency per se.'

'Not a lot of people do – I had to call in all kinds of favours to get this information. If there is a living expert on the After Dark Campaign and Frobisher and his reign of terror, it's Nathaniel Joel. He was tasked to investigate him and all of his activities back in the late nineties. I'm told he made some serious fucking headway, too, was seen as something of a rising star.'

'So why is Frobisher still active?'

'That's a very good question. My sources tell me that someone got to Joel – he was either paid off or frightened so badly he became very quiet and reticent. He's still paid a retainer, but he hasn't given any real information in more than a decade.'

'What good is he to me, then?'

'Just because he's not reporting doesn't mean he doesn't know anything. Why not have a cup of tea with him and see what develops? Can't hurt, can it?'

'No. It probably can't.'

'Look,' Tormey said, 'between you, me and the wall, I think Joel is as crooked as the day is long, but these days, so are you. You might just get along like a house on fire.'

'Where will I find him?'

'Joel is the writer in residence at the Universität Hamburg. And do you want to know something else?'

'I don't know – do I?'

'Hamburg is, according to the accepted wisdom, Ernest Frobisher's last known residence.'

'Interesting.'

'Isn't it?'

'Is there anything else I should know?'

'The fucking minister for justice is pushing for you to be fired and prosecuted, and not necessarily in that order. I can't do anything about it. I tried.'

'That's okay, boss. I understand.'

'The only thing that will make all this go away is conclusive proof Beth was framed and that it went to the top – no one really believes she was actively involved, but the brass are saying you should have let due process run its course.'

'Maybe they're right.'

'They're not.'

'We'll see.'

'You can do this, Davey. You have some good people with you – use their strengths and their skills and make this bastard pay for what he's done. We can collect the evidence when it's finished. I would love to serve it up to the minister on a silver fucking platter.'

'I'll do my best.'

'I know you will. Now listen, I'm going to text you an email address, and the password so you can access that account, which you should only do through internet cafés and public computers. As soon as you get the text, dump all your phones and buy new ones. You'll need to do that every couple of days – I'll do the same with the phones I'm contacting you on, and I'll send my new number to that email account. Check it regularly so you can contact me. We all need to be very careful. You don't know who's watching.'

'Good idea, boss. I'll tell the others.'

'I'll keep doing what I can at this end. Be good. We'll talk again soon.'

The line went dead. Dunnigan handed the phone back to Miley. 'I can't believe we're all together again,' he said.

Petru Kalash Volatov

They told him he was paranoid, but when one of your own men turns against you and removes most of the fingers on your left hand, it gives you a fresh perspective.

Yuri Chechnik had been a good soldier, and should have been collateral damage, but he had somehow survived an attack on one of their operations, and had come looking for Petru, believing he had sold him out.

Petru had no problem telling the angry and scarred Yuri that the decision to sacrifice him had not been his to make, it had all come down to Ernest Frobisher. Because while the average Irish person in the street believed organised crime was run by various gangs – a couple of notorious families in Limerick, Eastern Europeans hungry for new frontiers, pseudo-political factions from the North trying to fill the void left by peace (and the media, fools that they were, perpetuated this belief) – it was really Frobisher who ran it all.

Yuri's injuries must have affected him, because he left Petru mutilated but alive.

Since then the mob boss had upped his security considerably, and never left home without at least two bodyguards.

He had been for a drink at a private club in Inchicore, and, feeling the pleasant buzz only an expensive, correctly chilled vodka can produce, he and his two men got into the back of a Mercedes that had been waiting outside.

'Home now, please, Fyodor,' Petru instructed his driver.

The man (the back of whose head was all they could see) started the engine, and then, in a movement that looked slow but was still so fast none of them could do anything to save themselves, turned and shot Petru's two men in the head.

It was not Fyodor.

'Who are you?' Petru demanded, keeping admirable control of his emotions, despite the fact that he was covered in blood and bits of bone.

'You don't know me,' the driver said, operating the locking mechanism so the man in the back could not throw himself out as they drove. 'I need you to tell me how I can get in contact with Ernest Frobisher.'

'This again?' Petru spat.

'Someone else has been asking?'

'I told him and I am going to tell you the same thing: Frobisher went to ground more than a year ago. You won't find him. Nothing you can do to me will change that.'

'He's still at the top of the food chain, though?'

'There used to be an email address, but it went dead after that detective went to war on us.'

'Talk about this detective. I've been hearing a lot about him.'

'David Dunnigan. His niece was being held in one of our service depots. He took her back and brought the police down on us in force. I've heard there is a lot of bad blood between him and Frobisher.'

'This Dunnigan is a policeman?'

'A criminologist. He works for the National Bureau of Criminal Investigation.'

'And he has Frobisher on the ropes?'

'He has seriously compromised him, yes. From what I hear, he will rest at nothing until he finishes the After Dark Campaign.'

'Thank you, Mr Volatov. Now, would you please recite the email address you used to contact Frobisher? Dead or not, it may be useful.'

Petru did as he was bid, and the man drove on in silence.

'Where are you taking me?' Petru asked when the lights of Dublin faded behind them.

'Don't worry, we'll be there soon.'

Ten minutes later they pulled into a field somewhere in the vicinity of the Glen of the Downs – Petru saw another car (a non-descript Honda Civic) was parked there already. The man got out, closing and relocking the door behind him. Going to the boot, he took a cannister out and began to splash the contents all over the Mercedes.

Petru wasn't surprised when he smelled the petrol, nor when his captor struck a match and set the car alight.

He sighed bitterly. They told him he was being paranoid – well, he showed them, in the end.

Fumbling inside the jacket of one of his fallen bodyguards he found the man's handgun, and, placing the barrel under his chin, blew his own brains out before the flames reached him.

In the light of the burning vehicle, the dark-haired man got into the waiting Honda and disappeared into the night.

5

THE IRISH INTELLIGENCE SERVICE, OR J2 AS IT IS called by those within the corridors of government, was founded in the late 1930s by Éamon de Valera and his friend and spiritual advisor, John Charles McQuaid (later to become Archbishop).

Rumour has it that the mission of the organisation in the earliest days of its existence was to keep the less salutary aspects of the newly established Irish state under wraps – to suppress news of the murders, rapes and other violent and immoral crimes that plagued a population, the vast majority of whom were living in dire poverty with no discernible route out of it. De Valera did not feel such activities were beneficial to the image of Ireland he wanted to project: how could he govern a land of saints and scholars if those saints were raping and then eviscerating the scholars?

Agents were sent out to ensure all violent crime (including

that committed by the Irish overseas) was covered up or, if all else failed, reported only in the vaguest of terms.

As the times changed, J2 was brought in to address issues of terrorism and national security, and after the Good Friday Agreement, to get to grips with organised crime. In its current incarnation, Irish Intelligence is an offshoot of the Irish Army Ranger Wing (Diane's former unit), and is seen as one of the most skilled and effective intelligence-gathering forces in the world. Dunnigan, doing a bit of research in advance of his meeting, learned that John le Carré, the former spy and author, wrote that the proof of the brilliance of Irish Intelligence lay in the fact that most Irish people had no idea it even existed.

Dunnigan hoped that Diane's connection to the Rangers might inspire Joel to open up to them, and so, leaving Father Bill, Beth and Miley in Berlin, the two boarded the 8.03 from the city's Central Station, which was due to arrive in Hamburg at 9.48.

It was a warm spring day, and the train passed through small villages and pastoral countryside as it wound its way towards Hamburg's industrial sprawl. They ordered coffee and a pretzel for Diane from the food trolley and Dunnigan had tea.

'You know, if our lives didn't depend on this, I might actually be having a good time,' Diane said.

Dunnigan shrugged.

'You're doing it again,' she said, sighing.

'I'm doing what?'

'You're going into yourself.'

'I wasn't aware I was.'

'I know how serious this is – I just vocalised it. But there is also the fact that we are on this journey, wherever it might lead us, with the people we love most in the world. The band is back together again. That's something to cherish, surely.'

'I do cherish it.'

'Well, you hide it well. All I've seen is grumpiness and a harsh focus on the tougher aspects of what we're up against. God knows, we might not survive what's coming. We might as well try to enjoy ourselves while we can.'

Dunnigan smiled weakly. 'Okay. I'll try to do that.'

'Good. You are on a train with a beautiful woman, travelling to a city neither of us has ever been to before, to meet a spy. I mean, fuck it, Davey, if that isn't kind of fun, I don't know what is.'

'Well, when you put it like that ...'

They chatted and laughed for the rest of the journey. It was one of the last moments of levity either would remember for a long time.

6

NATHANIEL JOEL LOOKED TO BE IN HIS EARLY
sixties. He was probably five feet nine inches and was stockily
built, bordering on fat. His dark hair was thinning and
had been gelled straight back on his head, and he wore an
expensive tweed suit which he paired with a lime-coloured
shirt and a purple and black striped tie.

'I'm afraid you have me at a disadvantage,' he said when
Dunnigan knocked on his office door.

'My name is David Dunnigan. I am a civilian consultant
with the National Bureau of Criminal Investigation, in
Ireland, and I also lecture in criminology in the National
University of Ireland, Maynooth.'

'I'm very pleased to meet you,' Joel said, shaking his
hand.

'And this is Diane Robinson, formerly of the Irish Army
Ranger Wing.'

'I am honoured, Madam,' Joel said. 'I served briefly. A pleasure to meet you.'

The university was old-world, all wooden floors and faded paintings. Joel's office was no different. A portrait of W.B. Yeats hung on the wall above a huge, antique desk; the other three walls were lined, floor to ceiling, with books, some in English, some in Irish and some in German.

'I'm still not sure how I can help you, though,' the writer said.

'We have it on good authority that you are an expert on Ernest Frobisher and the After Dark Campaign,' Dunnigan said. 'My superior at the NBCI suggested I speak with you, as I have had some ... well, some rather negative experiences with Mr Frobisher.'

'Negative?'

'He abducted and tortured my niece and has tried to have me killed on several occasions.'

Joel sat down behind his desk and waved at two chairs opposite.

'I am sorry to disappoint you, but you have been misinformed,' he said.

'If you need to check my security clearance, you can contact Chief Superintendent Frank Tormey at Harcourt Street,' Dunnigan said.

'You misunderstand me,' Joel said, his voice flat and uninflected. 'I don't know what you're talking about. I sympathise with your circumstances, but I am not familiar with this person.'

'I know you work – or have worked, I'm not sure about your current status – for J2,' Dunnigan pressed. 'Your job was to investigate the activities of Ernest Frobisher, who has links to political corruption, industrial espionage and organised crime. All I want to do is have a conversation with you, off the record. I promise that not one word you say to me or Ms Robinson will be repeated outside these walls.'

'I don't know how to put it any other way,' Joel said, still in that odd monotone. 'I have never heard of, never mind worked for, any organisation called J2. I do not know this Frobisher person. I cannot be of any help to you. I'm sorry.'

'You were a Ranger,' Diane said sharply.

'For a time, yes.'

'So you know our code.'

'The cleanliness of our hearts, the strength of our limbs and our commitment to our promise,' Joel recited.

'Has your commitment to your promise waivered, Mr Joel?'

'I'm afraid I'm going to have to ask you to leave,' Joel said. 'I'm not feeling very well.'

Diane gave him a hard look. 'What was your rank, Mr Joel?'

'That was a long time ago.'

'I asked for your rank, soldier!'

'I was a regimental quartermaster.'

'An officer.'

'Yes.'

Diane reached over and took a pen from a jar sitting on the desk, and scribbled her phone number on a Post-it note. 'Think about that promise, quartermaster. Call me when you have.'

They left him sitting in his office, staring into space.

7

DUNNIGAN AND DIANE CALLED THE OTHERS TO
tell them they would be remaining in Hamburg that evening,
in the hope that Joel would change his mind, given time to
consider his moral obligations.

Father Bill told them not to worry and to enjoy their
evening. Then he went out to buy some cigarettes. There was
a tobacconist's a ten-minute walk from their hotel and he
made for it, enjoying the warmth of the evening sun and the
gentle flow of people. It occurred to him that it was more
than a decade since he had been out of Ireland, and he made
the decision to try and live in the moment and enjoy as much
of the experience as he could. He knew they were in mortal
danger, but he tended to place anxiety at the feet of his God
– he trusted that fate was in the hands of a higher power, that
what was destined to be would be. Him stressing would only
serve to distract him and make him more vulnerable.

The tobacco store didn't have his usual brand (Silk Cut Purple), so he bought a pack of Marlboro instead and he lit one from his Zippo as soon as he was back on the street. As he had nothing better to do, he decided to take a meandering route back to Gat Point Charlie and maybe take in some window-shopping on the way.

His nose was pressed against the glass at a leather worker's shop, examining a jacket made from treated calf's hide, when a reflection caught his eye. It was a tall, dark-haired man dressed in a loose-fitting white shirt and dark jeans. He was loitering in the doorway of a bar on the opposite side of the street, and seemed to be very pointedly *not* looking at Father Bill.

This in itself was not unusual, but for the fact that the priest was sure he recognised the interloper – hadn't he seen him outside their hotel as he was leaving earlier that afternoon? That said, the man wasn't unusual-looking, and Father Bill was prepared to admit he might be mistaken. Filing the image away for future reference, he turned his attention back to the leather jacket, and decided to go inside and try it on.

It didn't fit as well as he would like, but the assistant insisted he try on a couple of others, so it was a good twenty minutes before he left the store. When he did, the tall man was gone.

He reappeared two streets later, sitting on a windowsill, again not looking at the priest for all he was worth.

Father Bill paid him no heed and turned the corner that led to Rodrik Platz, then broke into a sprint, covering a hundred yards rapidly, slowing only to duck into an alley. He waited, just inside the shadows, for the man to pass.

It seemed to take him an age to catch up, but then he was there, hands deep in the pockets of his jeans. As soon as Father Bill spotted him, he reached out and caught his shoulder, spinning him into the mouth of the laneway, where he delivered a powerful right hook to his jaw.

The blow should have felled Father Bill's shadow, but in a move any boxer would be proud of he turned slightly just as the punch hit, lessening its force and putting the priest a little off-balance. As the cleric fought to regain his footing, the other man drove his elbow into his solar plexus. Pain exploded in his mid-section and he found he couldn't catch his breath, but he had no time to worry about such trivialities, as his attacker was reaching into his pocket – the priest assumed for either a gun or a knife. Father Bill cast about, spotted a crate of empty beer bottles, and grabbed one, smashing it into the side of the other's head. It made a satisfying *clunking* sound.

Once again, to his amazement, the man did not fall but instead staggered back against the alley wall. Thinking he must have disabled him, even temporarily, the priest stepped back for a moment, and this was his undoing. The man, blood now flowing from a cut in his temple, used the wall to launch himself at Father Bill, smashing his forearm into his cheekbone, causing the priest's world to be subsumed by stars, and this time knocking him onto his side.

By the time the priest got to his feet, his head pounding, the tall man was gone.

8

WHEN DUNNIGAN MET DIANE FOR BREAKFAST the next morning, she was grinning from ear to ear.

'Guess who called me last night?'

'You know I'm useless at guessing games.'

'Joel, you idiot. He's agreed to join us for coffee.'

'Good. There are one or two things I would like to say to Mr Joel.'

'Let's hope he has had a sleepless night and is anxious to purge his guilty conscience.'

'He might just feed us a pack of lies.'

'What did I tell you about focussing on the positive?'

'Sorry. I really am trying.'

'That's okay, Davey – it's not your fault you're such a miserable fucker.'

'Thanks. I think.'

*

Diane had arranged to meet Joel in a small café on Ballindamm/
Jungfernstieg, a junction of two of the city's most fashionable
shopping areas. He bustled in five minutes after they arrived,
looking flustered and annoyed.

'I can spare no more than half an hour this morning,' he
grumbled, ordering coffee and a strudel. 'I'm scheduled to
give a class at eleven.'

'I thought you were a writer,' Dunnigan said.

'Writers in residence do not just sit in their offices and
write all day. We are expected to give classes, meet visiting
dignitaries, do some one-on-one tutorials – I am a busy man,
Mr Dunnigan.'

'Davey.'

'I beg your pardon?'

'People call me Davey.'

'Oh. Davey, then.'

'How did you come by your residency?'

'The university was looking for an on-campus writer, and
as I was living locally, I was offered the position.'

'Because you're a successful and famous author?'

'Well, I wouldn't like to say ...'

'I will, then,' Dunnigan said. 'You're not. According to the
university website you have self-published two books, both
on the work of W.B. Yeats. Their combined sales, according
to my research, is 472 copies. I could only find one review, and
I think you might have written it.'

'I can assure you I did no such thing.'

'I did some checking,' Dunnigan continued. 'The residency
at the Universität Hamburg is a sponsored position. Meaning
someone put up the money. Someone outside the institution.'

'I do not concern myself with such things.'

'I haven't followed the money trail back yet,' the criminologist said, 'but when I do, I am pretty certain Ernest Frobisher is going to be at the end of it.'

'Now wouldn't that be a huge surprise,' Diane said, shaking her head ruefully.

'I did not come here to have my character maligned,' Joel said, turning a deep shade of purple.

'I just wanted to begin our conversation on even ground,' Dunnigan said, producing a sheet of paper from an inside pocket. 'We know you've been bought off. Let's get that out of the way so we can move on.'

Joel blinked and mopped some sweat from his brow, although it was comfortably cool in the café.

'Tell us what you know about Ernest Frobisher.'

'I don't know where to begin,' Joel said, his body-language and tone communicating he was resigned to the fact that he was going to have to talk, at last.

'The beginning usually works best,' Diane said.

And as Dunnigan took notes in his spidery hand, Nathaniel Joel painted a picture of Ernest Frobisher that surprised and perplexed them both.

Beth Carlton

She bought an Irish paper in one of Berlin's larger newsagent's, and was faced by an image of Wilfred Hubert staring up at her from the front page. It was just about the last thing she wanted to see.

Trying to remember what had happened in the hospital with Alfie Jones, attempting to focus her mind on the violence of that interaction had brought a lot of other experiences floating to the surface, too.

A few days after her fourteenth birthday Beth had been sent to a hotel in Amsterdam with Dova, another teenage girl. A party was going on there, and the two of them had been asked by Frobisher to entertain a short, violently tanned American man. This entertainment had involved Beth choking him with his own silk tie while he had sexual intercourse with Dova, strangling her with his small, perfectly manicured hands as he did so. Excited by the sex and emboldened by having taken far too much cocaine, Hubert had broken Dova's neck.

Beth, shocked and frightened at what had happened, was taken back to the apartment she shared with four other underage sex workers while the cleaning crew came to dispose of the body and hide the evidence. She was at home before she realised she still had Hubert's tie in her hand: soaked in blood and covered in all kinds of DNA – hers, Dova's and Hubert's.

Terrified of someone finding she had such an item (no one would believe she had taken it by accident), she put it in a plastic shopping bag and buried it in the apartment block's small garden.

It was only now, when her mind was so taken up with the

crime she believed she might have committed, that she began to wonder about that tie.

Hubert was, according to gossip among the girls she lived with, a regular patron, preferring his escorts to be in the midst of early adolescence. And Frobisher was the person through which he sourced these young girls.

Beth thought about that.

She didn't know if it would help her out of her own predicament, but it might. Hubert worked for Frobisher, and probably knew a lot of his secrets. The article said he was planning a run for the US presidency – maybe he would trade information to keep things out of the papers.

She had sworn to Frobisher, who threatened to kill her and everyone she cared about if she uttered a word of what Hubert had done, that she would never tell a soul. Now she began to wonder who she might share this information with.

There was really only one person. Miley Timoney.

9

AT PRECISELY THE SAME TIME AS DAVEY AND DIANE were talking to Joel in Hamburg, Beth, Father Bill and Miley were gathered around a table in the breakfast room of their hotel in Berlin,.

'Bar fight?' Miley asked the priest when he sat down: his left eye had come up in a glorious shiner.

'I wish,' Father Bill said, and told them about his adventure of the previous evening.

'It doesn't look like he was from the police,' Beth said when he was finished.

'If he was, we'd all be arrested by now,' Bill said, shaking his head. 'No, not police.'

'What about a bounty hunter?' Miley suggested.

'Doesn't make sense either,' the priest said. 'Why wouldn't they have just taken us in? He followed me from the hotel, so whoever he's working for knows where we live.'

'That only leaves Frobisher,' Beth said.

'But surely that toxic goblin wants us dead,' Father Bill mused. 'He had a chance to finish me in that alley last night, and he let me live.'

'Unless he's toying with us,' Beth said.

'Which is definitely his style,' Father Bill said. 'This didn't feel like Frobisher, though. It was too direct, too clean.'

'He tried to pull a weapon on you, and in return you hit him in the head with a bottle,' Beth said. 'Isn't that the very definition of fighting dirty?'

'That's not what I meant. From everything we've experienced of Frobisher so far, it seems to me he's not going to come at us head on like this. It's not his way.'

'It's a strange one, alright,' Miley agreed. 'No more going out alone, any of us. We travel in pairs or not at all.'

'Agreed,' Father Bill said, and Beth nodded.

'Did you notice anything about him, anything odd or unusual?'

The priest pondered that for a bit. 'He was very skilled – he'd been trained in hand-to-hand, and he was able to take a hit, that's for sure. Blows that would have put most people down, he shrugged off as if I was tickling him.'

'Anything else?'

'This is a harder one to put into words, but there was a … a very slight stiffness to him – it was barely perceptible, but it was there – that made me think he'd been injured at some point.'

'Injured?' Miley asked.

'Yes. When I was a young man I fought an English boxer called Bristol. In a previous bout he'd broken a rib, and even though it was healed up, he tended to favour his other side and was always protecting that spot, as if he was afraid he'd be hit there again.'

'And the man from last night was like that?'

'Kind of. You'd have to be a fighter to spot it, and it was only very slight. I think he'd been working really hard to put whatever happened behind him, but the body remembers these things and will instinctively try to protect weakened or damaged areas. It's almost subconscious. It's just a sense I had.'

'Does that help us?' Beth asked.

'Well, he still kicked my ass, so probably not,' Father Bill admitted.

'Anything we know is a benefit,' Miley said.

'Hell, I think I'm actually getting stupider as the days go by,' Beth said.

10

'I WAS SENT TO HAMBURG IN 1998 TO CARRY OUT surveillance on Ernest Frobisher,' Joel began. 'I had no real desire to do the job, but I had been out of the service for several years at that point, and my decision to try and make a career as a writer had not been successful. I needed the money, and I did not think following a businessman around for a few months would be a terribly challenging commission.'

'What did you know about him in the beginning?' Diane asked.

'Simply that he was a billionaire – it was old money, as the family had been successful in business for several hundred years – and in politics he leaned to the right. I was told he was active in a number of reactionary organisations and had been connected – though never with enough evidence to prosecute – to several murders.'

'But you didn't feel he was dangerous?'

'I saw no sign of it. I followed him to meetings, I sat outside restaurants when he went to dinner, I listened in on telephone conversations about stocks and shares and I intercepted his mail. Nothing seemed out of the ordinary. Well, almost nothing.'

'Can we cut to the almost nothing?' Diane said sweetly.

'His assistant seemed a bit ... a bit *off*.'

'The Yellow Man?' Dunnigan asked.

'Yes. His name was Norman Andrews. I witnessed one or two violent incidents where he was involved. I never thought Mr Frobisher approved, but he seemed somewhat in thrall to the man.'

'You know Andrews is dead, don't you?' Dunnigan asked.

'I had heard that, yes. A gang war on the Dublin docks, I believe.'

'Something like that,' Dunnigan said.

'What do you know about Andrews' past?' Diane asked. 'How did he and Frobisher get together?'

'I know almost nothing of him,' Joel admitted. 'It is as if he sprang into existence in the early 1990s. I have heard rumours that he was an assassin the British government couldn't control, but I don't believe it. I've always thought he was just a freelance psychopath.'

'And he became Frobisher's henchman,' Dunnigan said. 'What makes you think Frobisher was under his control?'

'Because everything I have seen and heard about Frobisher has led me to believe he is a good man.'

Dunnigan and Diane looked at Joel, stone-faced.

'Let me be very frank,' Dunnigan said. 'This "good man" you speak of instructed Andrews to put a knife in Diane's eye. Andrews didn't suggest it or propose it, Frobisher told him to do it and was visibly excited at the prospect. Does that sound to you like the actions of someone who is inherently good?'

Dunnigan and Diane's first meeting with Frobisher occurred after they had parked an old Volvo station wagon Diane owned right across the gate of his mansion in the Dublin Mountains, thereby making it impossible for anyone to get in or out of the estate. This drastic action was, in fact, a bid to draw him out. Dunnigan was convinced Frobisher was involved in people trafficking, but the criminologist's attempts to confront him had all been thwarted – it became clear Frobisher had bought off at least one government minister, who in turn had influenced Dunnigan's superiors in the Irish police to order his investigation be halted. Dunnigan had carried on in his free time, and Diane had agreed to help. Frobisher's people, led by The Yellow Man, had, in response, sandwiched their vehicular barricade between two jeeps, trapping them inside, after which the enforcer had smashed the windscreen in with a sledge-hammer, hauling them out and leading them to his employer, who had ordered they be killed. They had barely escaped with their lives.

'I believe he was corrupted,' Joel said earnestly.

'By Andrews?'

'No. By one far, far worse.'

'Who?'

'Have you encountered Doctor Phillipe Ressler?'

'I have had some dealings with him, yes.'

'I would say, with all due respect, that he is a bit of a cunt,' Diane added thoughtfully.

'I do not condone your choice of language, but I agree with the sentiment,' Joel said. 'Ressler is the monster in this tale.

Ernest Frobisher is a good man, some might say a visionary, who is beset by evil individuals. His wealth attracts them, and, alas, his inherent goodness does not permit him to separate himself from them.'

'Just hold on one moment,' Diane butted in. 'You are trying to tell us that Frobisher can't get rid of all these bad people because he's too good? Isn't that a contradiction?'

'I think there may be a psychological weakness to his character. His mother died when he was in adolescence. He has spent his life looking for people to trust. Ressler twisted and contorted him, taking advantage of his ill health and, I believe, ultimately taking charge of his business completely. Ernest Frobisher is barely functioning anymore. The evil you see is all coming from Phillipe Ressler.'

'If I didn't know better, I'd think you were suggesting Frobisher needs rescuing,' Dunnigan said.

'That may not be far from the truth,' Joel said, his eyes growing misty. 'The story of Ernest Frobisher may be one of the great tragedies of our age. If someone were to help him in these, his last days, and rid him of the demons who have beset him, well, I think that person would be doing the world a great service. Frobisher may still have some good to perform before he leaves this mortal coil, but for that to happen, Ressler will have to be neutralised.'

Dunnigan sat back, surveying his page, which he had now folded into a small square, writing densely covering it. 'So, to summarise your position – Ressler is responsible for all the crimes Frobisher is accused of, and before him, Norman Andrews, aka the Yellow Man.'

'That is the simplified version of events, yes.'

'Tell us the more complicated one.'

'Frobisher's businesses – which are many, varied, and all very profitable – employ hundreds, if not thousands, of people on a global scale. Do you not think that, within a barrel of that size, there are going to be some bad apples?'

'You're now going to tell us that the professional malpractice was all down to errant employees?' Diane said, the incredulity apparent in her voice.

'My knowledge of the man is that he is a micro-manager,' Dunnigan agreed. 'I've heard stories of him visiting maintenance yards. I don't think he's the type to miss what's going on at the executive level.'

'I agree that he has the common touch …'

'That's not what I meant.'

Joel ignored him. 'I'm just saying he isn't superhuman. It is perfectly reasonable that he would miss some things.'

'Could you give me an example?'

Joel finished his coffee and motioned the waitress for another. 'A man called Ambrose Harmon used to work for one of Frobisher's companies here in Hamburg. They specialised in the import and export of bespoke furniture.'

'Sort of a posh version of IKEA,' Diane offered.

'If you like. Harmon was having the books adjusted to show inflated profits in a bid to boost share prices. I spotted it during a random swoop through Frobisher's accounts.'

'But he didn't?'

'No. And there was more than that. Harmon was operating some very shady personnel policies – he refused to hire married women, he sacked employees he discovered were homosexual, he had very questionable policies around the role of individuals of certain … um … ethnic persuasions in his warehouses.'

'You're saying Frobisher knew about none of this?' Dunnigan asked.

'The same Frobisher who is a card-carrying member the British National Front and half a dozen similar groups with known racist and homophobic policies?' Diane scoffed.

'I do not believe his membership of those groups means he is a racist or a homophobic.'

'Now you're just being daft,' Diane said.

'I will concede that Mr Frobisher's politics are conservative, but that does not make him a bigot. The groups you refer to also support native businesses and free trade. It is these philosophies that attract him rather than their other activities, which are often exaggerated by certain factions within the press.'

'Are you for real?' Diane's tone was hardening now.

'Let's agree to disagree on this point,' Dunnigan said. 'The point you were making was that Frobisher did not know about this gentleman's actions.'

'Not at first. I found a way to let him know.'

Dunnigan paused, his pen hovering above his tightly folded notes. 'You're telling me you compromised your cover?'

'Yes. It was the right thing to do.'

'Please explain what you mean.'

'I felt Ernest Frobisher would want to know what was going on, that he would want to stop it.'

Dunnigan now realised what was happening. It is a well-recorded phenomenon. Ethnographers and anthropologists call it 'going native'. Sleeper agents refer to it as 'imprinting'. Whatever the name, it amounts to the same thing: an unhealthy over-identification with the subject of your research. Joel, it seemed, had become obsessed with an idealised version of Frobisher, and had allowed it to warp his judgement.

'What did you do?' Diane asked.

'I made an appointment to visit him in his offices in the Reeperbahn. I presented him with my evidence about Harmon, and Mr Frobisher was exactly as I knew he would be: shocked at the news of what was happening in one of his operations, and grateful to me for enlightening him.'

'He fixed the problem, then?'

'By the end of the day, Harmon was no longer in his employ.'

Dunnigan wrote something down. 'Do you know where Harmon is now?'

'Last I heard he was working for a liquidation firm in Prague.'

'Thank you,' Dunnigan said, adding this to the information he had recorded. 'Diane, is there anything else you want to ask Mr Joel?'

'There is,' Diane said. 'Mr Joel, did Frobisher pay you off at that first meeting, or was it later in your relationship?'

Joel scowled and stood up. 'I have been nothing but cooperative,' he said. 'I am not going to continue to sit here and be insulted.'

'*You* have insulted *me*,' Diane seethed. 'You are a disgrace to your regiment, to everything we are supposed to stand for.'

'Diane, please.' Dunnigan placed a hand on hers. 'Mr Joel, is there anything you want to add before you go?'

'I have given you the names of the people I know Mr Frobisher trusted but who let him down badly, who betrayed him, despite his goodwill and indulgence. But there is one person I know of whom Mr Frobisher truly despised. They had a very serious disagreement which got particularly ugly. Her name is Suzanna Merrick.'

'Frobisher had a falling out with this woman and she's still alive?' Diane marvelled.

Joel smirked in response. 'Once again you misjudge Mr Frobisher,' he said. 'He did not try to kill Suzanna Merrick. It was *she* who attempted to have *him* murdered.' The squat man turned for the door.

'Mr Joel,' Dunnigan called.

'What?'

'Where is he? Where's Frobisher hiding?'

Joel paused before answering. 'If I knew, I wouldn't tell you.'

11

THEY WENT BACK TO THEIR HOTEL AFTER meeting with Joel, and Dunnigan spent half an hour on the public computer in the lobby, after which he went to Diane's room.

'Suzanna Merrick is based in Portland, Oregon,' he said. 'She is vice president of a finance company called Global Economic Solutions.'

'And the other guy?'

'Ambrose Harmon. He is, indeed, in Prague. He is some kind of executive in a law firm that specialises in liquidation agreements between businesses and banks.'

'Sounds like a happy job.'

'I wouldn't know about that. What did you make of what Joel said?'

'I think he is completely full of shit, Davey,' Diane retorted. 'Frobisher paid him off and got him the cushiest job imaginable to keep him onside. Part of the deal is that he stops reporting to J2 at all, and he feeds anyone who does come asking some kind of bullshit line about Frobisher being the bastard love child of the Tooth Fairy and Santa Claus.'

'So you don't think there was any truth in it?'

'I think the Yellow Man and Ressler are definitely evil scumbags.'

'Of course.'

'But the rest? No.'

Dunnigan began to unfold the page of notes, checking and cross-checking information. 'Maybe a more pertinent question is: does *he* believe it?'

Diane, who was sitting on the bed, pulled her knees up under her. 'That's a more difficult question. I think he might *want* to believe it, because it lets him off the hook for being such a weak-ass pussy.'

'Agreed. I'm inclined to think we got some half-truths. A more reasonable take on his story is that Frobisher, or Andrews or Ressler, sniffed him out, and he traded information to save his own hide. The version of events he told us paints him as some kind of moral crusader who went over to the other side to strike a blow for human decency, which is much easier to live with than simply being a coward.'

'So where does that leave us?'

'With two fresh leads.'

'How do you want to play it?'

'Prague is an easy trip by rail from here.'

'Makes sense for the others to head stateside and for us to meet them there.'

'Don't you think we might be walking into a trap? Can we trust Joel?'

Dunnigan scribbled something onto his bit of paper. 'As long as it brings us closer to Frobisher, I'm prepared to risk it.'

Diane grinned. 'Would you like to call them and give them the good news?'

'I can do that.'

Nathaniel Joel

He got back to his apartment at 9.30 p.m. He had worked late in the library, and research for a new book he was planning on the mystical poetry of W.B. Yeats was almost complete.

He planned to have a glass of brandy and turn in. He was shocked when he turned on the light in his study to find a dark-haired man seated behind his desk.

'Good evening, Mr Joel,' the man said. 'You had a meeting earlier today with two individuals who were interested in Ernest Frobisher. I would like to know what you told them. And what you chose not to tell them.'

Joel began to protest.

His unexpected visitor stood, and came around the desk.

And Joel's protestations quickly became screams.

Part Seven

WHERE THE ROSES GROW

Wilfred Hubert

He blamed the cocaine.

He always tried to keep his wits about him when attending social functions (another product of his father's old rule about maintaining appearances) but back then, in the heady days of the economic boom of the first decade of the twenty-first century, he'd been so busy and spread so thinly, he found that a few lines of coke gave him an edge, made him feel more like the sheriff he was supposed to be.

Frobisher had sent him an email, inviting him to a very exclusive gathering in Amsterdam's select Andaz Prinsengracht Hotel. He'd already consumed 15 grams that day, and the stuff at the party was stronger than he was used to. When the maitre-d asked him if he would like to spend a couple of hours with one of the girls that had been laid on for the night, he immediately said he'd like two. 'I'm feeling particularly potent this evening,' he'd laughed.

The pair who looked youngest were just to his taste: one was some kind of Russkie – she had the sallow skin and mousy hair of her kind, and spoke hardly any American at all, but the other was (he was told) an Irish colleen – she was very pretty, with jet-black hair and big blue/grey eyes. She seemed unafraid and held his gaze and could follow his instructions without him having to speak loudly and slowly, as he often did with whores.

'What's your name?' he asked her.

'Whatever you want it to be.'

'Stop fucking around and tell me your name.'

'You can call me Sarah Jane.'

Alright, Sarah Jane. I am going to fuck your friend, and I want you to take my tie and wrap it around my neck and hold it tight while I do her.'

The girl shrugged. 'Whatever you want. It's your party.'

He hit her then, hard, knocking her flat onto her back on the carpeted floor. To his surprise, she didn't seem fazed. In fact, she laughed. 'Did that get your dick hard?'

'I could beat you some more and get it harder.'

'Like I said, it's your party.'

'Take your clothes off. Tell her to do the same.'

'I think she knows the drill.'

He toyed with them for a time, pushing them around and hitting them (though not too hard, he liked to save that for near the end), and then he mounted the Russian girl. 'My tie's on the floor,' he grunted at Sarah Jane. 'Choke me. Do it now!'

God, that little Irish hooker was good – she applied just the right pressure on the ligature to heighten his pleasure. Maybe it was her attitude, the fact that she knew how to take the hits and make it all seem like a game, but he was more turned on than he had ever been. He placed his hands around the Russkie's neck and began to choke her too. He saw her face turn purple, and she gripped his wrists and tried to pry them off, but he was nearing the moment of crisis, and there was no stopping him.

'I think she's had enough,' Irish said urgently.

'Shut the fuck up,' he croaked, and began to thrust harder and squeeze tighter.

The girl beneath him started to claw at his face, digging her nails into the flesh of his cheek, but that only drove him on harder, and he felt her pelvic bone thump against his, and in a surge of power that was both erotic and psychological he bore down on her with all his strength, and the bones in her neck crackled and popped and she bucked once, then twice, and was still.

In that moment he had the orgasm of his life.

'You *fucking* idiot!' Sarah Jane said, pushing him to one side and shaking the Russian girl. 'Dova – can you hear me, Dova? Jesus fucking Christ, you've only gone and killed her!'

'Stop whining and get the maitre-d to call for help,' he said. 'And while you're at it, fix me a drink, will you? The two of you have milked me dry.'

He liked being the sheriff.

He was still sprawled naked on the bed, sipping champagne, when the clean-up crew came.

1

BETH AND MILEY SAT SIDE BY SIDE IN THE HOTEL bar. Father Bill had gone to buy a book to read during their imminent flight to the States and was then intent on an early night, so the two had decided to spend their last evening in Berlin over a companionable drink.

'Miley?'

'Yes?'

'Can I ask you something?'

'You can ask me anything. I might not know the answer, but if I don't, I'll say so.'

The pair had become firm friends in the few days since their first meeting. Beth was aware that Miley was one of the few people Dunnigan trusted – which meant she could trust him, too.

'If we find Frobisher and Ressler ...'

'*When* we find them.'

'Okay, when. Well, it's been on my mind that no one is talking about what's going to happen after that. Are we going to sit down and have a chat? Are we going to call the police on them? Will Father Bill send his gangster mates to smoke them out?'

Miley pursed his lips, considering. His long hair was tied into a loose ponytail and his beard was cropped close. Beth thought he had a handsome, sensitive face. She realised, as she watched him, that they were similar ages, and had both led difficult lives – she at the hands of Frobisher's traffickers, he at the whim of his family and the state. She wondered if that was why she felt such a connection with him.

'I think what you're really asking me is whether or not we're planning on killing them,' Miley said after a time.

'Is that what I'm asking?'

'I reckon it is.'

'And what's the answer?'

Miley shrugged. 'We've all killed since we started this journey,' he said. 'Not because we wanted to, but because they gave us no choice. It's not something we've talked about, though. I suppose it's a truth none of us is ready to face up to yet.'

'What you're saying is that they're probably going to have to die, aren't you?'

'If they leave us no other option, yes. This has changed us, Beth. We've done things we wouldn't have thought possible a year ago.'

'You did those things for me,' Beth said. 'You and Father Bill and Diane went through hell, and you didn't even know me.'

'We did it for you, yes,' Miley agreed, 'but we also did it for

Davey, and we did it for ourselves. When I met these people, I found my family. You were and are a part of that. You do what you have to for your family.'

Beth laid her head against Miley's shoulder. 'I don't know if I deserve everything you've sacrificed,' she said. 'Sometimes it makes me really scared to think of what's been done for me.'

'No need to feel pressured by it,' Miley laughed. 'Just make sure that, as soon as this is over, you get started on finding a cure for cancer or solving the world hunger situation.'

'I'll get straight to it,' Beth agreed.

'In the meantime, just be grateful you've got so many people who love you. As someone who didn't for a *long* time, it's something I give thanks for every day.'

'Miley?'

'Yes, Beth?'

'Thanks for being honest.'

'Lying doesn't help anyone.'

'I wish everyone believed that.'

'Me too.'

They sat for a time in silence, the bar around them beginning to fill in the early evening with tourists returning from their day of sightseeing.

'There's something I need to tell you,' Beth said after a while. 'It's something I swore never to speak of, but I think I have to. It might be important. And if I'm going to tell anyone, I think it should be you.'

Miley sipped his beer. 'Okay. I'm listening.'

'Not here. Can we go for a walk?'

'Of course.'

He paid for their drinks and they went out into the city.

As they walked, she told him about a party in a hotel in Amsterdam, and how a man named Wilfred Hubert, who was, as they spoke, meeting with the Irish government as part of an historic trade agreement, had murdered an underage prostitute named Dova, and how Ernest Frobisher had warned her never to tell another living soul, on pain of terrible things being visited on those she loved.

2

WHEN BETH WAS FINISHED HER STORY, SHE FOUND she could not look at Miley. She had talked to her therapist, Harriet Grantham, about some of this stuff before, but never to her family or friends. Sharing something so sordid made her feel soiled and a little nauseous. Miley said very little throughout and made no immediate comment afterwards, and when she finally stole a glance at him she was horrified to see he was crying.

'Miley … I'm sorry – I didn't mean to upset you. God, I'm so stupid. Please forget I said anything.'

'Beth, you don't need to apologise. I'm not crying for me. I'm crying for you.' He stopped walking and put his arms around her. 'No one should have had to go through what you did,' he said, his voice still hoarse from tears. 'I'm so sorry you had to experience all that.'

Beth, overwhelmed, hugged him back. 'Thank you,' she said.

'What for?'

'For giving enough of a shit to cry for me.'

They walked on for a while, and somewhere along the way she reached out and took his hand. He looked over at her, surprised, but when he saw how uncertain she was, and how her eyes told him she needed this human contact, he grinned and gave her hand a squeeze and they continued like that, each getting comfort from the other.

*

They sat on a bench overlooking the River Spree. Couples strolled past, arm in arm. A busker was singing an Ed Sheeran song.

'Do you feel any better now you've talked to me about what happened?' he asked her.

'I do, but that's not why I told you.'

'No?'

'I think it's another way we can get Frobisher. It's like a second line of attack.'

'I can see where you're coming from, Beth, but it would be your word against his. I suppose there might be some hope of forensic evidence if you knew where poor Dova was buried, but even then, I suspect someone like Frobisher would use a cleaning crew who would dissolve the body with chemicals, like on Season 1 of *Breaking Bad*.'

'Never seen it.'

'When this is over, you and I are going to sit down and binge-watch the whole thing. It's brilliant. So dark and funny.'

'I'd like that.'

'It's a date.' He heard what he'd just said and felt himself blushing. He was glad he hadn't mentioned Netflix and chilling.

'Anyway,' Beth jumped in and saved him, 'I do have forensic evidence.'

'You do?'

'Yes. I have his tie. With both his and her blood on it.'

'Where? Back at the hotel?'

'No, silly. I buried it under a bush in the garden of the apartment complex where they kept us. I put it in a plastic bag, so it should still be there.'

Miley looked at her, amazed. 'Beth, that is brilliant. I mean, it's not conclusive, but along with your testimony, it would be enough to launch a serious investigation. And I think you're right – I have a feeling Hubert would do anything to save his own skin, including spilling his guts about all of Frobisher's nasty little secrets.'

'That's what I thought.'

Miley stood up, offering her his hand. 'And maybe, in all of that, we can find out how they framed you for murder. I mean, we know Ressler was behind it, which is just another way of saying Frobisher ordered it done.'

Beth lowered her eyes.

'What did I say?' Miley asked.

'I've remembered some of what happened.'

Miley blinked. 'And?'

'And I think I remember cutting Alfie's throat. I know I didn't want to, but it was like I couldn't stop myself. But I think I did it, Miley.'

'Nope.' Miley shook his head. 'I don't accept that for a minute. You know you didn't want to, and that's enough for me. Something messed up happened in that room, and we are going to find out what it was and clear your name. Now come on.'

'Where are we going?'

'We are going to tell Father Bill that he is travelling to Portland on his own. You and I have an appointment in Amsterdam.'

3

BETH WAS WORRIED THE BUILDING WOULD NO longer be there, but it was.

Situated in the Jordaan area in the central part of the city, it was a little the worse for wear, but the pieces of laundry hung out to dry in the many windows told her and Miley that the place was still inhabited.

'When I lived here there was always a building superintendent at a little counter in the main lobby,' she said. 'Frobisher owned the whole block, and everyone who lived here worked for him.'

'Is the garden out the back?'

'No, in the middle. The building is constructed like a tall stack of Lego bricks, with a hole in the centre. There were lots of rules for living here, and one of them was no smoking in any of the apartments. If you wanted to smoke, you had to go down to the garden.'

'Very civilised,' Miley said.

'For sure. They never brought clients here. Frobisher had this thing about not shitting where we slept. While I lived in Amsterdam, I would always go out to meet the men – in hotels, usually, but sometimes we would be sent to offices and private homes, too. But never here.'

'He wanted to keep the different parts of his business separate, I suppose,' Miley said.

'He told us it was so we felt safe here,' Beth said quietly.

'Did you?'

'No. I never felt safe from the moment the Yellow Man took me.'

Miley put his arm around her, and they went for lunch.

4

THAT EVENING THEY WERE BACK AT THE apartment block again, taking a position across the street.

'Do you think Frobisher still owns the building?' Beth asked.

'From what Davey has said, he didn't give up any of his businesses,' Miley told her. 'He had contingencies in place, and as soon as the heat was on, a kind of firewall clicked into operation.'

'How did that work?'

'Legal transfers signed all his interests over to hundreds of different shell companies and hedge funds, all managed by firms we believe are really his, but are all in different fake names. As you learned in the UK, if a name has a credit rating and a history, it's hard to prove it's fake. It would take years to unravel. Looks like the system was set up decades ago. His money is untouchable.'

'So this is still Frobisher property.'

'I'd be hugely surprised if it wasn't.'

The streetlights clicked on, one after another, as the sun began its journey below the horizon.

'How do you want to play this?' Beth asked.

'You know your way around the building. Can you get into the garden without a key card?'

'Yes. Or at least, you could.'

'Okay. I'll cause a distraction, you get in there, get the tie and get out.'

'How are you going to cause a distraction?'

'I'm going to play the ace in my deck.'

'What's that?'

'You'll see.'

Jan de Vilmers

Jan was fifty-three, unmarried and proud to be known as a misanthrope.

What he liked about his job as the super in the Jordaan Soud apartment block were all the rules. Jan liked rules: they created order and made life easier by limiting choice. If you knew exactly what mode of behaviour was expected of you, it made the myriad of little dilemmas each day presented so much simpler to deal with.

Jan had learned that first in the army and then when he was in prison – he hadn't coped well with civilian life after he was demobbed, and prison was a blessed relief – his time behind bars reinforced his belief that a well-regulated life is a happy and ordered life.

He carried this wisdom into the security job his parole officer set up for him on release by making sure all the rules were correctly upheld.

Even though his role was, primarily, to sit at his desk for the twelve hours whichever shift he was on dictated, he took it upon himself to do regular patrols in case any of the articles in the tenancy agreement all the residents had to sign were being broken. The most common of these was the rule against smoking – he would have been hard pressed to count the number of times he had been going about one of his patrols when his nostrils were invaded by the foul stench of tobacco, usually heavily laced with the even more unpleasant aroma of marijuana.

Jan had no time for either – he had always earned his living as a leg-breaker of one kind or another (either for the military or private interests), and while a liberal dose of growth enhancers (what the media referred to as steroids) every now and again was a necessary part of maintaining the size he needed for the purpose of intimidation, all other drugs were just plain evil, as far as he was concerned.

Jan operated a 'two strike' rule: on the first instance, once he had ascertained from which apartment the smoke was emanating, he would knock, inform the residents he had made a record of their infraction, and tell them that the next time it happened, he would be informing their landlord. Should it happen a second time, that is precisely what he did. Several tenants had lost their homes due to continued bad behaviour, and good riddance, as far as Jan was concerned.

Other rules regularly flouted were those relating to the number of people permitted to live in a single apartment (he strongly suspected certain tenants of sub-letting), and levels of noise after dark (he had bought a decibel meter to help gauge this one).

The final duty (and one he was not called upon to carry out very often) was to ensure vagrants and loiterers did not congregate in the lobby area of the apartments – if they did, he moved them on promptly.

So rarely did this occur, he was quite surprised when, at 8.25 on a Thursday evening the doors to the block were pushed open by a long-haired young man dressed in hippyish clothes, the purple and blue shirt of which was buttoned incorrectly, the trousers askew and only held up by a belt (the top button was undone and the flies wide open). Jan assumed he was either drunk or stoned, and heaved a heavy sigh. Jordaan was one of the better quarters of the city, and the ganja tourists and stag parties usually kept their festivities to the triangle around De Wallen, where the infamous red-light district could be found.

Sometimes, though, he had to deal with overflow.

'I wanna see my mommy,' the youngster said in English, and Jan realised he was not drunk but disabled, what he would have called a mongoloid, though he knew this term was no longer deemed politically correct.

There was a thin layer of drool coating the bristles of the unshaven face, and as he looked closer, he saw a lot of food stuck to the front of the garishly coloured shirt.

'Your mother doesn't live here,' Jan said, enunciating each word clearly so the dimwit could understand him – he knew his accent wasn't perfect.

'I need my mommy,' the retard said again. 'She meet me here. Tole me she would.'

'Please leave now, or I will have to call the police.'

'I want my mom!'

Jan stood up and was about to go around his desk and grab this annoying genetic mistake by the scruff of the neck, all the better to eject him onto the pavement, when the door to the street opened a second time, and a girl bustled in.

'Jamesie, are you bothering the nice man?'

'No,' the dullard said, looking guilty.

'I'm so sorry,' the girl continued. 'He got away from me. We've just been to his cousin's birthday party – we're visiting, you see – so he's a bit overstimulated.'

'Happy birthday to me, happy birthday to me,' sang the man-child, dreadfully off-key.

'No, Jamesie, it's not your birthday. It was Georgio's. Now come on, we need to get you back to the centre.'

'Toilet,' the scruffy lout said. 'Need go a toilet.'

'I told you to go before we left the restaurant.'

'Need go now!'

The girl, who was quite pretty, looked beseechingly at Jan. 'I'd be very grateful if we could use your bathroom. We'll be on our way then, I promise.'

Jan shook his head and gestured to a door on his left. 'Take him down there. Third door on the right. Then I really must ask you to leave. You should keep better control of him.'

'Thank you. And I will. Absolutely.' She took her dribbling charge by the hand and led him in the direction Jan had indicated.

'If he's not fit to be out in public, maybe he should stay in the asylum, huh?' Jan shot as they went past.

'I'll keep that in mind,' the girl said, and then they were gone.

Jan went back to a series he was watching on his tablet. (It was about these amazing American families who were preparing for the day society finally came asunder, either due to a nuclear strike or the fucking Muslim hordes or a hacker shutting down the grid using a supercomputer he'd built in his mother's basement – these guys had all constructed bunkers and stacked them with cans of beans and had set up solar panels and dug wells and created defence systems to keep the neighbours out. Jan thought it all very sensible.) Five minutes passed before he realised the girl and her pet simpleton hadn't come back.

Cursing his misplaced sense of human decency, Jan paused his show and got up, taking the sawn-off baseball bat he kept for the rare occasions he needed to use physical force to assert his authority.

When he got to the toilet door, he wrapped twice on it with the bat. 'Time to go,' he said. 'Come out right now or I'm coming in.'

There was no response, so he turned the handle, expecting to find the door locked, but it swung open easily. The toilet was empty. Where the hell had they gone?

Coming back out into the hallway, he stood, momentarily confused. They definitely hadn't passed back through the entrance lobby – which meant there was only one other direction they could have taken.

Slapping the bat against his thigh and muttering darkly, Jan strode up the corridor towards the garden.

5

AS SOON AS BETH AND MILEY WERE THROUGH the door and into the hallway beyond, Miley hissed at her, 'Do you know the way from here?'

'Yes – straight ahead. The door is always open. Come on.'

They ran the length of the hallway, at the end of which was a set of glass double doors, which Beth pushed open. Beyond was a square area about the size of a suburban back garden, surrounded on all sides by the four blocks that made up the apartment building. Ten floors above them, the sky peeped in, full of stars.

The garden consisted of a lawn that was mostly dead grass and compacted dirt. Two narrow raised beds bordered the right and left sides, in which someone (clearly years ago) had planted some bushes and shrubs which no one had bothered to care for. They looked badly in need of watering and had gone beyond the point where pruning would be of any help. They were scraggy, unloved things.

'Can you remember where you buried it?' Miley asked, remaining by the door to keep watch.

'I think so ...' Beth said, suddenly frozen to the spot.

'We'll only get one chance at this,' Miley warned her. 'It's now or never, Beth.'

The girl threw him an uncertain look, and then walked quickly over to what might once have been a rose bush, and, falling to her knees, began to dig beneath it with her hands. She got about a foot down before she hit the concrete at the bottom.

Shit – maybe it was one of the other bushes; no, she was sure it was this one.

She stood up and went to the other side of the bush and dug there.

'I think he's coming,' Miley said urgently.

'Just a couple more minutes,' Beth grunted.

Miley watched anxiously. The unpleasant security guard was standing at the door of the toilet, looking puzzled. Then, with a grim expression, he turned and began to walk swiftly towards them.

'You've got maybe twenty seconds,' Miley said.

'Nearly there.'

'So is he.' Miley stepped back as the double doors swung open and the building super marched in.

Jan de Vilmers

When Jan stepped into the garden, he found the girl kneeling over one of his prized flowerbeds, mounds of disturbed and desecrated earth all about her, and a ragged and faded plastic bag in one of her hands.

He didn't have to think very hard to work out what he was seeing. That asshole Berni, who worked the opposite shift to him, had obviously been sleeping on the job again, and had allowed this bitch to slip past him and bury her stash (it was probably heroin) under one of Jan's beloved rose bushes.

'Okay, drop the drugs, you little whore,' Jan said, taking a couple of threatening steps in her direction.

The girl stood up slowly, the bag still dangling from her fist.

'I said drop it,' Jan repeated. 'If I have to go over there and take it off you, I promise you right now that you'll be very sorry.'

He pointed the bat at her to show he meant business, but as he did, felt a tap on his shoulder. Turning, he saw the handicapped guy – only he somehow didn't look quite so handicapped anymore. It was something about the way he was standing, and there was a different cast to his eyes: where before Jan had seen an emptiness, now those eyes glowed with wit and warmth and intelligence.

'That's not a nice way to speak to a lady, now, is it?' he said, except the words were loud and clear this time.

Jan looked from the girl back to the strange young man. 'I don't know what's going on here, but I think I am going to call the police,' he said.

'I really would prefer if you didn't,' the mongoloid said.

'Don't move, either of you,' Jan said, reaching for his phone,

but to his disbelief the retard who wasn't a retard shot out a leg with shocking speed and accuracy, knocking the Samsung out of his grip.

It took Jan a second to process what had just happened, but by then the girl was sprinting across the lawn in an attempt to get past him and out the doors. He made to grab her, but the young man, in another unnaturally swift movement, caught the arm and twisted, somehow sending him off-kilter and spinning him in the other direction completely.

By the time he regained composure the girl was gone and it was only him and the disabled youngster. 'Who are you?' Jan asked, shrugging his shoulders to loosen them and swinging the bat back and forth in front of him, as they had been taught to do in the army – the idea is to make your opponent follow the weapon so they aren't watching you and can't anticipate your next move.

Except the boy seemed completely disinterested in the bat – he was looking Jan dead in the eye. 'Would you believe me if I said I was just passing through?'

'Doesn't matter what I believe. Your girlfriend might have got by me, but you aren't going anywhere.'

'I really don't want to fight you. What if I offer to fill in the holes my friend made and water the plants? They look like they could use it. I'll clean up the mess and then be on my way. How does that sound?'

Jan was no longer listening. In a single motion he stepped around the imbecile on his left-hand side (which Jan reasoned would be weaker), bringing the sawn-off bat up in a vicious arc, his intention to shatter the idiot's teeth and break his jaw. It was a simple, devastating move, and should have ended the altercation in one short, crushing blow.

The problem was, the handicapped guy somehow anticipated it and moved gracefully with Jan, as if they were dancing partners. As the security guard moved to his left, the youngster rolled sideways and the bat swung wide. As it did, the retard dropped low and kicked his leg out, sweeping Jan's feet from under him. The force of the swing caused him to literally go head over heels.

The last thing Jan de Vilmers felt before he was knocked unconscious was a dull thump as his head connected with one of the compacted patches of bare earth on his lawn.

A tenant, an elderly lady named Margaret, found him fifteen minutes later when she popped out for a cigarette. When he would not immediately awaken on being nudged by her slippered foot, she called the paramedics.

Jan noted, as they wheeled him out on a gurney, that the soil the girl had dug up had been replaced, and it looked as if the bushes had been watered.

6

THEY WERE SAFELY BACK IN BETH'S ROOM AT their hotel near the Oude Kerk before she took the bag from her jacket pocket. They sat on the single bed in the small, featureless space.

'Will you take a look?' she asked Miley. 'I don't think I want to touch it.'

He solemnly accepted the bundle. 'Do you want to go into the bathroom, or something? You don't have to watch.'

'No. I can look at the damn thing. I just don't want it in my hands again. Not after what it did. Can you understand that?'

'Of course I can. Let's get this open.'

The bag was made from thick plastic and was from a well-known local supermarket chain. It had once been blue, green and white, but was now quite faded, and grimy with soil. Miley saw that Beth had tied the top to seal it, and he fumbled with the knot for a moment. It wouldn't give. He tried to get his thumb under one of the folds, and the plastic tore. He looked at her guiltily.

'I don't think that matters,' Beth reassured him. 'It's what's inside that counts.'

Miley nodded and, taking a napkin so as not to contaminate the object with his own DNA, reached inside, his napkin-covered fingers coming out holding a pink and green silk tie. Placing the bag on the bed behind them, he held the tie up to the light. Speckles of black covered it, which Miley took to be mould, but there were patterns of raised clusters of another kind of residue, and these he knew were blood: he'd got enough of it on him during his hunting trips in Greenland to know the stuff when he saw it.

'And you're sure these are both his and hers?' Miley asked.

'I'm certain.'

'Okay, then,' he said, putting the tie back into the bag, folding that over, and placing the whole bundle into his suitcase.

'What should we do now?'

'The only thing that makes sense is to ring Uncle Frank.'

'Chief Superintendent Tormey?'

'Yes. He'll know how best to proceed. We can't do anything with it ourselves. Evidence like this only has power once it's with the police.'

Beth nodded.

'I'll make the call,' Miley said, and picked up the burner phone they'd bought on arriving in the city.

It rang out three times before Tormey picked up, and when he did, Miley knew there was something wrong right away.

'I've been waiting for one of you to call,' the detective told him. 'I need to speak to Davey.'

'I'm not with him just now,' Miley said. 'Do you want to talk to Beth? She's here.'

There was a long pause at the other end of the line. 'No. Ask Davey to get in contact as soon as he can.'

'Is it serious? Do you need us to come home?'

'It wouldn't make any difference. Why did you call, anyway?'

Miley outlined (as succinctly as he could) the piece of evidence he and Beth had recovered. Tormey listened without interruption. When his nephew had finished, he asked, 'Beth is absolutely certain about this?'

'She's positive, yes.'

'Alright. I'm going to make some calls and see if I can get someone trustworthy to you. Stay put and I'll be in touch.'

'Will do. And, Uncle Frank?'

'Yes, Miley?'

'Is everything alright? You sound stressed.'

'There's been some hassle with my superiors over here, Miley. I knew there would be. It's nothing you should concern yourself with. I've got it under control.'

'You're sure?'

'Absolutely. Miley, I'm really proud of you. You and wee Beth have just found a weapon that could turn this whole thing around – we can use it to leverage Hubert into giving us Frobisher and Ressler, which will bring the case against Beth crashing down. Let me do some work at this end, and I'll get back to you.'

'Okay. Talk soon.'

Beth looked at him expectantly. 'Well?'

'He thinks the tie could be really useful. He's going to call us back shortly.'

'That's good. Why do you look so worried?'

'I think something bad has happened in Ireland.'

'Why?'

'It's just a feeling. I'm probably wrong.'

He wasn't.

Beth Carlton

It took her some time to realise she was falling in love with Miley.

She did not think she would ever want to be with a man again after Davey rescued her from the sex trade. The idea of being with anyone in such an intimate way had been tainted, and she could not imagine herself entering into that kind of relationship.

There was also the fact that she felt no need for sex. Beth had been forced to indulge men's needs for so long, without ever giving a moment's thought to her own, that she had come to believe that part of her being had shrivelled and died. She was a physically healthy young woman in her early twenties, it would have been perfectly normal and natural for her to have a sexual relationship, but such a notion was alien to her.

She was not one of those damaged people who could not stand to be touched – in fact she craved hugs and cuddles from those she loved: her mother, Davey, Diane and Father Bill, and somehow, in a very short space of time, Miley had joined those ranks. But there was something about him that was different.

Part of it was his centredness. There was a physical confidence about Miley that made her feel incredibly safe with him. She felt similarly around Father Bill. She knew instinctively that when he walked into any room he was always confident that he was the toughest person there – the other people might not know, but that didn't matter. He did.

Father Bill was a priest, though, and was old enough to be her grandfather. Miley was young, and he was cool – she loved the way he dressed and the way he wore his hair and the fact that when he laughed, his whole face lit up and his whole body shook and he made everyone else who was around smile and laugh too. The fact that he had no idea that he was cool and would be deeply shocked to discover she thought so, endeared him to her even more.

And she just adored his face. She thought she could look at him all day long. It was warm and friendly and kind and handsome and there was just a hint of sadness in it too. She knew Miley had suffered. It was something they shared.

She hadn't told him she was in love with him yet. But she thought she might, soon.

And she had a sneaking feeling he felt the same way.

Part Eight

DANGEROUS CONTRACTS

Wilfred Hubert

The more famous he got, the more dangerous the world became.

In the early days of his celebrity, he could always depend on Frobisher to smooth out any ruffles and remove any flies in the ointment when it came to those he may have offended (advertently or inadvertently) through his daily wheeling and dealing.

If he sensed a threat (or – as was much more likely – one of his underlings reported one to him), a call was made to his benefactor and the problem disappeared.

But then Frobisher disappeared. Hubert received an email to an encrypted account only he had access to, informing him that he would from then on only file reports to a dark web site, and all funds were to be channelled through a numbered account in the Channel Islands. Frobisher, to all intents and purposes, was gone.

Only, of course, he wasn't. Two months after the email, Hubert got home to his apartment in Los Angeles to find the Yellow Man's replacement, Ressler, sitting beside his pool, drinking some of his forty-year-old Scotch.

Hubert had never liked the Yellow Man, but he loathed Ressler even more. With Andrews there was a sense of control, of an energy always kept in check – Hubert knew the man could end his life without so much as breaking a sweat, but the threat was always unsaid. Ressler, however, seemed to revel in making the danger overt.

He was a man of average height and build, his hair such a deep blue/black, Hubert always assumed it was not natural. His skin was a rosy pink, as if he always had a mild case of sunburn, and his eyes were a strange, amber colour, like a cat.

'Ah, it is my very dear friend Mr Wilfred Hubert, home from a day of financial hunting and gathering. How went your work?'

Ressler spoke with an accent Hubert always took to be Dutch, but the odd rhythm of it made him wonder if he was correct. What always unnerved him particularly about the man was his tendency to suddenly shout, or bang a glass, or violently knock over a piece of furniture. It was as if he wanted whoever he was with to be ill at ease. He seemed to thrive on it.

'Very well,' Hubert said. 'My staff didn't mention you were here.'

'That is because they did not know. I wanted to give you the biggest of surprises. It is fun, is it not? Ha!'

Hubert pulled up a chair and sat down opposite his visitor. 'What do you want?'

'To give you a timely reminder from my employer.'

'How is Mr Frobisher?'

'He is doing very well, under the circumstances.'

'What circumstances might those be?'

He didn't even feel the blow. One moment he was sitting upright, watching Ressler drinking his most expensive whiskey, the next he was flat on his back with Ressler's foot on his chest, the barrel of a handgun inches from his nose.

'Do not think for one single moment, friend Hubert, that just because my employer has been forced to take a less active role in his affairs due to some unfortunate legal matters he is no longer in control of them. It would be a grave mistake to make that assumption.'

'I ... I didn't think it for a moment,' Hubert said. 'I was just making small talk.'

'Well, please forgive me – perhaps it is my embarrassingly poor grasp of your American idiom, but it seemed to me that you were, in fact, talking big.'

The gun disappeared and one of Ressler's pink hands was thrust at him. He took it and was helped to his feet.

'Your last transfer of funds was both late and a poor reflection of the performance of Mr Frobisher's portfolios,' Ressler said, straightening the jacket of his pale linen suit.

'I'll check the figures and rectify them immediately if there was any error.'

'There was. See it gets done.'

And then he was gone.

When Hubert asked them later, none of his staff reported seeing Ressler either arrive or leave.

He didn't sleep that night. He tossed and turned until the wee small hours. Finally he got up and made a call to a security expert he knew named Kovack.

'What can I do for you, Mr Hubert?'

'I want to hire a bodyguard and I want the best there is.'

Kovack thought about it for a moment. 'There's a guy called John Chatham who is probably the scariest person I know. He was dishonourably discharged from the fucking Green Berets, but I am aware of several heads of state who are alive because of him. He is big and ugly and always in a bad mood, but if you pay John Chatham to be your bodyguard no one – and I mean fucking no one – will get by him.'

'So you'd trust him to protect you?' Hubert asked.

'I would trust him to protect the state of Texas. Look, do you want me to call him? He's between clients, but he won't be for long. This guy is in demand.'

'Yeah. Tell him I need him out here. Literally yesterday.'

'I should probably add that he's expensive. But he's worth every red cent.'

'Thank you, Max. I can't wait to meet the guy.'

John Chatham became Hubert's Yellow Man. His Ressler.

He was six foot six inches in height, weighed more than three hundred pounds and looked as if his face was made completely out of scar tissue. He had very little hair and wore dark suits with those ridiculous string ties cowboys always wore in films. He rarely spoke, but when he did, it was in a dry rasp that was hard to listen to.

Hubert loved him and was terrified of him in equal measure.

After agreeing terms of employment, Chatham asked his new boss, 'Do you have any particular concerns, sir? Are there any clear and present threats you're aware of?'

'As it happens, there are,' Hubert said, taking a photograph from a folder on his desk. He passed it to the enormous man. It was a picture of Dr Phillipe Ressler. 'If you see this guy, kill him.'

'Sir?'

'He is the reason you are here. Obviously, there will be other dangers every now and again, but I want your primary goal to be making sure that malignant little bastard never gets next nor near me. If you see him about any of my properties, if you spot him across the street while we are out and about, if we are at a party and you spy him through the crowd, I direct you to do whatever you have to do to eradicate him from the face of the earth. Are we clear, Mr Chatham?'

'As crystal, sir. Roger that.'

When Chatham came to work for him, Wilfred Hubert knew, once and for all, that being the sheriff was no longer a fantasy: it was a reality. Now he had his deputy, he was untouchable. No one would ever push him around again.

1

'I WANT TO HELP YOU, GINA, BUT I DON'T SEE HOW I can,' Tormey said.

They were in Wagamama, Gina's favourite noodle bar in Dublin, behind the Stephen's Green shopping centre. It was midday, and the place was reasonably quiet. They had a table to themselves and there were only a couple of other people in the long room.

'You know people,' Gina said. 'You're only a couple of rungs down the ladder from the minister, for God's sake.'

'Did you not hear me when I told you that I am currently persona non grata? I'm in disgrace. Out in the cold. How many more ways do I need to put it? I have no authority and no influence.'

'Okay, let's look at it from a different perspective.'

'Please enlighten me on what that perspective might be.'

'Maybe we should just take it as a problem that needs

to be solved. You're a detective. Solving problems is your job.'

'Catching villains is my job. Getting you in to meet an international dignitary who is here to chair a gathering of leaders of commerce and politicians from all over the world is just a little above my paygrade. And Gina, love, the whole crazy scheme is based on a hunch by this shrink. Don't you reckon you should at least talk to Beth about it first?'

'How? They're on the run, God knows where, changing phones almost daily, and we have no idea who is listening in on *our* phones. No, Frank. I'm going to chase this one up myself. If I'm wrong, I'll apologise and plead temporary insanity. I'm a mother who is beside herself with worry, after all.'

'That's all well and good after the fact, but it still doesn't get you in.'

They sat back, sampling their green tea.

'How would Davey tackle this?' Gina asked.

'The last time he wanted to talk to a minister he just barged right on into the room where the bloke was giving a speech and started shouting at him.'

Gina's eyes lit up. 'Hubert is doing several speaking engagements while he's here, isn't he?'

'I think so, yeah.'

Gina pulled her phone from her pocket and opened her web browser. 'He's giving a talk to the Literary and Historical Society in University College Dublin tomorrow night.'

'And you're going to stand up during the Q&A and ask him about his history with underage girls?'

'I didn't say I had a plan yet, did I?'

'My God, you really are like your brother.'

'You should order some food, Frank. You get very cranky when you're hungry.'

'I don't see anything I recognise as food on the menu.'

'Now who's being like Davey?'

And there wasn't much Tormey could say to that.

2

THE LITERARY AND HISTORICAL SOCIETY OF
University College Dublin is one of the oldest debating
societies in the world, and has hosted a dazzling array of
international figures, from philosopher Noam Chomsky to
porn star Ron Jeremy. It made sense to Gina that someone
like Wilfred Hubert would be invited (the society courted
most visiting celebrities in the hope they might make an
appearance) and neither was it a surprise he accepted: Hubert
was a popular figure who was as likely to be seen on a crass
reality TV show as he was addressing the American House
of Representatives, yet he clearly craved the approval of the
intelligentsia, and UCD's L&H was about as intellectual as
you could get.

Gina was a former student (she had done some postgraduate
studies at UCD), and though she had to pull a few strings to
get a ticket to the event, it didn't prove too great a challenge.

So it was that, at 7.30 the following evening, Gina was on one of the red felt chairs in the university's Garret FitzGerald Chamber when Hubert took to the stage.

He was everything she expected, and at the same time very different. On television, Wilfred Hubert's personality was front and centre: his barking delivery and loud suits, along with his often confrontational ideas about people, money and politics made him appear huge, larger than life. In person, however, he seemed absurdly small – he was probably five feet seven inches tall, and weighed about one hundred and thirty pounds. While the suit he wore that evening was an eye-watering blue and red stripe, the fact that it was in such a tiny size made it come off as less aggressive. Hubert's skin was its trademark deep orange, and his hair was, as usual, virtually static with hairspray and frothed out from his head in a bizarre loose perm. But in miniature, it made less of an impact.

The man could certainly speak, though. Within moments the audience was in the palm of his (diminutive) hand.

'I want to talk to you tonight about something you Irish aren't always very good at discussing,' he began. 'Success. Where I come from, you are encouraged to own your victories, to share the fact you have accomplished something. You celebrate your wins and you learn from your losses. One thing I've noticed in the few days I've been in your beautiful country is that, culturally, you guys don't feel comfortable with success. It's almost as if it's a sin to be proud of your achievements – in fact, it *is* a sin, isn't it? Isn't pride one of the deadly sins?'

There was murmured acknowledgement that Hubert's grasp of catechism was accurate.

'But I don't go for that. I really think it's important to give people credit where it's due. Let me give you an example. It's no secret that my father was a criminal. He was what these days would be euphemistically called a grifter – a confidence trickster. What he used to do was target isolated, lonely older women, call to their homes, befriend them, and then sell them insurance policies: life, home, and health, that weren't worth the paper they were written on. What my dad was really selling these ladies was himself – he would call and visit them on a weekly basis and he would sit and talk with them and drink awful coffee and eat old-fashioned cookies and when he was finished they would happily pay him their weekly instalment. He made them feel special, you see. As if he was their friend. He wasn't, of course: as soon as one of them wanted to cash in or needed a medical procedure paid for, my dad was nowhere to be found, but when everything was going well, he was very attentive.'

There was some nervous laughter at this. Hubert waved it off.

'I'm not looking for your approval or your sympathy. What my father was doing was immoral and disgusting, but he always owned that he was good with people. That was his success. And I'm prepared to give him that. He was the only wage earner in our home, and until he got prosecuted for fraud, we had a very comfortable lifestyle. Now, the object of this evening's address is not that crime pays – please don't go home tonight thinking that was my point.'

More laughter. People were enjoying themselves. Hubert had put them at ease.

'What I want you to think about is this: you might feel that you're just treading water, or that you're facing challenges that are impossible to overcome. You could have exams coming up that seem scary, or maybe you're concerned about your job prospects after graduation – I don't know what your bogeys are, but you do. We've all got them.'

Nods of agreement all around the chamber.

'Here's how I want you to tackle those worries. Tonight, before you go to sleep, have a think about what you're good at. What is it that you do really well? It doesn't have to be work- or study-related – maybe you make the best mashed potatoes in the whole of Ireland.'

A few good-natured cheers.

'Whatever your talent is, recognise it and celebrate it. Every morning from tomorrow onwards, I want you to look in the mirror when you're brushing your teeth, and say to yourself, "I'm Jim, or Martha, or Bill, or Janey" – fill in as appropriate – "and I'm damn good at making mashed potatoes, or programming computers or running the 5k", or whatever your talent might be. You see, what I learned really early in my career was that, once you know you're good at one thing, other skills follow. Having the confidence to admit you are successful in just one area will leave you open to success in other areas too. What you are doing is leaving yourself open to the universe, leaving yourself open to success. And I promise you – it *will* come.'

There was thunderous applause, which went on for almost a full minute. When it had died down, the chairperson of the L&H informed the audience that Mr Hubert was ready to take questions from the floor. Myriad hands shot into the air. Gina's was among them.

Most questions focussed on the fact that Hubert was in the process of setting up a branch of his business empire in Ireland, an undertaking that promised to generate hundreds of jobs and billions in revenue. Hubert answered each person in detail, and if he dodged any of the more thorny issues (the government's rather indulgent approach to corporation tax for foreign investors, for example, which meant Hubert would be paying virtually no tax at all), he did so with such skill and apparent grace, no one noticed.

Gina was beginning to worry that she wouldn't be chosen to ask her question, when a student appeared at her side, a roving mike in hand.

Hubert, who was still standing at the podium, smiled indulgently at her, showing impossibly white and even teeth.

'Mr Hubert, you've been very candid this evening about the criminal history within your own family.'

He smiled and nodded. 'It's common knowledge, and I'm not ashamed of where I come from. I don't think anyone should be. The sins of my father are not my sins. I hope I've learned from them.'

'Your father isn't the only criminal in your past though, is he?'

'I'm sure I've met plenty. I'm a businessman, after all.'

Laughter echoed around the chamber, and Gina spoke over it. 'What was it like working with Ernest Frobisher, Mr Hubert? Did you learn anything from him?'

Hubert's expression changed for a brief moment, but he recovered his composure quickly. 'I worked for Frobisher in the role of a stock and investment broker for one year in … I think it was 1986. I've met him at events a few times since then, but to be honest, he isn't the most sociable of men, and I doubt that his current status as a fugitive has improved his manner very much.'

Hubert paused, watching Gina through lidded eyes.

'Frobisher isn't a well-known figure. How did you come to hear of him, Miss?'

'He abducted my daughter and held her for eighteen years, putting her to work as an underage prostitute. And he continued to victimise her, even after we, against all the odds, managed to rescue her from one of his brothels.'

The words Gina had spoken sounded ugly in the hallowed room. There was absolute silence now, and all eyes were on Gina. No one had expected the discussion to take this turn, and it was clear from the demeanour of the chairperson and stewards that they were not altogether happy about it.

Hubert blinked, but again kept a veneer of control. 'I'm very sorry to hear that. But I'm not sure why you're sharing this rather personal information in such a public forum.'

'Frobisher is a wanted man, guilty of crimes of the most awful nature. But his wealth, which he still seems to have control over despite the best efforts of the police, has meant he has continued to evade capture.'

'Frustrating and tragic. Very bad.'

'A man of your resources could surely help the police by sharing what you know of his empire, which you helped build, after all. And while you were doing so, he must have paid you handsomely, which means he helped build your empire too?'

'It's not quite as simple as that, Miss,' Hubert said, but Gina was on a roll now.

'Don't you think that it might be a way of giving something back by using those funds to employ a collective of private investigators to look for Frobisher? I mean, the money you earned in 1986 came from the worst kind of crime. Why not put it to good use?'

All eyes now turned to Hubert. He paused, looking at

the sheets of paper he had in front of him as if he hoped an answer to Gina's challenge might be in there. Finally he said, 'If the police asked me – which they have not, by the way – to hand over any files I still have on Frobisher, I would do so without hesitation. As to sending private investigators after him – that's hardly my responsibility, is it? I'm not in that type of business, and I don't think I should be.'

'My daughter is in hiding because of Frobisher's continued vendetta against her.'

The student who had handed Gina the roving microphone tried to take it back, but she held on tightly.

'I bet, if you thought deeply about it, Mr Hubert, that you know something that could really help the police to bring this evil man to justice.'

The student was more tenacious than Gina had expected, and on his second attempt he got the mike away from her.

'I can see you're upset,' Hubert said. 'Why don't you and me have a sit down when this is over, and I'll see if there's anything I can do to help. How's that?'

'Thank you. I'd appreciate it,' Gina said winsomely.

She was in. She thought Davey would be proud of her.

3

WHEN THE Q&A WAS OVER, PEOPLE BEGAN TO file out of the chamber. This took about forty-five minutes because a lot of them wanted to stop and say a few words to Hubert, and there were a lot of selfies taken. He dealt with all of this with a smile and a thumbs-up (although Gina noticed he had a way of putting his arm around people's shoulders and pulling them down for the photos, so it never looked as if they were significantly taller than he was).

When the last of the audience left the chamber, she was still in her seat. Hubert was talking to an enormous man in a dark suit, a string tie knotted about his trunk-like neck. Both threw occasional glances at Gina, who smiled and waved back. After a few moments, Hubert sat down beside her. The giant hovered nearby, looking, it seemed at nothing and everything simultaneously.

'Now, Miss. Let's you and me have a look and see what we can do about your baby girl.'

Gina suddenly found herself unable to speak. She had been through a lot of therapy over the years, had spent hours upon hours exploring the devastation of losing her daughter. She was aware that her strategy for survival for almost twenty years had been to channel her energies into hoping Beth might one day be found, or at least that there would be some form of closure. That her twin brother was the lead investigator on the case (whether his superiors wanted him to be or not) helped her to retain a modicum of hopefulness.

When Beth was (despite overwhelming odds) found, she had struggled to accept this damaged, angry, sometimes violent young woman as the child she had lost, and forced herself to take a step back to allow her some independence and some space to create a new life. That meant forging a new role for herself. She could not be the mother she had wanted to be, because the child was gone, replaced by an adult. She wanted so badly to give Beth what she'd missed, but the time had passed and could never be reclaimed. Gina understood intellectually that this was so, but she was wracked with the guilt of it.

Now that child was in danger all over again, and here, sitting beside her, was one of the men who had abused and tormented her. Gina wanted to grab him by his absurd, coiffured hair and smash his face to smithereens against the wall. She had never been a violent woman, and she was shocked at the urge. She had to fight to control it.

'Her name is Beth,' she finally managed to say.

'Lovely name.'

'Thank you. What do you think the police will do when I tell them you raped her?'

It was a bluff, and she knew it, but as soon as the words were out of her mouth, and she saw the look on Hubert's orange face, she knew she had him.

'Miss, this conversation is over.'

'No, Mr Hubert, it is not over until I say it's over.' She spoke quietly, but the anger that welled up inside gave her voice a force that was almost physically tangible. She had lived for almost two decades wondering what might be happening to her little girl and who might be responsible, and now fate had delivered one of the culprits to her. She was not about to let him slip through her grasp. 'You abused my daughter, you sick and evil little troll. I am not stupid enough to think a man of your wealth will serve so much as a single minute in prison, but I promise you this: if you do not help me, I will make it my life's work to see that every newspaper and television channel has heard what you did. How do you think that will affect your market share?'

'Where I come from, this is called blackmail.'

'They call it that here, too. Not everyone will believe it (I'm sure you'll publish a denial and threaten lawsuits on the media outlets) but a cloud of scandal will follow you around for the rest of your life. Hard to address the UN on world debt when you're accused of using underage, trafficked sex workers. It somewhat lessens your credibility.'

Hubert's colour darkened under his fake tan. Gina wasn't sure what that meant, but she was sure it was some kind of negative emotional response.

'Now let me be very clear: I am not admitting to a single one of your allegations. However, I might be prepared to help you and your family. What if I said that I did know one or two pieces of information the police might find useful in their search for Frobisher – would that make you happy?'

'It's a start.'

'I don't see what else I can do.'

'The resources of the police are finite. I mentioned private investigators. You can afford to pay for the best and you could tell them things you might not wish to share with the police for fear of incriminating yourself, things that may well lead them right to Frobisher's bolthole.'

'You're asking a lot.'

'You raped my daughter.'

'Alright, settle down. I'll make some calls, set some things in motion. Where do I find you?'

Gina took a piece of paper from her handbag and scribbled a phone number. A part of her was wary of him cooperating so easily, but she pushed aside her worries – it was all for Beth, in the end. She would take whatever risks were necessary. 'You have one day, Mr Hubert, and then I will be visiting the offices of *The Irish Times*. I bet they would love to hear my tragic story.'

'I'll call. I give you my word.'

She stood. He followed suit.

'I'd like to say it was a pleasure doing business with you,' Hubert said, extending his child-sized hand. 'But it'd be a lie.'

Gina took the proffered appendage, but instead of shaking, she suddenly pulled the little man towards her and kneed him in the groin with all the strength she could muster. The huge man in the dark suit charged forward, but Hubert stalled him with a look as he sank to his knees.

'You get that one for free,' he said through gritted teeth. 'You won't get another chance.'

'Neither will you,' Gina said, and left him on the floor clutching his dignity.

On the way home she called Tormey to let him know how it had gone. He listened gravely when he heard about her parting shot, and told her to be *much* more careful in future – people like Hubert were not inclined to let such things pass.

The words would come back to haunt him.

4

DADDY JOE'S WAS A NIGHTCLUB ON DUBLIN'S North Wall. In the nineties it made its money holding raves and acid-house parties, and was now renowned for drawing the cream of Ireland's hugely popular country music scene. It also happened to be the base of operations for Tim Pat Rogers, Father Bill's close friend and associate, and a prominent player in the city's organised criminal underworld.

Chief Superintendent Frank Tormey parked his Toyota next to a black Lexus, the only other vehicle in Daddy Joe's carpark at noon on a weekday.

Tormey had never been to the nightclub before. He had occasionally crossed paths with Rogers, known in the less salubrious corners of the print media as the Janitor, due to the fact the crime scenes he left behind were remarkably clean, which meant Tormey had never been able to pin anything on him. The relationship the gangster had with Father Bill was one of the reasons the detective had little time for the priest – Tormey always considered Father Bill to be little more than a criminal in fancy dress, and it annoyed him that Miley and Dunnigan were so drawn to the charismatic cleric.

However, now that all other avenues were cut off to him, the detective had no option but to seek help from a man he considered to be an arch enemy. It galled him, but Tormey was, if nothing else, practical. He used the key fob to lock the car then approached the main door to the club, knocking smartly.

A tall, broad man in his mid-thirties, wearing a suit that cost several times what Tormey's had, answered.

'Good morning, Terry,' the detective said. 'Is the boss home?'

'He's busy,' the big man said. 'He's washing his hair.'

'I'm not here to give him a hard time,' Tormey said. 'This involves Bill Creedon. He'll want to talk to me.'

Terry gave him a look that suggested he was not entirely convinced. 'Wait there.'

The door closed and Tormey heard footsteps disappearing into the bowels of the building. Minutes passed, and then the door was reopened and Tim Pat Rogers, the Janitor, was standing before him.

Rogers was a couple of years younger than Tormey, but was significantly more fresh-faced. His hair, which he wore long and brushed back from his forehead, showed not a sign of grey, and his suits, which Tormey knew were all custom-made by one of Dublin's premier fashion designers, were of a modern cut.

'Well, this is a nice surprise,' Rogers said, smiling. 'It's been too long, Frank.'

'Not long enough, in my opinion,' Tormey said, accepting the gangster's hand.

'Can I offer you tea? Coffee? Something stronger?'

'I'm driving, Tim Pat. Tea will be fine.'

'Tea it is, then. I think my cleaning lady brought in some scones this morning. Can I tempt you with one?'

'Very kind of you. I haven't had lunch yet.'

They sat in Rogers' office, which was a large room at the back of the club, posters of various bands who had played there down through the years on the walls: Tormey recognised The Prodigy, Meat Loaf and Declan Nerney at a glance.

'So, to what do I owe the pleasure?' Rogers asked, once Terry had brought them tea and scones on a tray.

'Do you know where Father Bill is?'

'No.'

'But you know he's gone?'

'He told me he was off on sabbatical. He goes every couple of years. It's the clerical equivalent of study leave, or so he tells me.'

Tormey spread some jam on his scone and had a bite, nodding at Rogers in appreciation. 'I'm not here as a copper, Tim Pat.'

'I know. You've been suspended. Been a right bold boy, from what my contacts in the Bureau tell me.'

Tormey bristled, but didn't take the bait. 'Bill has gone with Davey and the others to try and bring down Frobisher and the After Dark Campaign. I know full well you have an axe to grind with Frobisher. He tried to hit you last year, didn't he?'

'He did. Why do you think I'm funding Father Bill's mission?'

'You're bankrolling them?'

'How do you reckon they've paid for plane tickets? Hotel bills? Food?'

Tormey had wondered about that, but assumed Toddy's crypto-currency was footing the bill.

'Tim Pat, someone very high up has buried the Frobisher case. I've been driven out because I won't cooperate with the cover-up. I'm worried that Bill and Davey are walking into a trap.'

'And what do you want me to do?'

'I want to make sure all the information they're collecting is valid. Can you see what you can learn using your own channels? I think that, if we cross-check and pool resources, it could give us a better picture. Right now there are very few people I trust and, God love me, you're one of those few.'

'You don't believe the intelligence they're gathering themselves? Bill is pretty astute. He's hard to bullshit.'

'Frobisher and Ressler have been one step ahead of us since the start. I want to come at this from every angle I can.'

Rogers poured more tea. He drank his black. 'You know what you're asking, don't you?'

'I think so, yes.'

'When Bill finds this man, he's going to kill him. It's the only way to end this war.'

'I wasn't aware it was a war.'

'Of course it is. Don't be so gullible. The moment you advised your protégé to run, you stepped over the line that separates your world from mine. You can't spend time on this side of the tracks without getting dirty.'

'There's lots of different kinds of dirt, Tim Pat.'

'Don't fool yourself. Dirt is dirt.'

Tormey felt himself stiffen. The hail-fellow-well-met routine both men had been adopting was rapidly disintegrating, old hostilities floating to the surface. 'Don't forget who you're talking to,' he said.

'How could I when I can smell the bacon from here?'

Tormey could feel the comforting weight of his private sidearm, a serviceable Glock 9 (which he had confiscated from a young gang member some years back and decided to keep in case of emergencies), in the small of his back. He had been aware as soon as he entered the room that Rogers had a drawer at his right elbow open, and he had no doubt a similar weapon was in there within easy reach. 'I didn't come here to throw down,' he said, keeping his tone even and his eyes on Rogers'. 'You and I have unfinished business, and we can get back to that when our friends are home safe. For now, how about we return to the matter at hand?'

Rogers smiled stiffly. 'That seems sensible.'

'Can you help them? I know you have people all over the world. I don't know what hole Frobisher and Ressler have crawled into, but I have a suspicion it would be hard for those two to find anywhere without an Irishman somewhere nearby on your payroll.'

The Janitor laughed. 'You flatter me, Frank.'

'Will you help?'

'As long as you're clear that you will owe me, Chief Superintendent. You will owe me big.'

'Right now, I am a civilian and not worth a whole fucking lot.'

'The powers that be will welcome you back to the fold sooner or later. You're an old-school policeman, Frank. They won't leave you in the wind for long.'

Tormey laughed cynically. 'Don't be so sure.'

'Have faith, my friend.'

Tormey stood and brushed crumbs off his trousers. 'Don't for a second start thinking we're friends,' he said, and left the gangster to his thoughts.

5

AT TEN-THIRTY THAT NIGHT TORMEY WENT
through the weekly ritual of leaving his bins out for collection.
He had lived in the same house, a modest semi-detached
in the quiet Dublin suburb of Clonsilla, since his marriage
almost thirty years ago, and while some may have described
his domestic arrangements as boring, he treasured the simple,
regular routines he and his wife shared.

They had never been blessed with children (he wasn't
certain whether the fault lay with him or with her, and he
didn't really want to know), but they had made a contented
life with one another. He wasn't a man to wax lyrical about
romance or any of that touchy-feely stuff, but if he were
forced to talk about it, Frank Tormey would have said that he
loved his wife dearly, and given the chance to live his life over,
would do it pretty much the same way.

He placed the last bag into general waste and wheeled that
receptacle to the front of the house, and went to the narrow

alley between his home and the one beside it to put some wine bottles in the glass recycling. There, he heard a sound behind him. He turned, to find himself gazing down the barrel of a handgun.

'I've been sent to give you a message.'

The man at the other end of the weapon was shorter than the detective, and dressed in jeans and a purple windbreaker which just about held a middle-aged paunch. He had stubble he was probably hoping to pass off as a beard and his receding hair was pulled back into a top-knot.

'I'm listening.'

'Leave the Frobisher case alone. You've been told once already. If the warning doesn't take this time, other people will be hurt, and no one wants to rough up your missus. She seems like a nice lady, but if you won't do as you're told, what other option do we have?'

Tormey was, in the main, an easy-going man. He lost his temper from time to time in Harcourt Street, but that generally involved shouting at a few people (often Dunnigan) and slamming the occasional door. The kind of physical confrontations frontline police work brought with it were, in the main, a part of his past, but in his day Tormey had been a force to be reckoned with. Looking at this ridiculous man with his stupid hair and adolescent beard, the detective felt a familiar red mist begin to descend across his vision.

'Would you care to tell me on whose behalf you are delivering this message?' he asked through gritted teeth.

'It doesn't matter.'

'Yes it does.'

'You're on fucking suspension. Play some golf or take up fishing or some other old-guy shite. Do you hear me?'

'My hearing is perfectly fine. I'm asking you again: who sent you?'

The man with the top-knot blinked uncertainly. The person being threatened wasn't supposed to ask any questions. He was just supposed to be afraid. Why wasn't this man fulfilling his end of the arrangement? Top-knot decided to terminate this confusing interaction. 'I'm going now. You stay right where you are and count to two hundred.'

'I can count pretty fast.'

'Three hundred, then.'

He backed away until he reached the corner and then turned to make a run for it, but he was too slow. Tormey used his long legs to bridge the distance in two strides and had the thug by the scruff of the neck. With his right hand Tormey slammed Top-knot's head into the wall of his house once, then twice, and with his left grabbed the man's gun-hand, the grip of which was already loosening as unconsciousness took hold. Shoving the weapon into the back of his trousers, Tormey caught the man under his oxters and dragged him into the alleyway and through to his back garden.

When he had him safely trussed up in his shed, he called one of the detectives on the squad he was no longer in charge of to come and pick up a man he had subdued as he tried to rob his home.

He then called Tim Pat Rogers. 'Looks like I'm going to owe you even bigger,' he said when the gangster picked up. 'I'm going to need a safe house. Tonight.'

It was then that he saw he had got a call from Gina Carlton. He tried to ring her back, but her phone seemed to be switched off.

6

AS TORMEY GRAPPLED WITH HIS INTRUDER, GINA was travelling up the lift in an apartment building on Grand Canal Dock, in Ringsend. Hubert had called her earlier to say he wanted to meet to discuss an agreement that would satisfy them both. She had tried to call Tormey to tell him where she was going, but had got no response.

'I've had some of my people draft a contract,' Hubert had explained. 'You sign an agreement asserting that you will not disclose any rumours about me to the media, and I will agree to pledge funds to employing a security firm to investigate Ernest Frobisher and Phillipe Ressler. That part of the contract will permit said investigators to share certain information I have within my files with law enforcement, both here and abroad.'

'I'd like to have a lawyer look it over before I sign anything.'

'That's fine. But there is a time limit. I'm completing

my negotiations on Friday. I want to begin this process tonight.'

'I don't think you're in the position to make any demands, Mr Hubert.'

'I don't like discussing this over the phone. I'm texting you an address. I'll be there in forty minutes. Come alone.'

A voice in her head had told her she was foolhardy to accede to this wish, that she should have waited for Tormey to answer and bring him with her, but the image of her daughter, on the run God knew where, facing constant danger, was always at the front of her mind. She had to act, to do what needed to be done to help her. She would make up for everything she had not been able to give Beth. If that meant facing demons alone, then so be it.

The building was surprisingly scruffy, and Gina assumed this was not Hubert's main accommodation during his stay in Dublin. She reached the fifth floor and, as per the instructions she'd been sent, went to the last door.

'It's open.'

The voice didn't sound like Hubert's, but he had sounded funny over the phone, too – very different to the confident and articulate man who had addressed the L&H a couple of nights ago. She paused for a moment, but then went inside.

There was a small hallway leading into an open-plan sitting-room/kitchen. The apartment was in semi-darkness; a single light bulb illuminated a table in the middle of the room, at which sat the enormous man who had been with Hubert in UCD. He was again dressed in a dark suit and shoestring tie. The bulb cast a shine on his shaven head. Gina wondered if he used some kind of polish on it.

'I'm here to see Mr Hubert?' she said.

The man said nothing, just took his right hand from below the table.

Gina saw the blue-black finish of the handgun, and turned to bolt, but it was too late. The man shot her in the chest.

She felt no pain, just a dull thump that took her breath away, and the force of it spun her and she fell against the wall and slid to the floor, coming to rest half-lying and half-sitting. For a moment she wasn't sure what had happened. There was a terrible pressure on her chest and when she tried to pull in a breath it was as if a weight was on her lungs and she had to use every bit of her strength to suck in a small amount of air. She started to panic, but somehow a calm began to drift over her and she pushed the anxiety away.

Her vision grew dim, and as if through a blue veil she saw the big, ugly man with the gun stand and come around the table.

'One of your lungs has collapsed,' he said, his voice a guttural rasp. 'That's why it's so hard to breathe.'

Gina tried to look up at him but the room began to spin, and she thought she would be sick. She knew what was coming, and didn't want to be found covered in vomit. She suspected the end would be messy enough as it was. To her surprise, she wasn't afraid, just terribly sad. This wasn't how it was supposed to go.

As she felt her life ebbing away, she realised that its rhythm and tone had been set all those years ago, when Beth had been taken. It seemed that in that single action, everything she was and would ever be was frozen, as in amber.

Her life had been about Beth.

She wanted to say something, ask this brute if he knew what he was doing, tell him she had a daughter and she was only trying to help her. But she didn't have the breath to speak, so instead she thought of Beth, and of Davey and of that last meal they had together, all those years ago, before everything had gone so terribly wrong.

'Time to go,' the huge man said, and shot Gina Dunnigan-Carlton between the eyes.

Part Nine

IMPROVISATIONS AND NIGHT TERRORS

1

'THIS IS NOT WHAT YOU FORESAW,' FROBISHER said, 'or what you promised me.'

These days he rarely opened his eyes, and there were times when Ressler was speaking to him when the dying man drifted off to sleep in the middle of their conversation, which was upsetting and frustrating.

But patience was a skill Ressler had spent a lifetime developing, and he always made a mental note of exactly where they had been in their discussion so he could pick things up right where they left off. Time was a luxury they no longer had, and he was not going to waste a second recapping.

Today, his employer seemed to be wide awake, even if his ragged eyelids were closed (or as closed as they ever got – one was shrinking as the tumour on the adjacent cheek ate more and more of the flesh on the right side of his face).

Ressler worded his response carefully. 'I will admit to you, my dearest companion, that I never believed the criminologist David Dunnigan would run away with his niece. However, I think we should view this as an opportunity to improvise. To expand the game.'

'Expand it how?'

'The police are after them, are they not?'

'Of course they are, for all the good that'll do us.'

'And we sent a team to Scotland, who have now taken their search to Germany.'

'Useless fuckers.'

'Quite so. I would like to suggest to you that we bring them to us.'

'You mean ...'

'Yes. I will lay a trail, as of breadcrumbs. Our perimeter guards should have them picked off long before they get anywhere near our inner sanctum.'

'No.'

'You do not approve?'

'I want Dunnigan and Beth alive – shackled and clawless, but alive. My fondest wish is that we get to play with them together. Wouldn't you like that, Phillipe?'

'I was thinking only of your safety. But yes, it is a wonderful idea. I shall begin the preparations. The clues should not be too obvious, of course. We don't want to scare them off.'

'I trust you to get it done, Phillipe.'

'That means a great deal to me, sir.' He waited for some kind of response, but when he looked over, Frobisher had drifted into unconsciousness again.

2

HE HAD A DREAM WHERE HE AND HIS MASTER were walking together through the Black Forest. The trees rose above them so high the sky was blotted out, and in the coolness of the woods it was dark and secluded, and they could be together the way they wanted to be.

In his dream, sometimes they were wolves and sometimes they were boar – apex predators who needed to fear nothing in their domain, because they were the most powerful and dangerous creatures in it.

The dream took different forms: sometimes they were chasing a naked girl through the trees. They would coax and harry her, letting her run this way before cutting her off, then giving her leave to flee back the way she had come before springing into her path and driving her deeper into the trees.

That dream always culminated with the two of them pouncing upon her and tearing her to pieces, beginning the feast while she was still alive and her screams echoed all about their feeding frenzy, a hymn to blood and violence.

There was another dream, that he had often enough to

have written it down for future analysis. He was the wolf and Frobisher the boar, and this time they were hunting one another. Equally matched as they were, there was an erotic element to the hunt as much as a bloodlust. Sometimes he came within a hair's breadth of sinking his teeth into the wild pig's side, but just as he was about to taste his flesh, Frobisher would leap away, squealing for him to follow. On other occasions the boar had him cornered, tusks bared ready to penetrate his tender belly, but just at the moment of crisis he managed to fling himself out of the path of destruction and flee into the darkness of a copse of trees, howling with arousal and hunger.

Sometimes the dream ended with his death, other times with Frobisher's. Once, he dreamed the boar mounted him, gouging him to death as they copulated. It was one of the most sensual things he had ever contemplated.

Ressler sat and watched his benefactor sleep, the machines blowing air into his lungs, injecting pain-relief into his blood, pumping food and moisture into his belly. He thought of the majesty of the boar, and knew what the dream meant: it was how he truly saw Frobisher —a magnificent, lethal force, unstoppable and beautiful.

Yet the world had broken that energy. Quelled it. Was this a life his employer was living, or was it a torment? Would Ressler like to end his days as much machine as man?

He walked slowly to Frobisher's bedside and stood over his master, pondering the mysteries of life and death. Slowly, tentatively, he reached out and stroked the dry, cracked, lined forehead.

Ressler didn't know if he wanted to live in a world without Frobisher in it. Soon, though, he would have no choice.

Or would he?

Part Ten

LIQUIDATIONS

1

DUNNIGAN AND DIANE WERE COMING IN TO land in Václav Havel Airport in Prague when the criminologist turned to her. 'Something's wrong.'

Diane looked at him in horror. 'What do you mean something's wrong? Do you think there's a problem with the plane?' The former Irish Ranger was not exactly phobic of flying, but she never enjoyed the experience, convinced as she was that placing yourself in a metal tube travelling at ludicrous speeds many thousands of feet above the earth where the lack of oxygen and freezing temperatures would kill you long before the fall did was, frankly, just plain reckless.

'No. It's not that. I just have a really horrible feeling. It's been growing since yesterday.'

Diane gave him a hard look. 'If you *ever* say anything like that to me again when we are on an aeroplane, I will make sure you have an even more horrible feeling. I can guarantee you that.'

As soon as they were through customs and had their bags back, Dunnigan went to a tech store and bought a new burner phone. They got a hotel on the edge of the Old Town, and Dunnigan used the computer in the lobby to log into their group email account, post his new number, and get everyone else's latest.

Once in his room, he called Miley, to discover his friend and Beth were in Amsterdam.

'What are you doing there?'

Miley told him.

'And this tie has Wilfred Hubert's DNA on it?'

'We think so. He worked for Frobisher for years, and used him to source underage girls. If we can bring him down, we can bring Frobisher down too, which should go a long way towards proving that Beth was framed by Ressler, and that Frobisher was behind it.'

Dunnigan was quiet for a moment. 'If he talks.'

'Uncle Frank thinks he'll say whatever it takes to lessen the impact on himself. Oh, and he wants you to call him.'

'I'll be sure to. I just want to check in with Father Bill.'

*

'I've located Ms Merrick,' the priest told him. 'Will I make contact or wait until you get here?'

'Hold off for the moment. Just keep an eye on her. I want to see how everything links up.'

'Right you be. Tormey has made a deal with Tim Pat. He wants us to cross-check all information with him.'

'That doesn't make any sense. And it'll slow things down terribly.'

'He's helped us before, Davey, and he has a *lot* of

contacts. It might not do any harm to have him do some fact-checking.'

'I don't like it. Look, I'm about to ring the chief anyway.'

'When will I see you?'

'I would imagine in a couple of days. It all depends on what we find here.'

'Okay. Talk soon.'

*

Tormey picked up before the first ring was finished. 'Davey.'

'Hello, boss. Miley said for me to call you.'

'Yes. He's a good lad, is Miley.'

Dunnigan heard something in Tormey's voice, and suddenly had a terrible sinking feeling in the pit of his stomach. 'What's wrong, boss?'

'I ... I'm really sorry to have to tell you this, Davey.'

Dunnigan was sitting bolt upright on the hotel bed, the phone pressed to his ear so hard it was actually hurting. 'What? What is it?'

'Davey, Gina's dead. I'm so sorry, son. I truly am.'

Dunnigan heard the words, but the message they carried seemed so absurd he just couldn't process it. 'No. That's not right, boss. It can't be. She's my sister, you see. My ... my twin. Tell me you've made a mistake.'

'I wish I could. I'm sorry.'

'No.' Something snapped in Dunnigan. He looked about the hotel room desperately for something familiar to anchor him to reality, but there was nothing and he felt himself begin to spin into chaos. At the centre of the chaos he found rage, and he clung to it.

'Is Diane with you?'

'She's in the other room.'

'Why don't you go and get her, eh? You shouldn't be on your own.'

'How did she ... how did my sister die?'

'She was ... someone shot her, Davey.'

'Who?'

'We don't know yet.'

The line went silent.

'Davey? Are you still there?'

'How did you let this happen?' The tone was cold, full of anger.

'I was distracted. I'm sorry. I should have been with her.' Tormey didn't try to evade Dunnigan's ire. He was angry with himself.

'She was my sister. She was all I had. For so long, she was all I had.'

'I'm sorry.'

'I can't be there. I can't go after them. So you have to.'

'I know. I'll get them, I promise.'

'You'd better.'

'I'm going to hang up, and I think you should go and get Diane.'

'Alright.'

'Bye bye, Davey.'

The line went dead, but Dunnigan remained with the phone to his ear for several more minutes. Slowly, by very small degrees, his hand began to drop, and as it did, his features started to crumple. Finally a wail emitted from his lips that was so loud Diane, who was two rooms down, heard it.

She hammered on his door but got no answer. 'Davey, for the love of God will you let me in?'

She could hear sobbing from inside, but received no other response. Finally, not knowing what else to do, she went to reception and told the clerk her friend was ill, and could they please let her into his room. A manager was summoned, and a brief listen at the door told him all he needed to know, and five seconds later she was inside.

Diane had known Dunnigan for a little over a year, and believed she had seen him at his best and his worst. But nothing could have prepared her for the well of grief her former partner seemed to have plummeted into. A full hour passed before he regained the ability to speak, and even then all she could get out of him was the strangled word: Gina.

2

WHEN A MERCIFUL SLEEP TOOK HIM, SHE USED
the burner phone to call Tormey, who filled her in on what he
knew.

'She was found in an alley not far from her house. Her
handbag was gone and her clothes were in disarray. It looks
like a sexual assault that went wrong.'

'Are you happy with that version of events?'

'No. I'm not.'

'I didn't think so,' Diane said. 'Because I'm not either.'

'The problem is that nobody wants to touch it with a
ten-foot pole,' Tormey continued. 'I mean, this is a teacher,
apparently walking back home in the early evening after
picking up a carton of milk in a middle-class residential area
– normally the press would be all over it and my boys would
be here, there and everywhere asking questions and gathering
evidence.'

'Except they're not.'

'Precisely. No one wants to know.'

They were both quiet, considering what it all meant.

'I should have been with her,' Tormey said, finally. 'They sent someone to my house, and I fell for it hook, line and sinker. I allowed myself to get distracted. I took my eye off the ball and Gina paid for it, God love her.'

'You can't blame yourself, Frank.'

'I can and I do. This is on me.'

'Feeling sorry for yourself won't achieve anything,' Diane said grimly. 'Do you have any thoughts on who did it?'

'A couple. Believe me, I have been thinking about very little else.'

'Frank?'

There were tears audible in her voice.

'Yes, Diane?'

'I need you to get the bastards. For me and for Davey and for Beth. Can you do that?'

'Yes. I can do that for you.'

'Good,' she said, and hung up.

That night she slept in Dunnigan's room, her arms wrapped around him. At three in the morning he woke sobbing, and she kissed away his tears.

3

DUNNIGAN SLEPT MOST OF THE NEXT DAY.

Diane tried to get him to eat something but he shook his head at the suggestion.

'You have to at least drink some water,' she said, and he took a few gulps, the liquid running down his chin before he collapsed back on the bed.

She took out a Lee Child novel she had been picking at, but the words wouldn't stay still on the page and she tossed it aside. She did press-ups and sits-ups for an hour until she had worked up a really good sweat, then got into the shower and stayed under the hot water for as long as she could bear.

Dressed in the complimentary bathrobe, she sat in the room's bucket chair and flicked idly through the television with the sound turned low.

Dunnigan lay with his back to her. She could see his shoulders rise and fall as he breathed. She loved him. She was bound to this strange, difficult man. All around them was darkness and death, and it had to be brought to an end. They had been on the run for almost two months, and it felt like they were just treading water. Gina was gone, and heaven knew which of them would be next.

Sitting watching reruns of *Only Fools and Horses* wouldn't help them.

'Davey,' she said, getting up and placing a hand on his arm.

He didn't reply, but she felt a change as he came back to consciousness.

'I'm going to head out and see if I can talk to Harmon. You'll be okay for an hour, won't you?'

He nodded, his eyes unfocussed.

'Okay. I'll be back soon.'

She got dressed and closed the door quietly behind her. She saw but didn't register the tall, dark-haired man who was pretending to look into a linen closet near the lift.

4

AMBROSE HARMON WORKED IN A LARGE OFFICE complex a five-minute walk from Wenceslas Square. Diane told the security guard at the door that she needed to see him on a personal matter, and had to wait twenty minutes before a skinny, balding man in an open-necked shirt and dark slacks arrived out of the lift into the reception area.

'I'm Ambrose Harmon,' he told her, offering his hand. He spoke in a well-educated English accent, a bit like a BBC newsreader. 'What is this in relation to?'

'It's a private matter,' Diane said. 'Is there anywhere we can speak discreetly?'

He brought her through a couple of doors to a conference room. 'No one will disturb us here. So, how can I help you?'

'I need to talk to you about Ernest Frobisher.'

Harmon sat down and motioned for her to do the same. 'That's a name I hoped never to hear again.'

'I hear he fired you.'

'Who told you that?'

'It doesn't matter. Do you know where Frobisher is?'

'His main offices are in Hamburg, but he has homes all over the world. I haven't had dealings with him in more than a decade. He ... well, he hurt me. Professionally. Emotionally.' The man's voice began to tremble. 'Physically. I still don't really know why.'

'I was told your management practices were a bit suspect.'

Harmon looked confused. 'Management? Miss ... sorry, I don't know your name.'

'You can call me Robyn.'

'Robyn, I'm an accountant. I had no management responsibility in Germany at all. My job was to collate the balance sheets from all of Frobisher's different companies and investment portfolios and file them with revenue.'

'So you didn't run a furniture warehouse?'

'There was some kind of store next door to us that exported furniture, but I never worked there. Frobisher leased the property, but that was it.'

'You say he hurt you?'

Harmon fiddled with his watch strap, looking uncomfortable. 'Why are you asking me these questions? Are you a police officer? A private detective?'

'I'm working with the police.'

'Do you have any ID?'

'Nothing I can show you. Frobisher has hurt some people who are very dear to me.'

'Yes. He does that.'

'I'm going to hurt him back.'

'You won't. No one can.'

'I promise you, Frobisher won't be able to cause anyone pain again when me and my friends are finished with him.'

'I wish I could believe that.'

Diane looked at the man, and realised he was shaking. 'You can trust me, Mr Harmon. No one will know I was here. If there's anything you can tell me that might help, I'd be very grateful.'

Harmon looked about the room, as if he was expecting to see someone hiding behind a potted plant, eavesdropping. Satisfied they were completely alone, he turned back to Diane. 'I told you my job was to collate his accounts.'

'Yes.'

'There was one book that came in every month. It was simply a numbered file. The documents I handled for Frobisher usually had names: Kaiser Care or Midden International or Doraack Research and Development. But this one was just a series of numbers.'

'The entries must have shown some detail, though,' Diane suggested.

'You'd think, but no. Numbered expenses: expense 2045, charge 3076, and so on. I was convinced these just wouldn't be accepted by revenue, but no one ever asked any questions. I figured someone like Frobisher had to have an arrangement with someone on the inside, but each year I flagged up the issue as one that needed to be rectified, even though I knew it wouldn't make any difference. That was my job.'

'So, no one ever addressed it?'

'No. In my third year working for the company, though, I came across a discrepancy.'

'What was that?'

'In accounting there's only one kind: the figures didn't

balance. It was quite significant, something I couldn't fix with a little creative accounting. I had to follow up on it, as it was down to me to make sure the ins and outs of each account matched up. The numbered file showed a spend that was more than one hundred thousand euro over what they had in their funds.'

'What would you normally do when you came across something like that?'

'The usual process would be to call the manager of that particular office and find out what had happened. Something of this magnitude would, more than likely, be a mistake. I think this was in the region of a hundred and fifty thousand – I assumed at least three of those zeros were typos.'

'So, who did you call?'

'That's the problem, you see – there was no one to call. I had no idea who ran this account.'

'So, what did you do?'

'I called head office and asked to speak to someone about the numbered file. I said there was a large overspend and I just wanted to make sure everything was tickety-boo.'

'Who did you end up speaking to?'

'I was put on hold for half an hour, and then informed someone would be in touch shortly.'

'And were they?'

'Oh yes. Shortly after I returned from lunch I was visited by the Yellow Man.' Harmon held up his left hand, which Diane saw was missing both the pinkie and ring finger.

'That was just the start of it,' the accountant said, and began to cry.

5

DUNNIGAN, WHO HAD GONE VERY DEEP INSIDE himself, was aware of the door to his room opening, but assumed it was Diane returning. He didn't move when he heard a heavy tread as the person walked around his bed and paused above him.

Even when the voice that spoke was obviously not Diane's, Dunnigan remained where he was, curled into a foetal position.

'You and I need to talk.'

The criminologist registered that the speaker was male and the accent had traces of the north of England, where he had recently spent some time. But this recognition was like a feather blowing across his mental landscape – he noticed it, but it was gone as quickly as it appeared.

'I said we need to talk.'

Dunnigan was thinking of his and Gina's thirteenth birthday. He had made a chocolate cake for her (it was always chocolate, her favourite) and had saved his pocket money to buy her an album: Lloyd Cole and the Commotions. There was a song on it about walking in the pouring rain which she listened to over and over until their mother threatened to break the disk in half. Dunnigan, who never had much interest in music but was delighted his twin was enjoying her gift, climbed up to the loft in the old Victorian house they grew up in, the sounds of the crows in the pine trees behind it a constant white noise. He had found an old set of earphones in a box up there and given it to her.

'You can listen any time you want now,' he'd told her.

'Are you deaf?'

He had forgotten there was a man standing over him. It didn't matter. Nothing mattered now.

A hand gripped his shoulder so hard, sharp pain shot right down his arm, but he was so far away it was a distant, insignificant sensation. He felt himself being flung to the floor. A rough hand gripped his face.

'Ernest Frobisher. You've been tracking him. That man owes me a debt which I am going to collect.'

Dunnigan opened his eyes. The man was slim, with dark hair. He was dressed in the uniform of one of the staff at the hotel. He had a hooked knife in his hand.

'You have been following his trail for some time now. I want you to tell me what you know.'

Dunnigan sighed and closed his eyes again.

Gina had always liked music. He remembered when she was fourteen, she had gone through a phase where she was obsessed with a band called The Cure. Their music tended towards the maudlin, and his sister had rooted out every single item of clothing she could find that was black and borrowed some of his, to boot. To their father's horror, she had mixed sugar and water into a syrup and used it to tease her hair into long spikes, and coloured her lips black with eyeliner.

My gosh, how angry their father had been.

'I'm going to ask nicely one more time,' the man said, 'because I know you've got your own argument with him. But if you aren't prepared to share information, I'm going to stop being nice. Do you understand me, Mr Dunnigan?'

'You're not leaving the house dressed like that!' their father had shouted.

Gina had stormed off to her room, and hadn't come out for three days. They had finally compromised, and his sister had been allowed a slightly tamer, modified goth hairstyle, which she had worn for a fortnight, by which time she had moved her musical affections to The Smiths, and was trying to get her hair to stay in a rockabilly quiff.

'Have it your own way, then,' the man said, and Dunnigan felt a sting on his cheek.

His visitor was cutting a jagged line across his face with the blade. He didn't care. He remembered when Gina was pregnant with Beth.

Beth … Did she know her mother was gone? Was someone looking after her? He struggled to get his mind working again. For a moment, he couldn't even remember where his niece was.

Then things began to click into place. Beth was with Miley in Amsterdam. He seemed to recall Diane telling him that Tormey had decided not to let the girl know – she had enough on her plate, and there was nothing she could do anyway.

But she would have to be informed, sooner or later. And then she would need all the people she loved around her.

The pain in his cheek throbbed and he felt a wetness as blood flowed from the wound. His hand shot up and grabbed the wrist that controlled the blade, stopping it in its work. Dunnigan's eyes snapped open, and the man looming over him saw determination and fury in them so great he almost took a step back.

'Who are you?' the criminologist asked, and his voice was steady and firm.

'They call me The Harpy. I haven't gone by any other name for a long time.'

'You're looking for Frobisher.'

'Yes. He killed someone I loved and I'm going to kill him.'

The criminologist stood up. 'What makes you think you can do it?'

'I kill people for a living and I do it very well.'

Dunnigan went to the bathroom and ran a facecloth under the tap, which he pressed to his cheek. The man was sitting on the bed now, clearly puzzled at the sudden, dramatic change.

'Maybe we can help one another,' the criminologist said.

And they were still talking an hour later when Diane got back.

6

THE FOLLOWING DAY, DUNNIGAN AND DIANE
boarded a plane bound for Portland, Oregon.

They hadn't talked much since she had returned to the
hotel and found him with the assassin. She was glad that he
was functioning again, but there was a coldness and distance
to him she found hard to deal with.

But he needed to know what she had learned. 'Harmon
seems to have stumbled upon what might be the root of
Frobisher's entire criminal operation,' Diane said as they
tucked into the risible airline meal (the flight attendant told
them it was penne and meatballs, but Dunnigan wasn't
so sure). 'The Yellow Man took two of his fingers, his left
nipple and, in a very Shakespearean twist, a large chunk of
one of his love handles, to make sure he never told anyone
about it.'

'But he told you.'

'I promised him we'd end Frobisher. I was also able to give him the good news that the Yellow Man is dead. I thought he was going to pass out with joy at that little gem of information.'

'So, what did he stumble upon?'

'They never told him, but he worked it out for himself. It was the business Frobisher used to launder the dirty money from the less than legal parts of his operation.'

'Where was the laundering done?'

'He didn't know, at first – it was all hidden behind anonymous numbered entries. But you see, even after the Yellow Man's visit, Harmon couldn't leave it alone. He worked out that the numbers of the expenses were all references for bank lodgements, and he followed the trail back.'

'Where did it lead?'

'To the United States.'

Dunnigan smiled a sad smile and put the plastic cover back on his meal. He had taken maybe four spoonfuls. 'Was he able to identify the specific business Frobisher was using to clean the funds?'

'Oh yes. And if you want to rinse clean large quantities of cash, this is the best kind of business to do it, bar none.'

'Are you going to tell me?'

'A casino. In the desert in Arizona.'

'That is clever,' Dunnigan agreed.

Diane speared a meatball on her fork. 'What kind of meat do you think this is?'

'I'm not sure it's actually meat of any kind. The texture resembles cardboard.'

She took a bite and grimaced. 'How's your face?'

The Harpy had stitched the wound for Dunnigan while

they had talked. Diane marvelled at how neat a job he had done.

'It's alright. Smarts a bit.'

'And you really trust your stabby friend? You're confident he won't knife us all in the back when we're not looking?'

'He wants the same thing we do. I think he'll do what he says he'll do.'

'Which is what, exactly?'

'Better you don't know. He'll be around. That's as much as I can say.'

'Don't start getting all mysterious on me again, Davey Dunnigan. The last time you played your cards close to your chest was in Greenland, and we all nearly died. Remember?'

'I gave him my word, Diane. It'll all become clear soon. I promise.'

'Alright, then. And how are you? In your head … emotionally …'

'To be honest, I don't feel anything.'

'You were hysterical, Davey. I thought you'd had a breakdown. You don't just snap out of that – believe me, it's something I know from personal experience.'

'I've set it aside for the moment.'

'How the fuck do you do that?'

'I know Gina is dead, and the pain and the sadness haven't gone away. I've taken them and put them in a place deep inside myself. When this is over and we have set things right, I'll revisit them and deal with them. At the moment, though, grieving is a luxury I can't afford. We have to avoid getting arrested and we have to find Ressler and Frobisher and there's Beth to think about too.'

'That's all very sensible, but I have to tell you, grief of

this magnitude doesn't fare well being put in a hole. It'll seep out, one way or another. And when it does, it'll make a mess.'

'I promise I will not let that happen. Not until it's safe to do so.'

'Famous last words, Davey,' Diane said, and, putting her seat back, went to sleep.

7

THE FLIGHT TOOK ALMOST THIRTEEN HOURS (including a three-hour stopover in Reykjavik) and when they landed in Portland International it was five thirty, local time.

Father Bill met them at the airport. He embraced them both, and told Dunnigan how sorry he was about Gina. 'My heart is broken for your loss.'

'Thanks, Father, but I don't think I can talk about it just now.'

'Of course, Davey. Whenever you're ready.'

The cleric had rented a car, and he drove them to a Quality Inn where he had booked rooms for them in advance. 'Beth and Miley arrived yesterday,' he said. 'They're watching Merrick at the moment.'

'How are they?' Dunnigan asked.

'Oh – they're good,' the priest said, and the criminologist thought there was an odd tone to his voice.

S.A. Dunphy

'You haven't told them about Gina?'

'I understood we weren't going to do that,' the priest said. 'Shouldn't Clive be the one to do it? He's her father, after all.'

'He hasn't spoken to her in months,' Dunnigan said. 'I don't know what he expected when we found her, but he couldn't cope with who she is now. They're … estranged.'

Gina and Clive had moved to London about a year after their daughter had been abducted, in an attempt to salvage what was left of their relationship. The change of scenery hadn't worked, however, and their marriage had sundered, never to be repaired. When Beth had been found, Clive had never been able to accept this gaunt, hollow-eyed young adult as the four-year-old he had lost. Beth had immediately picked up her father's confused (and often hostile) feelings, and her bond with her father disintegrated. In the weeks and months to follow, it had never been repaired.

'Let's keep it between us, then, for the moment.'

'As you wish.'

'How did they get on in Amsterdam?'

Father Bill explained about the tie and how they had retrieved it. 'Tormey organised for Davies, an Interpol operative he says you know, to meet them and take custody of the item. He's going to get it safely to Ireland, and Frank will decide how best to use it from there.'

'I don't know if it helps us but it certainly doesn't hurt us,' Diane said.

'Have you learned anything from watching Merrick?' Dunnigan wanted to know.

'She gets driven to and from work every day, including Sundays, where she remains until about eight in the evening.

After that she goes home and drinks,' Father Bill said. 'That is pretty much it.'

'No friends, family, dog?'

'Not that we've noticed. She seems to be very alone.'

'Where does she live?'

'She rents a brownstone in midtown.'

'Probably best to approach her there.'

'I'll go,' Father Bill said. 'I've been following her about for a few days. I think I've got a sense of who she is. We're also around the same age. Maybe I can bring a little charm into play.'

'Take Miley,' Diane suggested. 'He tends to have a calming effect on people.'

'You're right,' the priest said. 'And it's always best to have something to dilute my charm, otherwise ladies tend to hurt themselves in their rush to bed me.'

'Don't you mean in their hurry to fling themselves from the nearest window to get away from you?' Diane asked.

'Well, it happens less since I changed my aftershave,' Father Bill said dolefully.

8

FATHER BILL, DRESSED IN HIS CLERICAL COLLAR and a black blazer and jeans, accompanied by Miley, who had donned a tie-dye collarless shirt and loose-fitting cotton trousers and sandals, knocked on Suzanna Merrick's door at nine that evening. The priest told his friend that it was best to give her enough time to consume a sufficient quantity of the sauvignon blanc she favoured to make her happy, while keeping her coherent enough for a conversation.

She opened the door dressed in purple workout gear, a large glass of white wine in her hand. She was probably in her mid to late fifties, with long auburn hair, a large, friendly mouth and understated makeup. Miley thought she was very attractive – not as pretty as Beth, maybe, but then, no one was.

'Hello, Ms Merrick.' Father Bill smiled his best smile. 'May we come in, please?'

'My name is on the mailbox at the gate, so you don't earn any brownie points for using it," the woman said. 'Now, I'm going to save you some time by telling you that I have not found Jesus and I'm not about to start looking for him, either.' Her flushed cheeks hinted that she had drunk quite a bit already, but her voice was strident and confident, betraying nothing less than full sobriety.

'I can assure you we don't want to talk to you about our Lord,' Father Bill said.

'You're fundraising, then? Save me the sales pitch. How much do you want? I haven't made my monthly charitable donation yet. If you're prepared to give me a receipt so I can write it off against my taxes, I'll give you whatever you want.'

The priest and Miley exchanged a glance.

'Well, thank you very much,' Miley grinned. 'The parish trip to Medjugorje needs all the help it can get.'

'Come inside and I'll get my cheque book.'

They stepped into her hallway and she closed the door behind them.

'Will five hundred be okay?'

'You know, Ms Merrick, I have a confession to make,' Father Bill said as she padded barefoot through a doorway to their left, which seemed to be her home office.

'Whatever it is, I'm not interested. Can I just write this and see you on your way? I'm watching Season 6 of *Orange Is the New Black*. Have you seen it yet?'

'I haven't had the pleasure,' Father Bill admitted.

'That show has just gone from strength to strength,' their host gushed.

'I haven't caught up since Season 3,' Miley said.

'You have *got* to take the time,' Merrick replied from inside her sanctum. 'Who will I make this out to?'

'Ms Merrick, I'm not fundraising,' Father Bill said. 'I want to talk to you about Ernest Frobisher.'

This was met with silence.

'I apologise for the subterfuge. It's just that, when you mentioned making a donation, it seemed as good a way as any to get in here to chat with you.'

Suddenly Suzanna Merrick was in the doorway, the glass of wine gone, a frighteningly large handgun in its place. 'Get the fuck out of my house before I blow your fucking heads clean off,' she said.

9

MILEY RAISED A HAND AND SMILED AT THE woman. 'We don't want to cause any trouble, Ms Merrick,' he said. 'All we want to know, really, is if you can tell us where Frobisher is. I'm sorry if we alarmed you. We didn't mean to.'

The gun wavered for a moment. 'He's in fucking Arizona,' she said.

'I beg your pardon,' Father Bill said, 'but how do you know that?'

'I received an email out of the blue two days ago.'

'From Frobisher?'

'Actually, it was from someone called Ressler. He said he works for Frobisher. In the email it said that, should anyone named Dunnigan come asking about Frobisher's location, I was to give them an address and some GPS coordinates.'

'Dunnigan is our friend,' Miley said. 'We're here on his behalf.'

'How can I be sure of that? It has been twenty years since I had any dealings with Frobisher, that twisted, evil sonofabitch, and I do not want to give him any excuse to come looking for me again.'

'I'm going to put my hand into my pocket,' Miley said. 'I'll do it nice and slow.' He did so, and took out their burner phone. 'I'm going to dial a number. I'll make sure it's the right person and then I'm going to give it to you. You can ask him any questions you like to satisfy yourself that it's the person Frobisher was referring to.'

Luckily, Dunnigan picked up.

'Davey, Ms Merrick wants to talk to you.'

'Why?'

'You should speak to her yourself.' He passed over the phone.

'Are you Dunnigan?'

'I'm David Dunnigan, yes.'

'Why does someone called Ressler, who says he works for Ernest Frobisher, want to let you know where he is?'

'I suspect it's because he wants to kill me. You have his location?'

'Yes. Ressler sent it to me.'

'Can you give it to Father Bill and Miley?'

'Yes. Alright.'

'Thank you.'

'Are you planning on going there?'

'Yes, I am.'

'Why?'

'Because I'm going to kill him.'

'I tried to. It didn't work.'

'Well, nothing ventured.'

'I don't think he can be killed. I don't think he's human.'

'I am going to give it a damn good try.'

'Good luck.' Suzanna Merrick hung up and handed the phone back to Miley. 'You can wait in the lounge. I'll print out the email.'

The Email

Dear Suzanna,

You do not know me, but my employer, Mr Ernest Frobisher, speaks very fondly of you. He has told me about your relationship and how close you once were, and he has also expressed his regret at the way things ended between you both. It is a terrible thing when love dies, and even more tragic when that regard is replaced with bitterness and anger.

Mr Frobisher hopes you have overcome any feelings of negativity you may have once harboured towards him, and that this message finds you happy and well. Maybe he and I could come and visit you one of these fine days? I'm sure, from what he has told me of your last meeting, that it would not be difficult to rekindle some of the old passion! That would be fun, would it not?

In the meantime, perhaps you can help us with a little problem.

Another old friend of ours, a man named Dunnigan, is hoping to meet us, but circumstances have conspired so that we have no way of contacting him to tell him where we are currently situated. We have reason to believe he may be calling on you in the coming days. If so, perhaps you could let him know that we are enjoying the desert air in the beautiful state of Arizona, in our ranch adjacent to the Deep Dive Casino in the Sonoran Desert? Please furnish him with these GPS coordinates, to ensure he has no difficulty finding us.

Latitude: 33 15' 22.80' N

Longitude -111 10' 3.00' W

It is of the utmost importance to my employer that Mr Dunnigan receives these details – but please ensure that they do not find their way into anyone else's hands. As you, better than most, are aware, there are many people out there who wish Mr Frobisher harm. One can never be too careful with one's personal details.

Please allow me to wish you a fond farewell. Now that we have your contact details, I have no doubt we will be coming to see you very soon.

Best wishes,

Dr Phillipe Ressler

10

'THANKS FOR THIS,' FATHER BILL SAID, ONCE HE had read the email and passed it to Miley. 'Did you check the coordinates? Are they real?'

'Yes. According to Google Earth they show what looks to be a walled complex of some kind. There is a casino about five miles away, between it and Phoenix.'

'So after all this searching, he's just gone and told us where he is,' Miley said.

'Makes sense,' Father Bill observed. 'He's meeting us on his terms. This way, he'll be ready for us.'

'You don't mean to actually go,' Suzanna Merrick asked incredulously.

'We've come this far,' Miley said.

'But he's a monster.'

'You said you tried to kill him,' Father Bill said.

'I tried to have him killed,' the woman said, topping up her glass of wine. 'Where are my manners – would either of you like one?'

'Well, just to keep you company,' Father Bill said.

She bustled out and came back with a fresh bottle and two more glasses. 'Frobisher took my company in a hostile takeover,' she said when she was sitting down again. 'It is customary when such things occur for the CEOs to meet for a kind of handover. During that meeting, Frobisher raped me.'

'I'm sorry,' Father Bill said.

'That's awful,' Miley agreed.

'I'm not going to pretend that I was as pure as the driven snow when it came to my business practices. One of the areas my company dabbled in was waste management, and one of the groups we'd had some dealings with was a group called the Gambinis. Are you familiar with them?'

'I'm not, but I am going to buy into cultural stereotypes and assume they are a fraternal organisation with links to crime,' Father Bill said.

'Precisely. I made a call to Paolo Gambini, who had been my contact guy, and I told him what had happened. He was very sympathetic, and said it would be dealt with.'

Miley and Father Bill said nothing. This was her story. She would tell it in her own good time.

'Two days later I was at home – I was living in Salem, then – and my door was kicked open and it was that bastard the Yellow Man with what looked like three homeless guys. He held a gun on me while they took turns. When they were done, the Yellow fucker said to me that his employer was a wise man. Paolo had tried to kill him and had failed, but before he died, he had given me up. The Yellow Man was all for killing me, but Frobisher told him that a worse fate was to brutalise me some more, and let me live, knowing that he could come back any time and do it again. He told me that if I went to the police, he'd make sure they heard about my business dealings that were on the wrong side of the law. So I kept quiet.'

'And did he come back?' Father Bill asked.

'Once more. A year later. After that, I bought a gun. I decided I'd kill them or myself the next time they came.'

'But still you let us in – two strangers,' Miley said.

'You have a kind face,' Suzanna Merrick said. 'I didn't think someone who looked like you would work for Ernest Frobisher.'

'That's a very sweet thing to say,' Miley told her.

'When you go there, please kill him,' she said.

'That's the plan,' Miley said.

Part Eleven

DESERT STORMS

1

THE DEEP DIVE CASINO WAS SITUATED TWO
hours' drive from Phoenix, and was on land that bordered
the Gila River Reservation, home to a community of Native
Americans, principally the Pima and Maricopa tribes.

Dunnigan had never been in a desert before, and he found
the heat shocking. He could not tolerate being out in it for
more than a couple of minutes before he became light-headed
and had to get back into the shade, or ideally under an air-
conditioner.

The reservation reminded Dunnigan of the one he had
lived on with Diane and Miley in Greenland – it was made
up of a mix-and-match of modern, cheaply built structures
alongside traditional, bow-roofed houses. Instead of snow
and ice, the land hereabouts was scorched by the dry, arid
heat, the yellow and red sands broken here and there by
ironwood and mesquite.

It was both terrifying and beautiful.

The community had a population of 11,300 souls, and provided the water, electricity and mobile phone service for the entire region, as well as publishing a weekly paper, and boasting a modern health care centre.

Dunnigan noted, as he and Diane made a tour of the reservation, that it was also home to Gila River Memorial Airport, a private-use airstrip just north of the township of Chandler. 'Perfectly placed for someone with Frobisher's needs,' he observed.

'My thoughts exactly.'

Gila River sheriff's office was based in the Sacaton district.

'That's the only law between here and Phoenix,' Dunnigan observed. 'If we get into really bad trouble, they're the only support we've got.'

'Won't they arrest us on the spot?' Diane asked. 'We're here to kill at least one person – probably more.'

'If they attack first, it'll be self-defence.'

'If they attack first, we'll be too dead to defend ourselves.'

*

They found a rocky outcrop a mile from the cluster of buildings Frobisher had given them the coordinates for, and observed the structures through binoculars in the early evening when the heat was just about bearable. In the clear desert air, figures could be seen patrolling the walls.

'Google Maps gives it an area of a quarter of a square mile with sixteen buildings inside,' Miley said. 'There's a large block right in the middle, which is probably where they've got Frobisher.'

'Probably isn't good enough,' Father Bill said. 'We need

exact intelligence or we'll be lumbering around in there blind.'

'Which is a fabulous way to get picked off,' Diane agreed.

'Well, how do we secure that type of information?' Miley asked.

'He has to have staff in there,' Beth said. 'Medical, for a start, but I'll bet there's cooks and cleaners, and we can see the guards.'

'And where, pray tell, would he have found the people to fulfil those roles?' Father Bill asked.

'Only one place hereabouts,' Diane agreed.

'The Gila River Reservation,' Dunnigan said, following their line of reasoning. 'Even if Frobisher is bringing in his own people, he'll have had to take on some locals.'

'So they'll know the layout,' Miley agreed. 'The problem being we don't know anyone out here. And this isn't like Greenland, where we had people on the inside. We can't just roll up and tell them we're planning to break into a local ranch.'

'Is that what they're calling it?' Diane demanded.

'On Google Maps it's labelled as Desert Moon Ranch, yes.'

'A fucking fortified compound is what that is,' Diane said. 'A ranch! Jesus fucking Christ on a bike.'

'Ranch, compound or day spa, we're in the same predicament,' Dunnigan said. 'Miley, there's no way you could use your connections with the Inughuit to get the locals here on our side, is there?'

Miley gave his friend a hard stare. 'Davey, I don't want to suggest that's a racist statement, but it would be the equivalent of my thinking a Senegalese tribesman would have an immediate rapport with a member of the Zulu nation.'

'I'm going to take that as a no, then?'

'It's like when English people think everyone in Ireland knows one another.'

'Like I said, you're telling me no?'

'Or when someone from Kilkenny asks if you know their mate because their mate lives in Dublin too.'

'I think I get it, Miley.'

'Good.'

'Well, I'm fresh out of ideas, then,' Dunnigan said ruefully.

They all stood and stared at the walled area in the hazy distance, as if a floorplan would mysteriously materialise from the dusty air.

'I surely do wish someone had a friend, even one with a distant chance of helping us out,' Diane said.

'If I thought there was even a slim chance, I'd try it,' Father Bill said.

'Just one phone call could make all the difference,' Beth agreed.

'Alright, I'll call Tuntuk and see if he can have a word with one of the local elders,' Miley said testily.

'Good lad, Miley,' Father Bill said.

And they got into the car and drove back to the hotel.

2

TO MILEY'S SURPRISE (ALTHOUGH TO HIS frustration, his friends were not shocked in the least), Tuntuk seemed to think it was a perfectly reasonable request. 'Tribal people help one another,' he told Miley. 'You know the fella's name?'

'Wikipedia says the governor is man named Joseph Goldfoot.'

'You got a number?'

Miley gave him the listing he had for the reservation's administrative centre.

'Okay. When should I call?'

'We're six hours behind here.'

'So afternoon here, morning there.'

'Yes.'

'Okay.'

'Thank you, Father.'

'You being safe?'

'So far.'

'You gonna fight this bad man?'

'We have to. It's … well, it's the right thing to do.'

'You remember what I told you. Best way to fight is to use enemy's strength against him. That way, he fighting against himself.'

'I'll remember.'

'You my son. You come home soon, okay?'

'I will.'

And the line went dead.

3

JOSEPH GOLDFOOT WAS A BROAD-SHOULDERED,
angular man with a high forehead, a prominent nose and
long, dark hair. He wore a tailored dress shirt and faded
Levi's around the waist of which he had wrapped a red and
green hand-woven Pima belt.

His office was large, with a bay window that looked out
over the desert plain. Black-and-white photographs of the
local tribespeople were framed on the wall, and the original
document that established the community, signed by Franklin
D. Roosevelt in 1939, hung above his desk.

He looked sternly at Miley. 'You don't look like no ice
warrior.'

'You don't look much like a Red Injun.'

'The times they are a changin',' Goldfoot said.

'Is that a line from an old Pima war song?'

'Hell, maybe you are a tribal person after all,' the governor
said. 'You know our music.'

The two laughed and shook hands warmly.

Dunnigan, who was sitting beside Miley, heaved a sigh of relief.

'Your chieftain asked me to help you guys out,' Goldfoot said. 'He tells me you have a beef with the men in the compound over yonder.'

'They took my niece,' Dunnigan said.

'And they killed some of Tuntuk's people,' Miley added.

'They're no friends of ours, either,' Goldfoot agreed.

'Have they broken some kind of treaty by building on your land?' Dunnigan asked. (Miley put his head in his hands, waiting for Goldfoot's retort.)

'No. They're assholes and their pay is shit.'

'Oh,' Dunnigan said.

'Billie Jones was the last of our people I know of who worked out there.'

'Is she a nurse?' Miley asked.

'No. They don't use our medics, they bring in their own. They asked to borrow our echocardiogram machine once, and got awful pissy when we wouldn't give it to them, but it's a damned expensive piece of equipment, and we've not got but one of them in the clinic. No, Billie did some cleaning out there. She would've been all over that place. I'll get her to have a word with you.'

'Thanks a million,' Miley said.

'You gonna raise hell out there?'

'It's probably better you don't know,' Dunnigan told him.

'Hell,' Goldfoot replied, 'I'm just a simple Indian man.'.

4

GOLDFOOT INVITED THEM TO HAVE LUNCH IN the local diner, which specialised in a kind of Tex-Mex cuisine that Miley loved and Dunnigan loathed, but forced himself to pick at.

'You don't have much of an appetite,' Goldfoot observed.

'Apologies. I lost my sister a few days ago – which I'd prefer you kept to yourself, by the way. Some of my party don't know yet.'

'I'm sorry to hear it. That part of the reason you're here?'

'I'm not sure. Probably.'

'They start killing your family, they deserve what they get. You need any backup, you give me a call.'

'We probably shouldn't involve the police,' Dunnigan said.

'We're a self-contained force out here with full authority to act as we see fit. You're telling me that there's a criminal gang holed up just outside our land? I'm not going to ignore that. It would be criminal if I did.'

'I should probably tell you that the police back home are looking for us.'

Goldfoot sampled some of his burrito. 'Why would that be?'

'One of the men in that compound framed my niece for the murder of a police detective.'

'They say she shot him?'

'They say she cut his head off with a hunting knife.'

'You talking about the girl in the picture you showed me? The little thing?'

'Yes.'

'I'm guessing these police back in Ireland never tried to butcher a antelope.'

'You're probably right about that.'

'I expect you saw them out on the mesa on your way here – small, fast-moving deer. Trying to cut off the head of one of them is about the same as trying to cut the head off of a man. It's not one bit easy. You need the right tool and you need to know how to do it and you need the physical strength. Your niece do much hunting?'

'None I know of.'

Goldfoot shrugged as if the matter was settled.

'They reason that if she didn't do it, she helped the person who did,' Dunnigan said in the interest of full disclosure.

'What does she say?'

'That she doesn't know what happened.'

'And you believe her?'

Dunnigan put down his knife and fork and rubbed his eyes. He could feel the anger and anxiety and deep, deep sadness bubbling just under the surface, and with a conscious effort he pushed it down. 'I don't know, Governor. She's my niece. I love her. The only person who knows what happened is walled up five miles from here.'

Goldfoot grinned and took a swig of beer. 'Well, it seems I just experienced a bout of temporary deafness, and I didn't hear the last minute or so of our conversation. So unfortunately any confessions you might have made about being on the run from the law in this or any other jurisdiction will probably go unheeded.'

'You're not the kind of politician I expected,' Dunnigan said.

'Friend, I'm not the kind of politician *I* expected.'

5

BILLIE JONES LOOKED TO BE ABOUT FIFTY, HER long black hair greying at the temples and several of her teeth missing. Miley noted that her forearms, which showed below the rolled sleeves of her denim shirt, were densely muscled.

She sat beside Goldfoot in their booth in the diner and drank black coffee. 'I worked in that place for three weeks last summer. The old man was there, and that crazy doctor guy. They had a lot of men with guns with them, and a team of nurses. I cleaned and did some cooking. They paid four dollars an hour. It wasn't worth it, so I left.'

'How many guns?' Dunnigan asked.

'Ten. Twelve, maybe.'

'Where did they keep the old man?'

'Big shed in the middle of the yard. It used to be a garage, but they turned it into a hospital. He never comes out of there.'

'What about the rest of the buildings? Can you draw me an outline?'

She shrugged and pulled over a paper place mat. 'You got a pen?'

Dunnigan took one from the breast pocket of his shirt.

Billie drew a large square to represent the perimeter. 'These buildings,' she sketched a ring of structures close to the walls, 'are where the guards sleep. Bunkhouses. These ones,' she drew a second ring, 'are where they keep vehicles, fuel and weapons. And these,' a final ring, 'are where the kitchen, TV room and living area is. There's a gym in this section here,' she wrote the word GYM in one of the rectangles. 'Right in the middle is the medical facility, and that's where the old man is.'

'It's a fortress,' Miley said. 'We'll never get in there.'

'Come on, my Eskimo brother. This is just like the old days,' Goldfoot said.

'In what way?' Dunnigan asked.

'They've got the wagons in a circle. My people have been dealing with that crap for a couple of hundred years. We've developed some techniques for getting around it.'

'Such as?' Dunnigan asked.

'If I tell you, you have to promise not to tell all the other palefaces,' Goldfoot said, and winked.

6

WHEN MILEY AND DUNNIGAN GOT BACK TO THE
hotel, Father Bill was sitting in the lobby.

'We got a phone call from Ressler,' he said, when they sat
down with him.

'On the burner?' Dunnigan asked.

'No. Right to my hotel room. They know we're here,
Davey.'

'What did he say?'

'He wouldn't talk to me, says he will only deal with you.
He left a number.'

Dunnigan nodded. He supposed it was always going to
come to this. 'Okay. Let's go and do it.'

They walked to the lift.

'Beth is really upset,' the priest told them. 'Diane is with
her, but she's not good. She's scared half to death. She's
convinced they're going to come for us any second. It's why I
sat down in the lobby – she wanted me to keep watch.'

'I'll talk to her,' Dunnigan said. 'Let's make the call first.'

Father Bill put his hands on Dunnigan's shoulders and turned him so they were eye to eye. 'We're coming to the endgame, Davey – you get that, don't you?'

'Of course I do.'

'It's just, sometimes I think this has been a bit like a chess match for you, a battle of wits between you and these evil men. Well, that may be the case, but the stakes are really, really high. It's life or death. I am here for you, right to the bitter end, but I have to be sure you understand what we're doing. It's more than just you and Frobisher. We're all in it – you see that, don't you?'

Dunnigan stared back at the priest. Miley stood to the side, feeling uncomfortable.

'Tell me you understand what I've just said.'

'I understand,' Dunnigan said.

'Do you?'

'It's them or us,' the criminologist said. 'And I promise you, I won't let it be us.'

'That's what I wanted to hear,' Father Bill said. 'Now, let's go and talk to this creep.'

7

RESSLER ANSWERED AFTER THE FIRST RING. 'MR David Dunnigan the criminologist and wanted man, it is so very nice to speak to you again after such a long time.'

'What do you want, Ressler?'

'Are your good friends there with you? Is little Elizabeth safely by your side?'

'We're all here.'

'Good, good. Now, my employer, the very generous Mr Ernest Frobisher, is prepared to make you an offer, a way to end all the unpleasantness for good and proper. Are you interested in hearing the terms of this once-in-a-lifetime opportunity?'

Dunnigan looked at the others, who were all clustered around the receiver so they could hear what was said. 'I'm listening.'

'Ha! Most excellent. Here is the proposal. You and little Elizabeth present yourselves at the gate to our lovely Arizona residence tomorrow morning at eight o'clock and we will let Diane and Miley and your associate the priest Father Bill live. How does that sound to you?'

'No deal. Not under any circumstances.'

'Mr David Dunnigan, you are all staying in the Sonora Desert Star Hotel, in rooms 101 to 105. I could have a team of men go out there and bring you to me within ten minutes flat. It is only due to the generosity of my employer that you remain breathing at all.'

'You can have me,' Dunnigan said. 'Beth hasn't been responsible for any of your problems – they've all been my fault.'

'That is true – so you would come here with no arguments or fighting, and give yourself to me and Mr Frobisher?'

'Yes.'

'No!' Beth shouted, an edge of panic in her voice.

'Oh, I hear someone is not so pleased with this suggestion. Alright. I will see what my employer thinks. Wait one moment.'

The line went quiet.

'What the hell are you thinking?' Beth asked, shaking him. 'I am not letting you do this.'

'I'll be okay,' Dunnigan said. 'You have to trust me, Beth.'

'They'll tear you apart,' Beth said, tears streaming down her face. 'And worse. I thought we came here to fight, Davey, not to give in to them.'

'Eight o'clock tomorrow.' Ressler's voice chimed in his ear. 'I shall look forward to spending some time with you.'

And he was gone.

'That gives us fourteen hours to prepare,' Diane said.

'We'd better get started, then,' Dunnigan agreed.

Part Twelve

COPS AND ROBBERS

1

ALAIN DAVIES, A DETECTIVE FROM INTERPOL who had helped Dunnigan and Tormey in Greenland a little over a year ago, spoke to the suspended chief superintendent on the phone from Amsterdam. 'You got the package?'

'Yes, thanks, Alain. It arrived by courier yesterday.'

'Good. I got our lab guys to take samples and run some tests before I sent it.'

'And?'

'There was some black mould, which was a result of the bag the tie was in being slightly porous, so some spores managed to work their way in and take root. But there were also skin particles and blood.'

'Could you find matches?'

'Oh yes. Most of it belonged to – and this is going to cause a shitstorm unless I'm very much mistaken – Wilfred Hubert.'

'She was fucking telling the truth ...' Tormey said quietly.

'Sorry?'

'Just talking to myself, Alain. Sorry, mate.'

'I mean, this is *the* Wilfred Hubert. His DNA is on record because since 9/11 you have to provide a sample when you go into the House of Representatives and the UN buildings in the United States. I had them double check the results. It's him alright.'

'You said most of the samples?'

'There were skin cells and a blood pattern consistent with asphyxial spray from another person. We had to run this through several databases, but we finally got a hit. A kid named Dova Ibrahimi went missing from outside her home in Lithuania twenty years ago. She was presumed dead.'

'I'm sorry to say that she is,' Tormey said.

'What is this, Frank? What are we dealing with here?'

'Can you leave it with me for a few days, Alain? I'll bring you in at the end, I promise.'

'Is it part of that business in the Arctic?'

'Yes.'

'Alright. I can give you a week, maybe, but the searches I ran are going to set some alarm bells ringing in The Hague. I can't keep a lid on this for long.'

'You won't need to. Can you email me the test results?'

'I already have.'

'Thanks, Alain.'

'This is big game you're hunting. Make sure it doesn't turn around and bite you.'

'I'll be careful. We'll talk soon.'

2

THE MINISTER FOR JUSTICE, MAURICE MCDONALD TD, agreed to see Tormey out of courtesy, but informed him he could only spare fifteen minutes. They met in a quiet corner of Buswells Hotel, right across the road from Leinster House, the seat of the Oireachtas, Ireland's parliament.

'We could just as easily have talked in my office,' McDonald grumbled. He was a corpulent man in his late forties, tipped to be Taoiseach, Ireland's prime minister, within the next ten years.

'Less chance of any unwanted listeners over here,' Tormey said.

'You're getting paranoid in your old age.'

'Not paranoid. Just sensible.'

'I have to get back, Frank. What's this all about?'

'Did you read the paperwork I slipped under your door?'

'I did.'

'And?'

'What the fuck, Frank? I mean, really, what are you playing at?'

'I'm trying to do my job, Maurice.'

'You don't have a job at the moment. And you won't have one to go back to if you keep playing silly buggers.'

'I sent you evidence of a crime, minister. A man our government is about to climb into bed with is clearly guilty of the murder of a child. I also believe he is guilty of the death of Gina Carlton. At the very least, I want him taken in for questioning.'

'We are about to close a deal with this gentleman that will earn untold billions at a time we sorely need it. Do you know what that money is going to be spent on? They are finally going to build some decent social housing. A new and properly resourced juvenile detention centre – there hasn't been once since St Pat's closed. New schools are needed all over the country. Do you get what I'm telling you, chief?'

'That you don't want to arrest the goose that lays the golden eggs.'

'If we haul him in and start asking him about some kind of sexual indiscretion he may or may not have committed, we can kiss the deal goodbye. I'm not going to be the one responsible for that. I mean, Jesus, Frank – there's talk of this guy running for president.'

'He had sex with and killed a young girl called Dova Ibrahimi. That was her name, minister. I have a witness.'

'Even if you pursue this, do you think it'll stick? This is one of the richest men in the world. His lawyers will bury it under a mountain of paperwork and we'll lose the deal and he'll never see the inside of even the most luxurious open prison.

It's a waste of time, Frank. I know it's not right, but that's the way it is. You've been around long enough to know the score.'

'And that's your last word?'

'It is.'

Tormey nodded, almost to himself, and leaned in so the minister could hear him as he whispered, 'If you or anyone else in your office sends another leg-breaker to my home to threaten my wife, I'll rip your arm off and beat you to death with it. Am I clear, Maurice?'

The minister for justice nodded silently as Frank Tormey patted him smartly on the cheek and left him to his thoughts.

3

HE KNEW IN HIS GUT THAT HUBERT WAS responsible for Gina's death, but he had to be certain.

A woman had come to the safe house to do his wife's hair, which meant she would be occupied for most of the day. She had been upset at having to move, but she was a copper's wife, and he told her a guy he'd put behind bars had made threats, and she needed to go somewhere safe for a week or so. She was annoyed, but seemed to understand. She'd always been a good old girl.

He went to Pearse Street Station and found Toddy sitting on one of the benches on Platform 2, reading a John Grisham novel. He brought the nervous man back to Clonsilla, and sat him in front of his laptop. 'Can you check Gina Carlton's phone records for me, Toddy? I want to know the last couple of calls in and out to her number.'

It took the programmer five minutes to get the details up. 'Here they are.'

Tormey sat down and ran through the numbers Gina had been in contact with on her final day, cross-checking them with a list her ex-husband Clive had given him. Only one didn't match – it was the last number on the list, and a call and text had come from it to Gina's handset. 'Can you tell me who that number belongs to?'

'The police can do this, can't they?' Toddy asked as he rattled at the keys.

'They can, but not for me just now, Toddy. I'm not well liked within the department at the moment.'

'The number belongs to an unregistered pay-as-you-go phone,' the homeless man said.

'A burner?'

While all phones are traceable to an extent, smartphones leave much greater trails as to their movements, as they are all now fitted with GPS trackers and modems. A smartphone made for a much easier target.

More rattling keys.

'No.'

'So it's a smartphone? Can you tell me where it was when the call was made?'

'Toddy can do that. But it will take … a bit longer.'

'How about I make us some lunch and you crack on with it then?'

'Okay. Do you have minestrone soup?'

'I don't know – but if I don't, I'm sure I can get some.'

*

A trip to the supermarket later and Toddy was contentedly enjoying spoonfuls of soup between bouts of furious keyboard work. An hour passed, and he suddenly turned the screen around so Tormey could see. 'The call to Ms Carlton pinged off this tower here,' he said. 'Stephen's Green.'

'I thought that might be the case.'

'Toddy can pinpoint where the sim card was to within a few streets. It looks like it was somewhere between Dame Street and Kildare Street.'

'Which fairly accurately describes the location of the Shelbourne Hotel, which is where Hubert was staying,' Tormey said.

'The phone didn't stay there, though.'

'No?'

'A text message – this text message – was sent to Gina, and the phone travelled. The address in the text matches the location it went to.'

Tormey looked at the message Toddy had opened in a window in the corner of the screen, and at the map he had pulled up in another. 'You've done some good work, Toddy. Can I drive you anywhere? If you'd like a few nights in a hotel, I'd be glad to treat you as payment for your services.'

'Can I go back to Pearse Street?'

'You're sure?'

'Toddy is sure.'

'Come on, then. I'll drop you on the way.'

'Where you going?'

'Ringsend.'

4

THE TEXT MESSAGE GINA HAD RECEIVED
contained the address of an apartment block in Grand Canal
Dock. Tormey parked on the street outside and loitered at the
bus stop opposite the building until he saw a woman wearing
a hajib, loaded with shopping bags, approaching the door. He
hurried across. 'Here, Miss, let me help you with those.'

'Thank you, you're very kind.'

The woman tapped a code on a keypad and the locking
mechanism buzzed. She pushed, and the door swung open.
'I'll take those now, thank you again,' she said, and Tormey,
sticking his foot in the door to prevent it closing completely,
handed them over. He gave her a minute, then stepped
inside.

The text message had specified the very last apartment on
the top floor, and he took the steps three at a time. The door
was locked, and he knocked. No response. He tried again.

Satisfied that there was no one home, he took a step back and kicked the door in.

The first thing that struck him was the smell of paint and the new carpet. This was incongruous in itself, as the rest of the building was in poor repair and had not seen a paintbrush in many years. The apartment was an empty shell except for a folding table and a single chair that sat in the middle of the open-plan living area. Tormey walked slowly around the room, his eyes taking it all in. Nothing at first occurred to him – it looked for all the world like an apartment that had recently been renovated, probably in advance of new tenants moving in. He pulled over the chair and sat down.

There was a trick his first supervisor, an old-school country guard named O'Connor, had taught him when he was fresh out of Templemore, and he tried it now. He sat back, allowed his eyes to go slightly out of focus, and emptied his mind.

'Often, Francis,' O'Connor would say, *'we get bogged down with everything that's going on in the front of our heads. Sometimes, you* need *to* shut that down. *Let the little voice in the back of your mind do the work for you.'*

He sat, in a kind of meditative trance, for several minutes before the thing that was staring him in the face revealed itself. It was the plastering.

The summer after he left school, Tormey had done some labouring on building sites in London. He spent a month helping out a plasterer from Offaly who had patiently showed him the secrets of his trade. Almost forty years later the detective still found himself admiring good plastering work. There was some of it on display in this very apartment. In one area in particular.

Tormey got up and walked to a patch of wall just to the

right of the entrance hallway. He could see, now, that the entire apartment had not, in fact, been repainted, just this wall. And it was this wall that had been replastered by someone who knew what they were doing, while the rest of the surfaces looked as if the plaster had been thrown on by hyperactive chimpanzees.

The chief took a penknife from his pocket, pried open the blade and began to scrape away the fresh plaster. It came away easily enough, and soon he was through to the plasterboard beneath. Within ten minutes he had cleared a good section of the wall and was through to the wooden frame.

And there, in one of the crossbeams, he found what he was looking for. A bullet hole. He sat back on his heels – it was the final piece in the puzzle.

Hubert had lured Gina here to have her killed. There was no longer any doubt of that.

5

HE SAT ON THE FLOOR OF THE EMPTY SPACE AND dialled the number that had sent the text message that summoned Gina to a lonely death.

He didn't think anyone would pick up, but to his surprise, someone did. They didn't say anything, but he could hear breathing and vague background noises.

'I'm sitting at the scene of the crime,' he said. 'You did a good clean-up job, but not quite good enough. It's the little things that always give the game away.'

Still no response.

'You covered your tracks pretty well, but the trail leading back to you was still visible if you knew where to look. I should also add that I now have hard evidence of the crimes Gina Carlton talked to you about. I am talking to Wilfred Hubert, aren't I? Or someone in his employ.'

'What do you want?' a voice growled in his ear.

It wasn't Hubert – it was whoever he paid to do his dirty work.

'I want to meet.'

'Where?'

'There's a place called Hall's Wharf,' Tormey said. 'It's an abandoned shipyard on the quays. We can have a nice conversation without anyone disturbing us.'

'When?'

'Tonight. Ten o'clock. Bring Hubert or there's no deal.'

A growl Tormey took to be a 'yes' ended the phone call.

The chief hoped he hadn't overplayed his hand.

6

HALL'S WHARF HAD BEEN USED BY THE AFTER
Dark Campaign to ship slave workers out of Dublin until
Dunnigan, Father Bill and a small army provided by Tim
Pat Rogers had shut down their operations. Tormey thought
there was a poetic justice in confronting Hubert there. It was
also technically in Ringsend, which gave it a second layer of
significance – parts of it could be seen from the window of
the apartment where Gina had died.

At ten o'clock at night the docks were still busily pounding
and hissing with activity, but Hall's Wharf seemed in a bubble
of its own. The Dodder had been rerouted in the 1930s when
Dublin Docklands had reclaimed a chunk of land to extend
its operations, making the wharf one of the more isolated
sections of the waterfront.

Tormey was already standing with his back to the water
when a black-windowed limousine drove down the narrow

access road and parked beside an empty storage container. The rear door opened and Hubert's gigantic bodyguard, whom Tormey knew was called Chatham, got out. He walked around to the other rear door and opened it. Wilfred Hubert, literally dwarfed by his associate, emerged.

The chief marvelled that, even in the dim light, the American looked like a tangerine in a business suit.

'Did you get him to do it?' Tormey asked as the two approached.

'I'm a very fucking busy man,' Hubert said. 'You mentioned evidence of some kind. I presume you want money. Can we cut to the chase so I can get away from this filthy stinking waterfront?'

'I don't want your money,' Tormey said. 'I just want to look you in the eye when I tell you you're finished. I have a sequence of evidence that will definitely stand up in court linking you to two murders. I have an eyewitness for one of those, and while we're talking about witnesses, I have a friend who is accessing security footage of the apartment building where I know you killed Gina Carlton. I haven't seen it yet, but I suspect it will put this big bastard at the scene, and will show Gina walking in but not coming out, although I'll bet we find images of Chatham there carrying a person-sized bundle as he exits.'

Tormey was bluffing – he doubted a man like Hubert's bodyguard would be so sloppy, but he could see he was rattling the businessman. Which was exactly what he wanted. Hubert shuffled from foot to foot. Tormey knew he had him.

'My bosses tell me they don't want to pursue this, but the beauty of modern law enforcement is that I have friends in a number of different police forces all over the world. I promise you that one of them will take this and run with it. I'd start putting your affairs in order, if I were you.'

'John,' Hubert said. 'This man is beginning to get on my nerves. Make him stop talking, please.'

Chatham didn't respond verbally. He just charged.

Tormey had come prepared for such a turn of events, and he drew his Glock 9 from its holster on his right hip. 'Stop or I'll drop you.'

Chatham kept coming. The Glock 17 is so named because it carries a magazine containing seventeen rounds. Tormey fired two into giant's mid-section, but these didn't even slow him – he was wearing a Kevlar vest. He fired again, catching him just at the neckline, and blood erupted from a hole in the bodyguard's throat, but there still seemed to be no other effect. Adjusting his aim, the chief took out the man's right knee-cap, which disintegrated in a shower of red and white pulverised bone. This caused him to falter slightly, but he kept coming.

'Will you please go down?' Tormey said, and shot Chatham in the head.

A flap of scalp peeled off the top of the man's skull, and he fell on his face right at Tormey's feet.

'You dumb Mick fucker,' Hubert said.

Tormey looked up to see that the little man had a gun almost as big as himself pointed at him.

'What is that, a .357?'

'It's a Magnum .460.'

'Are you planning on encountering a rhinoceros or something? I'd be careful, a man of your size. That's going to have quite a kick.'

'Shut up! Will you for fuck sake stop with the commentary?'

'Am I getting to you, Hubert?'

'You just wouldn't leave it alone, would you?'

'Not in my nature.' Tormey took a step back towards the lapping water.

'All you had to do was mind your own business. None of this concerned you. That girl – it happened years ago. It was a mistake, for fuck sake. I didn't *mean* to kill her. The coke was too strong, made me crazy.'

'But you meant to have Gina killed.'

'She was going to ruin me. Her allegations wouldn't have had much of an impact on my business, but they would have killed any chance at the presidency. You can get away with a lot of scandal these days, but a dead whore? That would have stuck.'

'Her name was Dova,' Tormey said. 'You should know her name.' He went to take another step (his plan was to keep Hubert distracted long enough to throw himself into the water below) but found he couldn't. Chatham, not quite dead, it seemed, despite having lost half his cranium, had his left foot in a vice-like grip.

'I don't give a damn about her fucking name,' Hubert said, and shot Tormey once, twice, three times.

The first shot took away most of the chief's left shoulder and knocked him backwards. He would have been blown into the water and might have survived but for the fact that the giant had him by the leg. He staggered under the blast and tried to pull his leg free before being caught by the second shot, which obliterated his chest, blowing most of what was inside out through his back.

The third bullet went right through the cavity made by the second, doing very little harm at all, but by this time Chief

Superintendent Frank Tormey was dead. He fell onto his side, his ankle, still in Chatham's fist, twisted and broken.

Hubert walked briskly over and searched around until he found Tormey's gun, which had flown from his hand and landed a few feet away. Picking it up, he stood over his bodyguard and looked down at the huge man. 'Good work, John,' he said, and, taking aim with the Glock, shot him through his left eye before taking a handkerchief from his pocket and wiping down the Magnum, which he put into his dead employee's hand, manipulating Chatham's index finger to squeeze off a round into the air.

This done, he scurried back to the limo and got in, a broad grin on his face.

7

AS THE VEHICLE WOUND ITS WAY ALONG THE narrow pathway from the wharf, Hubert pressed the intercom button so he could speak to his driver, Bob, who was up front behind a screen. Hubert always brought Bob with him when he travelled, because Bob knew how to keep his mouth shut and he never asked questions. Hubert liked that in an employee.

'Take me right to the airport, Bob,' he directed. 'And would you call the hotel and ask them to have my bags sent on?'

Satisfied with the evening's work and pleased to be homeward bound, he opened the car's minibar and poured a miniature bottle of Jack Daniel's into one of the Waterford Crystal glasses he'd purchased to use while in the Emerald Isle. Glassware aside, Ireland had proved to be a washout. He had already decided that, tax incentives or not, he and his money were going elsewhere. The natives were nowhere near as friendly as he'd been led to believe.

He finished the bottle and reached for another, thinking that, before boarding his jet, he would have to mention to someone that Chatham was missing. As the bodies were in a disused part of the docks, it could be several days before they were found, and he would be on the other side of the world by then. And the problem would be someone else's.

He was about to call one of his minions to inquire if they knew of his bodyguard's whereabouts when he realised the car was stopping. He rapped on the screen that divided him from the driver. 'What's going on, Bob? I want to go directly to the jet.'

The door beside him opened and he looked out to see a man whose most significant quality was that he was not Bob. Bob was a solidly built black man in his late sixties whom he had never seen dressed in anything other than his chauffer's uniform, while this guy was white, in his thirties and wore what looked to be an expensive dark suit. Behind him was another, older guy, similarly attired but with long dark hair.

'Hello, Mr Hubert,' the older man said, with a smile that was not one bit friendly. 'I'm afraid that, while you were busy on the docks shooting guns and such, Terry and I had to have some harsh words with your driver. Please allow me to introduce myself – I'm Tim Pat Rogers. Welcome to Daddy Joe's.'

The man he had called Terry reached in and dragged Hubert out of the limo by his carefully coiffured hair. Hubert tried to go for his gun, but Rogers already had one pointed at him. 'Now, now, Mr Hubert. That's not very clever, is it?'

'What do you want? Why am I here?'

Terry was frog-marching him towards a large building that looked a bit like some of the roadhouses Hubert had seen back home. Rogers used a set of keys to open a big wooden door, and they moved through darkness along a corridor and down a flight of steps. A light came on, and he saw he was in a windowless cellar, surrounded by barrels and crates. Terry pushed him into a chair and proceeded to secure his arms and legs with cable ties.

'Mr Hubert, you don't know me,' Rogers said, pulling over a crate and perching on it. 'But as we're going to be spending a little time together, I should tell you that I am a bad man. I sell drugs, I steal, and I kill people. There are very few lines I won't cross, in fact.'

Hubert gazed at him, eyes wide.

'Your taking it upon yourself to shoot Frank Tormey is going to upset some good friends of mine, but if it were down to me, I'd probably let it slide. Just between us two, you might actually have done me a favour. I came pretty close to shooting him myself a couple of days ago.'

'I … well, you're welcome. Cut me loose and I'm sure I can help you in lots of other ways.'

'Sorry, Wilf. Can I call you Wilf?'

'Yes, of course.'

'Good. I'm afraid we won't be releasing you any time soon. By which I mean: ever. You see, you've done some things that require a reckoning.'

'What things?'

'Now you're just stalling for time. Like I said, Tormey and me weren't pals, but the points of order he wanted to address with you are the same ones we will be deliberating upon at our leisure for the next while. Gina Dunnigan was like family to someone who is like family to me, which placed her under my protection. You murdered her, and I can't let that slide. So that's point number one.'

'I didn't know!' Hubert, sweating profusely, virtually screamed the words at Rogers, squirming and wriggling in the chair as he tried to get loose of his bonds. 'If I knew, I wouldn't have touched her. Let me make it up to you. Just set me free and we can come to terms.'

Rogers nodded at Terry, who punched the American right on his orange nose. The blow wasn't hard enough to break the bone, but it caused blood to flow and brought tears to Hubert's eyes.

'Your bad behaviour is bringing us to the rough stuff well ahead of schedule,' Rogers said, shaking his head sorrowfully. 'Are you going to sit still while we talk? There'll be time enough for the physical side of our discussion later.'

Sobbing, Hubert froze.

'The second reason you find yourself in this situation is the death of a young lady named Dova Ibrahimi and the sexual abuse of Beth Carlton, Gina Carlton's daughter. Like I said, I'm a bad man, but when I do bad things, I do them to adults who entered into the criminal life with their eyes wide open. People who made a series of choices that brought them to my attention. One thing I absolutely abhor is people who prey on kiddies. It makes me really, really angry.'

'Me too,' Terry said, examining his knuckles, which, Hubert saw, were large and misshapen from regular harsh use.

'Something I've always liked about working with Terry is that we are of one mind on this issue. Isn't that right, Terry?'

'It is, Mr Rogers.'

'This is a mistake,' Hubert cried, genuinely terrified now. 'I have money – lots of money.'

'I know you do,' Rogers said. 'And I'm sure we can relieve you of some of it over the coming days.'

'Anything. Just tell me how much and it's yours.'

'All things in good time. Now, Terry, show Wilf the tools we're going to be using on him as we progress towards his demise.'

The younger man pulled a table on wheels out of the shadows. When Hubert saw the array of implements on it (some pointed, some edged, some with pincers and prongs), he began to scream.

It took him three days to die. They never found what was left of his body.

Part Thirteen

CLOSING GAMBITS

1

DUNNIGAN GAZED OUT THE WINDOW OF HIS
hotel room at the rolling desert beyond. A star-scape that
seemed impossibly vast wheeled above the moonlike sandy
floor. With the window open, he could hear occasional
animal cries: he had no idea what they were, he assumed
coyote and mountain lion, but they made him feel less
alone.

It was two in the morning. Jetlag had prevented him from
sleeping more than a couple of hours since they had arrived
in the United States. With the ordeal of the following day
looming, he knew the night would hold no rest for him.

Someone knocked on the door.

'Who is it?'

'It's me. Miley.'

'Come on in.'

His friend was dressed in a Chris de Burgh t-shirt and

shorts, his hair hanging loose about his shoulders. 'I thought you might need some company.'

'Have a seat.'

Miley pulled up a chair beside him. 'We have been to some amazing places, haven't we?' he said. 'Look at that sky.'

'I know. It's really quite beautiful.'

'Are you scared?'

'Yes.'

'I am too.'

'I don't want to lie to you, Miley. I haven't a clue what the morning will bring. All I do know is that, by this time tomorrow, it will all be over and we'll be free of Frobisher and Ressler, or we'll all be dead. That's all I've got. I'm sorry if it's not a lot of comfort.'

'That's alright, Davey.'

They sat for a while, then Miley said, 'I love Beth.'

'I know you do.'

'No – I mean I'm *in* love with her.'

Dunnigan shifted uncomfortably in his chair. 'Does she know this?'

'Yes.'

'And how does she feel about it … about you?'

'She says she loves me, too.'

The criminologist scratched a spot behind his ear. 'I don't know what to say.'

'Are you mad at me?'

'No. Not exactly.'

'Well, how *do* you feel about it?'

'I'm not sure. Have you … like … done anything together?'

'Do you mean …?'

'Yes.'

It was Miley's turn to look uncomfortable. 'Yeah. We kinda did. In Berlin when you and Diane had gone to Hamburg. And again in Amsterdam. And in Portland before you arrived ...'

'Yes, I think I get the picture.'

'Well, I wanted to be honest.'

'I appreciate that,' he said, although his tone suggested otherwise.

They were quiet again. Miley was clearly on tenterhooks, throwing glances at Dunnigan every few seconds, but the criminologist wasn't ready to let him off the hook yet.

'Is it serious?' Dunnigan asked eventually.

'Yes! It's, like, *really* serious. We're mad about each other.'

'Have you talked about what you're going to do when all this is done? Where you're going to live? *How* you're going to live?'

'We've talked about very little else.'

Dunnigan stood up and leaned against the window frame, breathing in the heady desert air. It smelt like nothing he had ever known before – it was sweet and musky and was almost intoxicating. 'She's the only family I have left,' he said.

'I'm your family. So is Diane and Father Bill.'

'I know that. I mean blood.'

'I'll look after her, I promise. I would give my life for her.'

Dunnigan reached over and placed a hand on his friend's shoulder. 'If she were to be with anyone, I'm glad it's you.'

Tears sprang to Miley's eyes. 'Thank you,' he said.

'Go on now,' Dunnigan said, lying down on the narrow bed. 'I think I might sleep for a bit.'

Miley left without another word.

And Dunnigan did drift into a dreamless sleep.

2

RESSLER CALLED AT DAWN TO SAY THE criminologist was to come on foot, unarmed and without a phone. 'You can try subterfuge if you wish,' the psychiatrist said, 'but you must know that we will be searching you before we are letting you inside, so it really is a waste of your time. Defying us will just make me angry, and I already have enough aggression to take out on you. Do you really need to give me more reasons to be cross?'

Father Bill and Diane walked the winding, dusty track with Dunnigan until Google Maps told them there was only a mile left to what the former Ranger had christened Shit Creek Compound. It was early morning, but the heat was already crushing.

'Take care of everyone for me,' Dunnigan said to the priest as they embraced.

'You know I will.'

He turned to Diane.

'I love you,' she said.

'I love you, too.' The words came almost as a reflex.

'If we get out of this ...' she said.

'Yes.'

'You know what I'm suggesting?'

'I think so.'

She kissed him, a long, tender kiss, and held him tightly. 'Go,' she said, and turned away.

Dunnigan nodded at Father Bill, and began to walk the long, winding mile towards Desert Moon Ranch and the horrific death he knew Frobisher and Ressler had planned for him.

3

BY THE TIME HE GOT TO THE GATE HIS CLOTHES
were soaked through with sweat and he was sick and dizzy
from dehydration.

Up close the structure was impressive, reminding Dunnigan
of films he had seen about the Alamo, the mission Davey
Crockett, Jim Bowie and a motley assortment of soldiers and
backwoodsmen had tried and failed to defend against the
might of the Mexican army during the Texan war.

A handsome, dark-skinned man with a mohican, and a fat
woman with a crewcut were on the wall above the gate, some
sort of machine-guns slung about their shoulders.

'You him?' the woman asked.

'I don't know,' Dunnigan said. 'Who are you expecting?'

There was the sound of muffled conversation, and then
Ressler appeared, a white fedora set at a raffish angle on his
head.

'Mr Dunnigan! Good of you to come, and so punctual too.'

Dunnigan said nothing, just stared up at the psychiatrist.

'Now, you will remove your clothing so we can see you are not carrying any weapons.'

'I'm not. If you know anything about me, you'll know I never carry weapons of any kind.'

'If he does not strip by the time I count to ten, shoot him in the belly,' Ressler said brightly to the guards. 'One. Two. Three ...'

Dunnigan began to unbutton his shirt.

'Do you see, my friends, how Mr Davey has learned, through a long process of dealing with me, that I am consistent in my punishments and rewards? We have established a relationship where he trusts that I will do what I say I am going to do. Is this not so, Davey?'

Dunnigan ignored him, and began to unlace his boots.

'I asked you if this is not so?' Ressler snapped. 'Answer or there will be painful repercussions.'

Dunnigan pulled off his right boot. 'I know you are a psychopath,' he said, unbuttoning his trousers. 'And I trust you to behave accordingly.'

'Psychopath, sociopath, these are terms people bandy about these days with so little real understanding of what they mean. I will need you to remove your charming boxer shorts also and your socks.'

Gritting his teeth, the criminologist did as he was asked. He could feel his back starting to burn under the sun's blaze already.

'Good work. Now, I will operate the gate mechanism, and

you will come inside. Then Miguel will commence the next phase of our search. What fun.'

Ressler disappeared, and moments later there was a grinding noise and the large metal gates in front of Dunnigan began to rise.

The dark-skinned man who had been on the wall came out, his automatic weapon trained on the now naked criminologist. 'Step in,' he said, sounding bored. 'You're gonna burn to a crisp out there. Didn't you put on no sunscreen?'

4

THERE WAS A KIND OF ARCHED TUNNEL THAT
ran through the wall to the compound within. The shadow
it provided was a glorious relief, and Dunnigan hoped they
would leave him there long enough to recover somewhat.
'Can I have a drink of water?' he asked the guard.

The man shrugged and took a bottle from a pouch on his
belt and handed it to him. 'Gonna have to give you a cavity
search. He's insisting on it.'

Dunnigan gulped the water, which was lukewarm and had
muddy after-taste and might have been the best drink he'd
ever had. 'I really don't have any weapons. I wasn't lying.'

'Dude, anything you've swallowed or put up your ass isn't
gonna be much help if I decide to open fire, anyway. But
the boss wants you searched, so I'm afraid you're gonna be
searched.'

The sound of someone whistling 'The Blue Danube'

interrupted their discussion, and Ressler strolled in from the yard. 'Welcome to Desert Moon Ranch, Mr Davey,' he said. 'Now, would you be so good as to step into the sunshine so Miguel can examine your orifices?'

'Sooner we get started, sooner it'll be over,' Miguel said, taking some latex gloves from a pocket. 'I'll be as gentle as I can be.'

'But perhaps not too gentle,' Ressler grinned.

5

THE CAVITY SEARCH WAS HORRENDOUS, BUT HE
closed his eyes and went somewhere else in his head until it
was over.

'He's clean,' Miguel said after what felt like an age of
probing and insertions.

'Bring him over here, then,' Ressler said.

Miguel, who struck Dunnigan as a man who had taken
what he thought was a standard security job and was
gradually finding out it was something other than standard,
took his arm in a loose grip and walked him over to the
psychiatrist.

'Mr Frobisher is anxious to meet you,' Ressler said, 'but he
has told me that I may have a little fun with you first.'

Dunnigan didn't see the other man's hand move, but one
moment he was standing and the next he was sprawled on his
back in the dust of the compound yard.

'Oops,' Ressler laughed. 'It looks as though my hand must have slipped.'

The criminologist tried to get his legs underneath him, but before he could, a foot was planted in his gut and all the air was driven from his lungs.

'Oh no! You have fallen over again.'

Knowing he was in for a beating, Dunnigan rolled into a ball, pulling his knees up to his chest and tucking his chin in. Kicks and blows rained down on him, but they were more uncomfortable than painful. He allowed his mind to wander back to childhood with Gina, and the chiding from Ressler and the abuse his body was taking seemed to be happening to someone else.

'Pick him up. Pick him up right now!' Ressler's voice had reached a pitch that hovered close to hysteria.

'You keep beatin' on him like that, he'll just go numb.' Miguel's voice came from somewhere above. 'That guy needs to get some clothes on him and rest out of the sun for a time, maybe drink some more water. You want information or whatever it is you're after, he ain't in no state to give it to you.'

'Pick him up, I said.'

Sighing, Miguel got his arms under Dunnigan's and dragged him upright.

'Take him to the hitching post.'

Dunnigan looked at the inside of the compound for the first time. As Billie Jones had said, it was a rough square, with three concentric circles of buildings, a large, low structure set in the middle. Quads, a couple of jeeps and machines he took to be generators and water pumps were dotted here and there, and Miguel was half-dragging, half-walking him to a tall wooden post with metal hooks protruding from the sides – it had probably originally been used to tether horses.

'Tie his hands to it,' Ressler ordered.

'What with?' Miguel asked. 'I don't got no rope or nothin'.'

Muttering in annoyance, Ressler stomped off to one of the buildings to their right, and returned with a length of rope and another of barbed wire, the end of which he was holding with some kind of heavy glove. 'Tie him.'

Miguel paused. 'What you're plannin' will most likely kill him. You know that, right?'

'Do you have a degree in medicine, Mr Security Guard?'

'No. But I do have some experience with ...'

'Do you have a degree in medicine?'

'No, I do not.'

'Then kindly shut your mouth and tie that man to the pole like I asked.'

Miguel did as he was told, lashing Dunnigan's wrists to a hook just above his head. 'I don't want no part of this,' the dark-skinned man said, and, giving Ressler an evil look, he walked back towards the wall.

When he was gone, the psychiatrist came over to Dunnigan and put an arm around his naked, sunburned shoulders. 'Alone at last. Now, I don't want you to be alarmed – I am not planning on flogging you to death. That would be far too quick an end. I just want to ... soften you up a little. Okay?'

Dunnigan gazed at Ressler, unblinking.

'Shall we begin?'

At that moment, a dim buzzing sound coming from overhead interrupted Ressler's flow. He stepped back, looking at the pale sky, and as he did so, something dropped from above and hovered, right in front of his nose.

It was an electronic drone, with what looked to be a canister dangling from a claw below it. In a rapid whoosh the mechanism shot upwards to a height of about forty feet and dropped the canister, which exploded in a shower of dirt and gravel, spraying Ressler and Dunnigan alike.

Suddenly the sky above was full of the machines, and packages were dropping all around them. Explosion after explosion followed. Dunnigan twisted in his shackles to try and gauge the destruction: he noticed that some of the drops contained explosives, while others released smoke, some seemed to contain gas, and still others some sort of flare, probably magnesium, which temporarily blinded anyone within range.

People were running here, there and everywhere. One of the quads was ablaze and a generator was smouldering. Machine-gun fire sounded on the other side of the compound – some of the guards were trying to shoot the invading contraptions out of the air.

Suddenly Ressler was pressed up against him, a knife in his hand. 'I am certain this inconvenient interruption is down to you and your friends, Mr Davey.'

'Wouldn't be surprised,' Dunnigan said.

'I am going to have to speed things along.' Ressler cut the rope that fastened Dunnigan to the pole. 'But please believe me, this is only bringing you closer to the end we had planned, Mr Frobisher and I. You have prevented nothing.'

The blade pressed to Dunnigan's throat, the psychiatrist led him to the single-storeyed building where he knew Frobisher was waiting.

6

IN A HOLLOW HALF A MILE FROM THE COMPOUND, Goldfoot, Father Bill, Diane, and a group of men and women (some from the Gila River Sheriff's Department, others recently deputised) were controlling the fleet of drones with laptop computers and remote control devices.

'Ancient Red Indian fighting technique,' the governor said, attaching a tear gas canister to his returning drone. 'Used in many battles with the white devil.'

'We're almost out of stuff to drop on them,' Diane said, 'and one of the guys on the wall seems to be a pretty good shot. Sooner or later, they'll take out all the drones.'

'I am ready to begin the next stage of my plan,' Goldfoot said.

'Which is?'

'Pow-wow.'

'So we go down and try to negotiate a surrender?' Diane asked.

'Kinda.'

'Is there a complex, cultural aspect to this I'm missing?'

'I am the last in a long line of chiefs, stretching right back to Antonio, the great Pima warrior, who won many battles against the blue soldiers. I have been given the wisdom of my fathers, and can use methods the red man utilised when the pilgrims first came across the ocean in their wooden ships.'

'Didn't the pilgrims screw you over and take your land?'

'They sure did. To be honest, I was just gonna go down there and tell them we'll blow them to hell if they don't open the gate and throw down their guns.'

'I like your style,' Father Bill said.

'Let's go,' Diane agreed. 'Davey's been in there with them for too long already.'

7

BACK AT THE HOTEL, BETH WAS PACING THE
floor of her room, while Miley watched American wrestling.
He'd never seen it before, and was fascinated by it. The bout
he was watching featured a massively muscled character called
the Undertaker, who was supposed to be some kind of undead
zombie. His opponent, a bald guy with impossibly broad
shoulders and a goatee, named Goldberg, was hitting him
repeatedly with a chair, but The Undertaker seemed unfazed.

'Is this supposed to be a sport or is it a kind of fantasy
game?' he asked Beth, who stopped her circuits of the room
every now and then to watch. 'I don't know if they've decided
before they began who was going to win, or if they're actually
competing. It's weird.'

'Maybe it's like MMA for old guys,' Beth suggested.

'They do as much talking as they do fighting, so you could
be right,' Miley said.

They were interrupted by someone banging on the door.

'Didn't you see the Do Not Disturb sign?' Miley called. 'We're indisposed.'

The knock sounded again.

'We won't be needing clean towels today, thanks,' Miley said, standing up and nodding at Beth, who pushed open the window quietly.

The knocking sounded a third time, so loud now the door shuddered in its frame.

'Okay, I'm calling the manager,' Miley said. 'As a paying guest, I'm entitled to a little privacy.'

The door exploded inwards and a man dressed in camouflage appeared in the space. He didn't get more than two steps into the room before Miley jacked a shell into a pump-action shotgun Goldfoot had provided, and blew him off his feet. The two who were behind fell back, and Miley dived onto the floor, using the bed for cover.

Beth was already out the window, hanging by her fingertips before dropping the single storey to the ground below.

Miley reloaded and poked his head above the mattress in time to see more figures lining up outside the room – he counted six now. 'This is only going to end in tears,' he called. 'Can't we just have a discussion like civilised people?'

A hail of automatic fire was the only response he received.

'Well, if you put it like that,' he said, and pulled the pin from a grenade before tossing it out the door.

He heard a flurry of footsteps as his attackers scattered just as the blast sounded, and then made a dash for the window himself.

8

THE AIR CONDITIONING IN THE CONVERTED shed where Frobisher lay was so strong, Dunnigan found himself shivering. As Ressler shoved him inside, a male nurse was hanging an IV bag on a stand.

'Leave us now,' the psychiatrist spat at him.

The medic nodded and disappeared swiftly. As soon as he did, Ressler hauled his prisoner over so they were standing right beside the old man's bed. Dark eyes turned upon Dunnigan, and something that might have been a smile creased the wizened features. 'You have a tiny dick,' Frobisher said.

Dunnigan looked down at this man who had destroyed almost everything in his life. He knew he should have pitied him, should have felt some sense of empathy that nature had cursed him with a living death, but in truth, his evil was so great, mortality and decay had done nothing to temper his poisonous influence. When he became too ill to perpetrate depravity himself, he found others like Ressler or the Yellow Man to do it for him.

As he perceived the husk Frobisher had become, Dunnigan understood two things profoundly: firstly, that the man had to die – it truly was the only way he and the people he loved would ever be free of him; and secondly, that perhaps the greatest harm Frobisher had done him was to force him to become a killer, too. The thought made him furious.

'You, Dunnigan, are an annoying little fucker,' Frobisher said. Tubes ran up his nose, pumping oxygen into his lungs, and every now and again a hiss sounded as a blood pressure machine monitored his vital signs. 'We had a whole series of entertainments planned around you, and now we are going to have to cut them short. It seems you broke your word to me, and informed the local savages who I am. I'd paid off the real governor in Phoenix, but it never occurred to me to clear things with Big Chief Pissing Bull too. Looks as if that was an oversight. Oh well. By the time they get in here you'll be dead, dismembered and in the fucking freezer. And not necessarily in that order, either.'

'I want to know how you framed Beth,' Dunnigan said.

Ressler stepped around him, a look of mild surprise on his face. 'You are still wondering about that?'

'She loved Jones. She wouldn't have hurt him.'

Something exploded loudly outside.

'We don't have time for your gloating, Ressler,' Frobisher growled. 'The natives are getting restless.'

'Did you wonder if your niece might have carved up your friend?' Ressler asked, ignoring his employer. 'Were you worried she might be too damaged to save?'

'If she is, it's because of you,' Dunnigan said.

'I went to the detective's room disguised in hospital scrubs – I covered my face with a surgical mask so even little Beth would not know me. I said Jones needed an injection, more antibiotics. But when he held out his arm for the needle, I stuck it in her instead.'

'They didn't find any drugs in her system.'

'This was a blend of my own concoction, a special cocktail that I created just for the occasion, undetectable by your doltish police chemists. It put her in a kind of semi-conscious state, just for a few moments, a trance from which she remembered nothing. The poor injured policeman, he tried to fight me off, but he was too fat and weak to prevent me from slicing his carotid artery – oh my golly gosh, but the spray went everywhere. He died very quickly. Then I took your little Beth's hands and I placed them on the handle of the knife, and together we cut and we sawed and we carved the fat detective's neck wide open for all to see. I put some fibres from her clothes on the knife for good measure, but it was hardly necessary, to be honest.'

Dunnigan was breathing heavily, his anger building to an almost uncontrollable level.

'I know you all wondered if she committed the murder. The truth is: she almost did. She was a very docile helper.'

'Enough!' Frobisher snapped. 'You might as well cut *his* throat now. All this talk has given me a hankering for it.'

'Before I kill you,' Ressler said, stepping behind the criminologist and pulling his head back, 'I want you to know that we have sent men to your hotel to collect little Beth and Miley the idiot boy.'

'When we get rid of the local ethnic police I'm going to

have Ressler flay Miley while Beth watches, then we're going to cut out her tongue and bury her alive out in the desert,' Frobisher crooned. 'I want you to have a good picture of that in your head as you go.'

Ressler raised the knife to Dunnigan's throat and pressed its edge to his skin, but at that moment the entire back wall of the medical wing came in on them with a deafening boom. Frobisher's bed, which was on wheels, was blown right past Dunnigan and thudded against the wall in front.

Dunnigan felt Ressler let go of him for a second and, turning, drove his heel right into the psychiatrist's stomach, knocking him backwards, but as he did so a huge pile of masonry fell from the ceiling, separating the two of them. Chunks of concrete and shards of adobe continued to rain down, and the dust was so great Dunnigan was temporarily blinded.

He grabbed a piece of bedsheet that was in the rubble at his feet and wrapped it around his mouth to help him breathe, and as he did so, a lone figure stepped out of the chaos.

'Hello, Mr Dunnigan,' the Harpy said.

9

THE GILA RIVER SHERIFF'S DEPARTMENT, ITS numbers swollen from its recent batch of new recruits, along with Father Bill and Diane, lined up outside Desert Moon Ranch. Now that the drone shelling attack was over, the guards all gathered atop the wall to face them.

'I thought your woman on the inside reported ten to twelve guns,' Father Bill said to Goldfoot quietly. 'I count thirty.'

'We Native Americans always downplay the odds,' Goldfoot said. 'It's because we're so brave.'

'Are you sure you're not just shit at counting?' Father Bill retorted.

'Well, there's that.'

'What's the reason for this attack?' a man called down from the wall.

Diane noticed his hair was cut in a mohican and he had a strong, finely boned face.

'We have reason to believe you've got a hostage in there,' Goldfoot responded through a loudspeaker attached to the roof of his jeep. 'We'd like you to open the gates so we can come in and get him.'

'You got a warrant?'

'I'm the fucking governor,' Goldfoot called back genially. 'I'm the one who signs the warrants.'

The air was split by a huge explosion from within the compound, a cloud of dust rising into the air.

'Would you like me to do that again, or are you going to let us in?' Goldfoot asked.

The men and women on the roof looked at one another uncertainly.

'You don't have any idea what caused that, do you?' Diane whispered.

'Not a clue. I'm just improvising,' Goldfoot admitted.

'We've got enough food and water in here to last for months,' the man with the mohican called down, although he sounded a lot less sure of himself than he had a few moments ago.

'Tough audience,' the governor sighed. 'Time to bring out Tonto.'

'Who's Tonto?' Diane asked.

'You'll see,' Goldfoot grinned, and pulled a walkie-talkie from his belt.

10

BETH SPRINTED FULL TILT DOWN THE DESERT
path that led from the back of the hotel towards the open
mesa beyond. Behind her, she heard a grenade exploding and
muffled gunfire, and she hoped Miley would have the sense to
make good his escape, too.

She paused for a moment to get her breath back and a jeep
suddenly topped the ridge and sped towards her. She turned
and began to run up the steep incline of a nearby hill, the jeep
and its four occupants in pursuit.

Her lungs were burning and her legs ached, but adrenaline
pushed Beth onwards and in a matter of seconds she reached
the top and flung herself over, disappearing from view. The
jeep's driver gunned the accelerator and increased his speed,
taking the peak at a jump. The jeep came down with its front
wheels half in and half out of the three-foot-deep trench Beth
and Miley had dug there the night before.

The driver pumped the gas pedal, but the front wheels were jammed and the rear ones spun uselessly in the air.

'Hey, fellas,' Beth called.

They all looked up to see the girl standing a short distance away, a Heckler & Koch MP 7 machine-gun in her hands.

By the time Miley jogged up five minutes later, she was walking back towards the road and the four men in the jeep were dead.

11

'SO YOU GOT FOOD AND YOU GOT WATER,'
Goldfoot said to the forces gathered on the wall.

'Yup,' mohican said. 'What we have will do us about
a month. Month and a half if we ration it out. By then, I
figure you'll've had to call in the Feds or whatever, and then
there'll be lawyers and the press and suchlike involved, and
as soon as folks in suits start in on a situation, it surely does
get more complicated. For example, I got a powerful sense
my democratic rights is being violated, what with you all
dropping fucking grenades on my head without so much as a
warning. That don't seem right. What do you think a lawyer
could do with that?'

Goldfoot scratched his head and glanced at Diane and
Father Bill, who were both beginning to look worried. 'We
seem to have a bit of a misunderstanding,' the governor said.

'We do?'

'Oh yes. You see, you seem to be under the impression that this is an old-fashioned siege. But see, it ain't.' He said something into the walkie-talkie.

Seconds passed, and everyone could hear a dull engine sound, and a speck appeared on the horizon, coming from the direction of the reservation. A minute later, a Chinook helicopter, complete with a deputy seated at a Gatling gun that had been mounted in the doorway, heaved into view. It hovered just above the men on the wall, looking for all the world as if one of the drones had been enlarged to nightmarish proportions.

'We call her Tonto,' Goldfoot said to Diane. 'Picked her up at a sale in Iowa.'

'She's a beauty,' Diane said in admiration. 'You have a *lot* of firepower and weaponry to hand: the guns, the drones, the explosives ...'

'All legally bought from reputable sources. Constitution says I'm entitled to have it so long as I've got the correct papers.'

'God bless America,' Diane marvelled.

Goldfoot turned his attention to the people on the wall. 'Does anyone have any questions?'

Mohican stepped forward and dropped his gun onto the desert floor below.

'Good choice,' Goldfoot said as the other guards followed suit.

12

'YOU TOOK YOUR TIME,' DUNNIGAN SAID TO THE
Harpy as the tall man strode past him, making a bee-line for
the orthopaedic bed on which the prone figure of Frobisher
lay, surrounded by the various medical machinery he had
pulled with him as he slid across the room.

'You seemed to have things under control,' the assassin
said. 'I wanted to make sure the guards were distracted by the
goings-on out front. Your friends in the local constabulary
have done a marvellous job at drawing their attention.'

He was wearing a khaki shirt over a green vest, and he
shrugged it off and tossed it to the criminologist. 'So this is
Mr Ernest Frobisher,' the Harpy said, pulling the bed around
so he could look the dying man in the face.

'I don't know where Ressler's gone,' Dunnigan warned
him.

'He'll have his turn,' the Harpy said, oblivious to anything other than the person he had spent years hunting, the knife he was named after suddenly in his hand as he cut the tubes feeding Frobisher oxygen. 'You probably haven't got a notion who I am,' he said, turning to the invalid, 'but that doesn't matter. All you need to know is that you killed the only man I have ever loved.'

Dunnigan heard the gas escape into the dusty atmosphere of the room.

The sheet that usually covered Frobisher had been blown free, and for the first time Dunnigan saw the devastation the cancer had wrought upon him: he was more a skeleton than a man, every bone clearly visible through his paper-like skin. The beating of his ravaged heart was visible within his concave chest, and one of his legs had been amputated above the knee where cancerous tissue had necrotised. Dressings covered several locations where tumours had suppurated about his person, and he reeked of human waste and disinfectant.

'You should have had your Yellow Man kill me when you had the chance,' the Harpy said. 'Because now, I am going to do you the mercy of killing you.'

Frobisher seemed incapable of words. He hissed at the assassin, snapping at him with blunt, yellowed teeth, more like an animal than a human being. Dunnigan wrapped the shirt about his waist and peered around the ruined ward, looking for Ressler, who was still nowhere to be seen.

'I don't even need to touch you, do I?' the Harpy was saying. 'All I have to do is disconnect you from all these machines, and your own body will do the job for me.'

He unplugged something from the wall, and removed one of the drips from Frobisher's arm. 'This one is for the painkillers, isn't it?' he asked, tapping a pump that was connected to a catheter in Frobisher's chest with the hooked blade. 'I'm guessing you're on a pretty heavy dosage, too. The pump probably delivers a payload every ten minutes or so.'

With a single swift motion, he cut the tube joining the mechanism to the man's body and precious pale fluid began to dribble onto the rubble-strewn floor. 'Once the morphine in your system wears off, the pain will start building. It might take some time, but eventually your body will go into toxic shock, and your heart will give out.'

He leaned in as close as he dared, because Frobisher snarled like a cornered dog and tried to bite him. Dunnigan noticed he was wheezing now – breathing was already becoming a struggle. 'I'll see you in hell, Mr Frobisher. We'll continue our discussion there.'

The Harpy was just straightening up when Dr Phillipe Ressler leapt over a pile of fallen rubble, a syringe in his hand, and wrapped his arms around the bigger man's neck. He stuck the needle in the assassin's shoulder, and sank his teeth into his cheek, thrashing his head from side to side like a shark to better tear the flesh.

The Harpy brought his knife down on the psychiatrist's arm, burying the blade up to the hilt before drawing it out for another strike. Dunnigan rushed over to help him, but the Harpy, his eyes bloodshot and misty from whatever poison Ressler had used on him, shook his head. 'Get out of here,' he said, his words slurring.

With the last vestige of strength he had, the assassin grabbed Ressler by the hair and threw him over his shoulder onto the ground. He didn't stay down for long, though, and was up and upon his foe in a second, a piece of fallen brick in his hand which he used like a hammer, clubbing the rapidly failing Harpy repeatedly on the head.

Dunnigan looked on helplessly for a moment and then turned and ran for the hole the explosion had made in the wall. Just as he reached it, Father Bill and Diane came charging in.

'We have to go – he's rigged the place to blow,' Dunnigan shouted at them. Together, they fled.

The last thing Dunnigan saw as he chanced a look over his shoulder was Ressler and the Harpy locked in mortal combat over the body of Frobisher, who had already started to wail as his tortured metabolism used up the last of the morphine in his system and he was forced to endure the agony it had kept in check for so many years.

Shouting to Goldfoot and his men to follow, Dunnigan, Diane and Father Bill sprinted for the safety of the desert. As they reached the gate to the compound, the medical centre went up like a roman candle, the plastic explosives the Harpy had used combining with the oxygen tanks inside to create a conflagration that could be seen in Phoenix.

And David Dunnigan sat down on the rough sand of the Sonoran Plateau and wept.

Part Fourteen

ALL THAT YOU CAN'T LEAVE BEHIND

1

DUNNIGAN RECEIVED A PHONE CALL THE DAY after the battle in Frobisher's compound. It was from the number they had been using to communicate with Tim Pat Rogers.

'I have some news I thought you'd want to hear,' the gangster told him.

'Good news, I hope.'

'I wish it was. Frank Tormey is dead.'

Dunnigan had been standing at the window of his room gazing out at the desert, and he sat down on the bed, suddenly feeling more tired than he thought possible.

'I know you were close,' Rogers said. 'Him being your boss, and what have you.'

'He was more than my boss,' Dunnigan said, having to force the words out. 'He was my friend.'

'I'm very sorry for your loss.'

Dunnigan cleared his throat. 'Thank you for calling.'

'Don't mention it. They're going to try and crucify you when you come home, you know that, don't you?'

'I barely care anymore,' Dunnigan said, and hung up.

He didn't tell the others until they were back in Ireland.

*

Two days later they all sat in Goldfoot's office. The clean-up operation out at Desert Moon Ranch was still ongoing, and those irritating men in suits from various federal agencies had arrived and, as Miguel had so astutely observed, done their utmost to make a complicated situation even more complex than it needed to be.

'It's taken this long for the area to cool enough for anyone to go in, but they recovered some bodies from the medical building out at Desert Moon this morning,' Goldfoot said. 'One is definitely Frobisher, and the other, judging by height, is your friend who set the explosives.'

'What about Ressler?' Dunnigan asked.

'Haven't found him yet. We're still looking but ...'

'I don't believe it,' Beth said.

'It looks like the bank of oxygen tanks had all been rigged with plastique,' Goldfoot said. 'If he was close enough to that, he would have pretty well disintegrated. I'm reliably informed that could have happened.'

'But you don't believe it any more than we do,' Diane said.

'How did he get out, though?' Miley asked. 'It doesn't seem possible.'

'My brother's right,' Goldfoot said. 'There's no way he could have got out past my people. We Injuns are famous for being cunning and observant. Our name, Pima, means "eyes like the eagle" in the language of my people.'

'I thought it meant "river tribe",' Father Bill said.

'It has many meanings,' Goldfoot replied, mysteriously.

'I'm pretty sure it just means "river people",' Dunnigan said.

'The mystical Indian act isn't working on you guys any more, is it?' Goldfoot said, grinning.

'I still kind of like it,' Miley said. 'Although I did think naming the helicopter Tonto was a bit much.'

'Come on, everyone knows Tonto – he's one of our most beloved folk heroes. He was the hero of that TV show back in the sixties; he had the sidekick who wore the mask.'

'You know Tonto was the sidekick, right?'

'No, he wasn't.'

Dunnigan smiled as his friends laughed and joked, trying to ignore the fact that, in the morning, they would be flying home to bury a sister and a beloved friend.

And his niece still did not know her mother was dead.

2

THE US AUTHORITIES HELD THEM FOR
questioning for a week before allowing them to travel home.
As soon as they landed, they understood why: they arrived to
a shitstorm of trouble.

Dunnigan, Diane and Beth were arrested as soon as
they touched down, but luckily Goldfoot had foreseen this
and sent an email to the US embassy, explaining how they
had been invaluable in helping him deal with Frobisher's
attempt to equip and train a small army of terrorists on land
adjoining the Gila River Reservation (an action that resulted
in Frobisher making the decision to blow up the compound,
killing himself and at least one of his people into the bargain).

Father Bill swore an affidavit that he had heard Ressler
admit to killing Jones and framing Beth, testimony that could
have been picked apart by a good barrister, but by then the
two police forces had bigger fish to fry: the Mother Joan case

was technically still open, as she had never been found after the events in Kielder Forest. That said, no further deaths had been linked to her after Jones's demise, and the fact that her blade had clearly been used by Ressler in the commission of that crime hinted at a sinister connection The case would remain open, but there were whispers that the woman who had once been called Hester Kitt was dead.

The disappearance of Wilfred Hubert forced the historic trade negotiations to come to a premature halt, and Davies spearheaded an investigation into Dova Ibrahimi's death, which implicated a number of big names within European political and business circles, and prominently featured both Frobisher and Ressler as major figures in the abduction and monetisation of young people from all over the world. The British and Irish police decided, on foot of these revelations, not to pursue further charges against Dunnigan, Diane and Beth.

*

'Why didn't you tell me about my mother?' Beth spat, her eyes red with tears.

Dunnigan had not told her until just after they arrived back in Ireland, thinking they would have lots of time to talk it through. They had, however, been arrested literally minutes later, which had somewhat compromised his plans. They were now sitting opposite one another in one of the interview rooms in Harcourt Street. The detectives interviewing them had just finished their final questions and told them they were free to go. They had agreed to let Dunnigan use the room for a bit, and he had asked Beth, who was still furious with him, to come in and sit down.

'You had enough to deal with,' he said, choosing his words carefully. 'Letting you know wouldn't have made any difference – you couldn't be here, we couldn't try and track down her murderer – we had other things we needed to do, and Gina would have wanted us to focus our attentions on them.'

'So you lied to me? All of you? Did Miley know?'

'No. Just me, Diane and Father Bill.'

'So you left him out in the cold too? Now it makes sense: poor, simple, disabled Miley and fucked-up, mental Beth?'

Dunnigan took a deep breath. 'That's not true and you know it. I suppose I didn't want to admit it to myself, but I think I knew you and Miley were getting close, and figured he'd tell you. I needed you to keep your mind on what we were doing. It was the only way to clear your name and set us all free of Frobisher.'

'You still kept me in the dark. I thought we were supposed to be a family. Families don't lie.'

'I'm sorry, Beth. The last thing I wanted to do was hurt you. I was trying to protect you. We all were.'

As if those words were all she was waiting for, Beth's features creased up into a mask of grief, and she put her face in her hands and sobbed. 'Oh God, Davey. My mam is gone … what are we going to do?'

He went around the table and held her. He needed the comfort as much as she did.

*

Tormey's death was written off as a tragedy: he had, the papers reported, got into an altercation with Chatham, a dangerous man with a history of violence (he was dishonourably discharged from the US Army's Green Berets for torching an Afghan village, and barely escaped court martial by claiming he did so through poorly deciphering a coded order). The chief superintendent had, according to those investigating his death, followed the American to a deserted part of the docks, probably on intelligence that the man was about to commit a crime, and the two had shot one another in the ensuing firefight.

Tormey received a hero's burial.

At her mother's funeral, Beth sat with Miley on one side, and Dunnigan on the other, Diane beside him – the only family that mattered to them anymore.

To complete the picture, Father Bill officiated.

3

BUT THE FALLOUT WENT DEEPER THAN THAT.

Dunnigan's insomnia returned with a vengeance. At first, he wrote it off as jetlag and hoped it would rectify itself within a few days. This did not happen, and in the rare moments he did manage to catch an hour of rest it was troubled and filled with terrifying dreams: he would be back in the medical wing of the compound, or lashed to the pole in the yard, and this time no one came to his rescue, and Frobisher's laughter became an evil cacophony as Ressler went to work on him.

Even when he was not asleep, the faces of Gina and Frank Tormey were never far away from his mind, two people he had loved who had become collateral damage in the battle of wits he had entered into with the After Dark Campaign.

He told himself it had been for Beth, or for the greater good, but there remained a part of him that wondered if this was true. If he was really honest, had it been a matter of pride? Had he felt a desire to prove he was smarter, tougher, wilier than his adversaries?

He paid Harriet Grantham a visit, ostensibly to set up some sessions for Beth, and had ended up staying for an hour himself. She listened sympathetically, and suggested he make some regular appointments. 'You have been through a deeply traumatic experience, and lost two very significant people in your life,' she told him. 'The fact that Phillipe Ressler's body was never found has also denied you the chance of any real closure. You're experiencing the symptoms of post-traumatic stress disorder, Mr Dunnigan. It's perfectly understandable.'

'Is there something I can take for it? A pill?'

'I can certainly prescribe a mild sedative to help you sleep, but the only real cure is therapy and time. Are you prepared to commit to that?'

'I'll think about it. Could you write me the prescription?'

That night he was sitting in his flat, gazing up at the poster of Patrick Troughton as the second incarnation of the iconic sci-fi character, Doctor Who, which he had in a frame above his fireplace. It had been with him since boarding school, and he thought of the picture as his oldest friend.

He was just about to make some tea when the buzzer sounded, meaning someone was on the street looking to come in. He went to the intercom.

'Who is it, please?'

'Hello, Mr Dunnigan. It's Tim Pat Rogers. I hope I haven't called at an inconvenient time.'

'No. You can come up.' He pressed the button to release the door lock and footsteps sounded on the stairs.

Rogers was dressed in a long woollen overcoat over a deep blue suit, a purple shirt with a small collar open at the neck. He smelt of expensive aftershave and cigar smoke. 'I just wanted to pay my respects,' the gangster said as he shook Dunnigan's hand. 'Frank and I were not friends, but I know you and he were close. As coppers went, he was a good one. Your sister I never met, but Father Bill spoke very highly of her. You're in my prayers.'

'Thank you,' Dunnigan said. 'I will do my best to repay the money you gave us while we were ... when we went after Frobisher. If you just let me know how much, I can set up a direct debit or something ...'

'That's not necessary,' Rogers said, 'and there's no need to mention it again. Father Bill and I go back a long way, and there are debts I owe that man I can never clear. Money is something I have more of than I will ever spend in my lifetime. I was happy to offer what small help I could.'

Dunnigan sat stiffly down on his threadbare couch. 'You know I work for the NBCI.'

'Of course.'

'This can't mean I'm beholden to you. I will happily pay back the money, but I won't turn a blind eye to any crimes you're involved with that I come across as part of an investigation.'

Rogers looked at Dunnigan with a wry smile. 'Are you trying to tell me that I shouldn't think that you're, to use the vernacular, in my pocket?'

'That is what I'm saying, yes.'

'Consider it noted. Now, before I take my leave, I have one more thing I want to give you. I hope you take it in the spirit it's intended and that your last point doesn't apply.' He handed Dunnigan a USB stick.

'What's this?'

'It contains the final fifteen minutes of the man who murdered your sister and Chief Superintendent Tormey. I thought it might ease your mind to know he spent those last moments in an advanced level of discomfort.'

Dunnigan paused for a moment then took the pen drive. 'How did you come by this?'

'I have my sources. I will bid you goodnight, Mr Dunnigan. I'm sure our paths will cross again soon.'

*

Dunnigan sat for a long time after the gangster was gone, simply looking at the small piece of plastic in his hand. Beth was staying with her father for a few days, and Diane was not due to call over for a while yet. Finally he pulled over his laptop and opened it, plugging the memory stick in and waiting for his computer to download the appropriate software so his operating system could run the footage it contained.

*

Diane arrived at Dunnigan's flat an hour later. She found him curled up on his couch, tears drying on his face. 'What's wrong, Davey?'

'What have we become?' he asked her, his voice full of pain and unhappiness. 'What has all this done to us? To me?'

She looked at the screen of his laptop. The criminologist had been watching an MP4 video which she saw he had paused after twenty-five seconds. The image that was frozen in place was of a man – or what might once have been a man, tied to a chair in a cellar she thought she recognised. 'Do you know who that is – or was?'

'I think it's what's left of Wilfred Hubert. Rogers thought I would want to see it, and part of me does but ... oh God, Diane. I don't know who I am anymore.'

She took him in her arms and let him cry.

4

TWO NIGHTS AFTER GINA'S FUNERAL, THE FIVE friends were in the Widow's Quay Homeless Project sitting in the lunch room, drinking tea that Father Bill had sneakily laced with whiskey. This had become a routine – they would meet in the evenings to share their day and just be together.

'They never did find Ressler's body,' Diane said. 'Do you think he's still out there?'

'We'd be idiots to think he's not,' Dunnigan said. 'But we've got to hope that losing Frobisher and all the power and resources he had will have hurt him enough that he'll hide away in some dark, squalid corner of the world and leave us alone.'

'We won,' Miley said. 'We beat him. Him and Frobisher both.'

'Yeah, we won, but we lost an awful lot in the process,' Beth pointed out.

'We did,' Father Bill agreed. 'But we have to believe that your mum and Frank would want us to be happy. To make a good life for ourselves. That way, they won't have died in vain.'

'So, what now?' Diane asked.

'Beth and I have something to tell you all,' Miley said.

'You're not getting married?' Diane asked excitedly.

'Well, we plan to, eventually, but not for a bit. I'm going back to Greenland next month, and I'd like Beth to come with me.'

Dunnigan put down his mug, feeling as if he'd just been slapped in the face.

'Before you get upset, hear us out,' Beth said, putting her hand on his. 'We want you and Diane to think about coming with us.'

'But ...' Dunnigan said, 'my life is here. My job with the police and at the university.'

'They have a police force in Faringen,' Miley said. 'And Tuntuk has been talking about setting up a sheriff's department out on the res for ages. There's some kind of grant he can draw down to pay for it. You and Diane could help them set it up – train in some of the Inughuit.'

'Have you even talked to Tuntuk about this?' Diane asked. 'Doesn't it smack a bit of colonialism having us sail in and set up shop?'

'I have, as it happens. Last night. If it isn't you training some of his people in, it'll just be some other non-tribal person. At least he knows and respects you both.'

Diane looked at Dunnigan, and he grinned. 'I suppose it would be a fresh start,' he said.

'We could all do with one,' she agreed.

'What about you, Father?' Dunnigan asked.

'My mission is here – the shelter, the inner city – this is where I belong. But it doesn't stop us being family. I'm always just a phone call away. And I can be there in a day or so if you really need me.'

And they knew he was right.

They started preparing for the move that night.

Epilogue

FRESH STARTS AND NEW BEGINNINGS

1

DAVID DUNNIGAN LOOKED AT THE IMAGE ON the screen of the ultrasound machine, but to him it showed little more than a series of misshapen blobs and swirls. The speaker attached to the device, which was supposed to be picking up sounds from inside Diane, seemed to be broadcasting a mix of whale song and gurgles.

'Okay,' the Faringen medical centre's nurse, Illsa, said, smiling broadly. 'I've got some news for you both.'

'The machine's broken?' Dunnigan offered.

'No, sheriff, that's not it. Maybe you should sit down.'

*

Miley and Beth were in the waiting room when Dunnigan came out, looking ashen-faced.

'Oh my God, is everything alright?' Beth demanded, standing up and grabbing him. 'Is the baby okay?'

'Babies,' Dunnigan said. 'Diane's having twins.'

He looked as if he was going to keel over, so Miley grabbed him and steered him over to the water cooler, where he filled a paper cup.

'Could Illsa tell you the genders?' Beth asked as she jumped up and down, squealing with delight.

'A boy and a girl,' Dunnigan said, sitting down in shock.

'Perfect,' Miley grinned, slapping him on the back. 'You can call them Miley and Elizabeth.'

'I was thinking more along the lines of Frank and Gina,' a beaming Diane said, as she came out to join them. 'Are you okay, Davey?'

'I just can't believe it,' Dunnigan said, and tears of joy sprang to his eyes and he hugged his wife and kissed her.

Miley and Beth came in for a group hug.

'We're obviously going to be the godparents,' Beth said, pulling up her hood as they walked out into the blizzard.

'We never had anyone else in mind,' Diane said. 'And don't forget, we're going to need babysitters when we get called out at night, too.'

'I'm sure we can negotiate a good hourly rate,' Miley said.

Laughing, they crossed the ice-rutted street to the Faringen Hotel, where they had a celebratory dinner.

Dunnigan checked the snowmobiles for explosives before they started the drive home, and Diane had rigged the entire area around the Inughuit camp with security cameras as soon as she and Dunnigan had officially taken up their positions as law-keepers on the res.

They kept a guard dog named Chewie, a huskie/wolf hybrid that Dunnigan trained to only accept food from his hand and who had free run of their house at night.

If he came for them, they'd be ready.

Other than that, life had never been so good.

2

ZAMKOVA CORRECTIONAL FACILITY NUMBER 58 sits atop Zamkova Hora Hill, five miles outside Kiev, and is home to 500 prisoners, 25 of whom are housed in a two-storey block built from stone hewn from the bare hillside.

This square cellblock is situated away from the general population, out the back near a storage shed. The structure is referred to by the correctional officers who work in the prison as *budynok bozhevilni*, the madhouse.

Inmate 24 had been incarcerated in the prison's madhouse for three years, though she had committed no crime. She was a small, wiry-haired creature, non-verbal and prone to fits of profound rage and violence. No one knew who her family was or where she was originally from. She had been found living deep in Holosiivyskyi Forest, naked and covered in scars, by a group of hunters a decade ago.

Boris, the hunter who had first spied her running through

the trees and who had coaxed her to his camp by leaving a trail of cured meat, had named her Katya, and indeed she seemed to answer to the title, but the foster parents she was placed with decided they did not like it (they had a maiden aunt they detested called Katya), and they named her Delia.

She thrived in the foster home, potty-training successfully and coming along in leaps and bounds at a school for children with learning difficulties. Then Karl, her foster father, was killed in an accident at the factory where he worked, and Dite, her foster mother, said she could not cope with grieving and caring for a disabled daughter – the state did not pay her enough to make it worth her while.

The next people she was moved to called her Sybil. That placement lasted three months. The next one four weeks. By the time they ran out of foster families, she had stopped responding to any names at all.

Her behaviour proved too challenging for the children's institution she was finally placed in, and her trajectory through the care system eventually brought her to a juvenile detention centre (she overheard the social worker tell one of the guards that there just wasn't anywhere else to put her). It was from there she graduated to Zamkova 58.

No one in the prison bothered with her much. Food was passed through a slot in her door and she was brought to the yard for exercise every other day (this amounted to a leather leash being fastened about her neck and one of the guards dragging her outside, where she sat sniffing the air like a dog before being led back to her cell).

A student doctor tried to teach her to say some words during her first year in the madhouse, and indeed she made a few noises that sounded promising before he got too close and she tried to bite his ear off. Since then, she'd been left alone.

Inmate 24 awakened one morning from a dream, in which she was back in the forest, to hear a conversation outside her cell door. One of the voices she knew well enough – it was the warden of the madhouse. The other was new.

'You're sure you want to go in there? We usually drug her food if we have to deal with her. She can move really fast when she wants to. Don't be fooled because she's small and looks harmless. That one's a killer.'

'There is nothing on her file that says she has killed anybody.'

'Give her time. She's still young.'

'I am certain. Just leave me the keys. I'll lock up when I'm finished.'

Inmate 24 could understand most of what was said to her, although she pretended not to. The new voice spoke Ukrainian with an accent, pronouncing some of the words oddly.

'Don't come running to me if she mauls you,' the warden's voice said as his footsteps grew dimmer. 'They say she was running with a pack of wild dogs in the woods when they found her. Whatever happened to her, she's never got over it.'

'I will heed your warnings. Now, please, leave us. I wish to get to know my patient.'

Keys rattled and the door opened, revealing a strange man. He was smiling, and Inmate 24 didn't like it. None of the guards smiled.

He was dressed in a tweed suit and his hair was so black the girl thought she could see blue lights in it. His skin was very pink, as if he had been standing out in the cold, and she noticed there was a lot of scar tissue on his left cheek, as if he had been burned and the wound had only recently healed.

'Hello, my dear girl,' he said.

She growled, to let him know to stay right where he was.

He raised a hand to show he understood, and squatted down on his haunches, so they were at the same level. 'People hereabouts call me Vladimir, but my real name is Phillipe. You and I are going to be great friends. I have been so lonely this past year.'

And he told her of how he wanted to help her get her life back.

All she had to do in return was help him reclaim his.

AUTHOR'S NOTE

When I sat down to write *After She Vanished*, the first book in what I have come to call The Dunnigan Series, I had no idea where it would lead me. That, I have discovered, is the joy of writing fiction – it takes you to the most unexpected places.

As I typed the first few words of my initial outline for that story, certain things were clear while others remained distinctly cloudy. I always knew, for example, what had happened to David Dunnigan to bring him to the self-destructive place we find him in the prologue of the first novel – I knew his niece had been abducted and that his life had gradually fallen apart in the years after this traumatic event, the guilt eating away at him until there was very little of him left. I knew his parents were pretty awful and that he and his sister had more or less raised one another.

I envisioned him as a loner, so I was surprised when I discovered he was going to have friends: when I sat down on that sunny Saturday afternoon to draft an outline of my first fiction title for Hachette Books Ireland, Miley, Father Bill and Diane poured out with the same level of detail that Dunnigan did. They had, it seemed, been living in my head for a long time. I was glad to finally meet them

I had a lot to learn, you see, about this world I was creating and the people who lived there.

I didn't really have a sense of Dunnigan's personality. I knew what he looked like and I knew what things he enjoyed and I knew the car he drove and how he dressed and where he lived (I had gone to Phibsboro and stood on the street and looked up at the window where his flat would be – I had even drawn a crude map of that flat). That he was the distinctly difficult person he turned out to be evolved as I started to write him. In some ways, Dunnigan told me who he was. And I loved him for it. Dunnigan is a man who lives life on his own terms. He has often found the process challenging and he has been hurt – sometimes very badly – by the slings and arrows of fortune. But Dunnigan is a survivor. Despite everything he has kept going.

That and his unerring sense of what is right are, I believe, his most admirable character traits.

Maybe the greatest theme of the series is that sometimes the kindness of others can save your life. Kindness certainly saved David Dunnigan's – I occasionally play a mental game and wonder where my character would be and what he would be doing now if hadn't met Father Bill and Diane.

And, perhaps most profoundly, if he hadn't met Miley.

Miley Timoney's story was one I approached with great care. I knew Dunnigan needed someone who would act as his conscience (the Jiminy Cricket role, as one reader has described it). But Miley's true strength and inner beauty were only gradually revealed to me as the books progressed. When I first came up with the idea for Miley, I didn't know how amazingly strong he was going to be. Sometimes it has felt that the harder and darker Dunnigan became, the truer and braver Miley grew.

I had no clue, even as I began *When She Was Gone*, that Dunnigan's best friend would end up staying in Greenland at the close of that book, or the impact that would have on the series as a whole. Looking back now, I realise how that passage of the story threw the world of the books wide open, and laid the ground work for action to move out of Ireland in *If She Returned* and this book. It was important to me that Dublin still remained the central location of the story (many readers have told me how much they enjoyed the fact that Ireland's capital is almost a character in the books), but it was great fun to put Dunnigan into strange and uncomfortable locations just to see how he coped with them.

And, I'm delighted to say, he usually managed to adapt. He is a Mighty Warrior, after all.

But back to Miley for a moment. He is, without question, the character I get asked about more than any other. I receive more emails and messages about him than I do about any other character I have ever written. And (to answer the question about him I get asked the most) I can tell you that he is based on a couple of individuals I have met and worked with in my career in social care. All the information about Down Syndrome in the books is one hundred per cent true and accurate, and the idea of Miley being stuck in a nursing home (despite not yet being thirty years old) as we find him in *After She Vanished* is based on a real case I was involved in, and was (thankfully without having to receive the beating Dunnigan endured) able to bring to a favourable conclusion.

I am deeply grateful that I was given the opportunity to breathe life into Miley by the amazing people in Hachette Ireland. That we find him (and indeed Dunnigan, Diane and Beth) in such a happy place at the end of this book gives me a very warm feeling.

Which brings me to another question I get asked a lot: did I know, back at the beginning of it all, that Beth would be found alive? The honest answer is: no, I didn't. I sketched out a few scenarios, and I still have a file on my laptop that contains fairly detailed outlines of possibilities for Beth. And if I am to offer full disclosure, I was very tempted to finish the series with an open ending, in which we are left wondering. But in a conversation with Ciara, my editor, we decided that while that may be realistic, and the most likely outcome of a case like this, it was just not fair on my loyal readership.

I was going to have to come down on one side or the other.

And I was just as surprised as Dunnigan was when he got that phone call from Father Bill at the end of *When She Was Gone*, informing him Father Bill thought he had found her. And that was that.

Getting to know the woman Beth has become has been a tremendous challenge and a great adventure. I am so proud of her. She is tough and courageous and loyal and fragile and damaged and beautiful and, just as I hope Miley is a character people with special needs can see as a powerful and affirming role model, I would love it if Beth could be perceived in the same light by survivors of abuse.

The reality of what she would have been through is unthinkable and just fucking horrible, but with love, support and a lot of hard work there can be life on the other side of it.

And speaking of trauma …

We say goodbye to a couple of important and well-loved characters in *Why She Ran*. I can assure you that I thought long and hard about who was going to leave us (Father Bill came close to a nasty end, but got a last minute reprieve).

But let's pause for a moment and remember those we have lost.

Frank Tormey swaggered into the text of the series very early on, and I have loved how his relationship with Dunnigan evolved. I did not initially see him as being more than a man behind a desk, barking at Dunnigan occasionally, but he just wouldn't stay there. And I soon understood that Dunnigan needed him as much as he needed any of the others in his strange little family. He was probably the father Dunnigan should have had, and I have no doubt that he loved Davey like a son.

Gina, whose humanity, love and loyalty were so crucial to Dunnigan's emergence as a person, has been a special joy for me to write (she wasn't initially Dunnigan's twin – that came out of some editorial conversations, but her personality and the relationship she and her brother shared were all there from the beginning). I must disclose that she is very much inspired by my own sister, Tara, who, just like Gina, refused to give up on me when I probably deserved it, and through love, determination and grit, ensured we have a close friendship in adulthood.

Ernest Frobisher, that most evil of men, was in my initial pitch, but if you were to ask me about him in those first days I could have only told you that he was dying. It has been a sometimes surprising journey becoming acquainted with him. And a lot of fun. The great thing about a character who is so dark is that you can throw all limits and restrictions of behaviour out the window. There have been times during the writing of the series where I would come to a scene and have to pause. No, I would think, Father Bill just wouldn't do that. Or that doesn't ring true... Davey Dunnigan would draw the line there. Never, on a single occasion, did I run into such recrimination with Frobisher. Even my blackest imaginings could appear mild when seen through the lens of this man's persona.

I like how he has come full circle, too: in the first book of the series we learned a lot about his childhood and youth, while in *Why She Ran*, we meet him at the end of his days.

And I think he gets the death he deserves, this man who has caused so much torment to so many.

I like the symmetry of that.

Why then, does Ressler live to fight another day?

Doctor Philippe Ressler has (along with Miley) been the breakout character of the series, and I must say, for all his being a thoroughly unpleasant piece of work, I have become quite fond of him. So fond, in fact, that I couldn't bring myself to kill him. I needed to know he was out there somewhere, doing what he does. I have no idea what that says about me as a person – and maybe I don't want to know! We all like to root for the bad guy from time to time, don't we? Don't we? Or maybe it's just me...

In the end, I suppose, it doesn't matter. The people who have populated these novels have become very important to me over the past five years. I have laughed with them, cried for them, cheered them on and mourned their losses.

I'm going to miss them.

ACKNOWLEDGEMENTS

A lot of people have contributed to the writing of this novel, and indeed to the Dunnigan Series.

I want to thank Ciara, Joanna, Elaine and all the people at Hachette Ireland. I've said it before and I'll say it again, this series would not have happened and been the success it has been without your faith in me, an untested fiction writer with a weird idea for a series that really didn't make a lot of sense on paper. I am deeply grateful you stuck with it.

Jonathan Williams and Marianne Gunn O'Connor each played a part in representing me during the writing of the Dunnigan Series, and I want to thank them both for their contributions to my career. But I particularly want to take a moment to write about the man who represents me now and who, I sincerely hope, will continue to do so for a very long time to come. Ivan Mulcahy and the people at MMB Creative arrived at a point on my writing journey when I was very close to throwing in the towel and changed my life completely by forging a future for me that I had scarcely believed was possible. Every now and again someone comes along who you just know you were supposed to be working with, and you wonder why it took so long for the two of you to find one another.

That's how it felt when I met Ivan. I want to thank him, Tilly, Sallyanne, Adrienn and everyone at MMB for making the past year such an exciting and productive one.

While I'm at it, I need to thank the person who introduced me to Ivan, and who is truly one of the kindest and most supportive people in the literary world in Ireland. Vanessa Fox O'Loughlin (Sam Blake) is not just a great crime writer in her own right (which she most certainly is) and a powerhouse of activity and productivity (she runs Writing.ie, the Inkwell Group, is a founder and organiser for Ireland's best crime writing festival, Murder One, plays a major part in running the Dublin International Literary Festival and has her own podcast) she is also a true and dear friend. Vanessa, thank you.

2019 was the year of the Underground Writer. Myself, Sheila Forsey and Caroline Busher, (two amazing writers, by the way – if you haven't read their work, do yourself a favour and seek them out), formed a society for people who wanted to bring their writing out into the light. We held workshops and gave talks and did readings and played some music and it was really special. Through the Underground Writers Society Sheila and Caroline have become two of my most treasured friends. Life kind of got in the way as the Autumn of 2019 rolled around and we all became outrageously busy, but I live in the sincere hope that we will get together again soon to have more writing adventures. This strange thing we writers do can be lonely, so having Caroline and Sheila, and indeed all of our Underground Writers, to share the journey with has been wonderful. Thanks to you all.

Carmel Harrington, another great writer, remains a huge source of support and inspiration and a wonderful friend whom I don't get to see half often enough. I want to thank Orla MacAlinden, Casey King, Andrea Carter, Patricia Gibney, Liz Nugent, Maria Duffy, Andrea Hayes and all the other amazing Irish writers who have encouraged me so much. It feels wonderful to be part of such a vibrant writing community.

I am blessed to have a fabulous family, without whom none of what I do would be possible. My wife, Deirdre, is truly the best person I know. She is genuinely the love of my life and she supports me in too many ways to mention here. My children, Richard and Marnie, are a constant source of pride and joy, and my grandson Rhys makes me smile every time I think about him.

My sister, Tara (whom I've already mentioned) is also one of my best friends, and delivers a regular kick to my proverbial behind to bring me back down to earth when I need it. Her husband, Gerry and my nephews Jack and Conn are some of my favourite people in the world.

I have known Ronan Lowney for as long as I can remember, and he is still one of my closest friends – in fact at this stage he is really a member of the family. He has been there for my best and worst times, and I am so grateful to have him in my life.

My dogs, Lulu and George, sat at my feet during most of the writing of this book, and are currently asleep in front of the fire as I type. They accompany me on the walks I use to sort through plot points and decompress after a long day at the keyboard, and are, therefore a very important part of the writing process.

Last, but by no means least, thanks to you, dear Reader. If it weren't for you, there would really be no point in any of this at all. Thank you for your support, kindness, and for putting Dunnigan on the bestseller lists. I couldn't have done it without you. And I mean that literally!

Why She Ran is the last instalment in this series of Dunnigan's adventures. I'm going to leave him, Diane, Miley and Beth to live their lives in peace in Greenland for a while. After all, they're going to be busy with two new babies on the way. And maybe the break will give Ressler time to regroup. Or perhaps some new threat is developing, unseen. We'll have to wait to find out. Suffice it to say this book is the end of this part of their story. I hope to return to these characters, but other books and other stories are calling me just now.

I hope you'll join me when I share them.

Wexford
November 2019